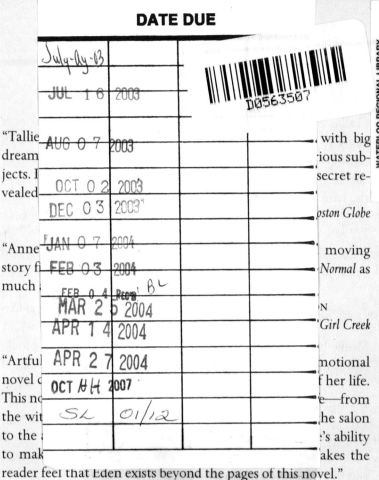

"Tallie . . . with big dream . . . rious subjects. . . . secret revealed . . . . oston Globe

"Anne . . . moving story f . . . Normal as much . . .

. . . N

. . . Girl Creek

"Artful . . . motional novel . . . f her life. This no . . . e—from the wit . . . he salon to the . . . 's ability to mak . . . akes the reader feel that Eden exists beyond the pages of this novel."

—*Romantic Times*

"Tallie is an endearing character, and the Southern banter of the ladies at the beauty parlor where she works is pitch-perfect. . . . LeClaire's homey storytelling goes down easy."

—*Publishers Weekly*

Please turn the page for more reviews. . . .

leaving
eden

Anne D. LeClaire

BALLANTINE BOOKS • New York

A Ballantine Book
Published by The Random House Ballantine Publishing Group

Copyright © 2002 by Anne D. LeClaire
Reader's Guide copyright © 2003 by Anne D. LeClaire and The Random House
Ballantine Publishing Group, a division of Random House, Inc.

The epigraph from "Dream Boogie" by Langston Hughes is from *The Collected
Poems of Langston Hughes* edited by Arnold Rampersad, published by
Alfred A. Knopf in 1994.

www.ballantinebooks.com/BRC/

Library of Congress Control Number: 2003091797

ISBN 0-345-44575-9

Text design by Jaime Putorti
Cover illustration by Aleta Rafton

Manufactured in the United States of America

First Hardcover Edition: September 2002
First Trade Paperback Edition: May 2003

1 3 5 7 9 10 8 6 4 2

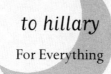

to hillary

For Everything

Good morning, daddy!
Ain't you heard
The boogie-woogie rumble
Of a dream deferred?

—LANGSTON HUGHES
"DREAM BOOGIE"

i was asleep the night Mama left us, but I remember every detail of the moment she came home. June 21, 1988. Hot enough to poach perch in Bald Creek and officially the first day of summer, although I had already been swimming for weeks. Country 99.7 was on in the kitchen, and I was forming a trio with the Judds. "Girls Night Out."

Daddy had already departed for the mill when Mr. Tinsley's taxi pulled up to the curb, belching blue. I peered through the kitchen window and saw the passenger door open and a dark-haired girl step out. She wore black flat-heeled shoes, black pedal pushers, a red and white striped sailor shirt and, cinching her waist, a black leather belt. Before I even got to wondering who she was and what she was doing here, she looked directly up at our house and—although I had been praying steady for just this moment—I couldn't believe what was laid out right before my eyes.

Mama had come home.

"Thank you, Jesus," I said. Just that. Back then I still had faith that what you asked for would surely come if you prayed with sufficient fervor, and I sincerely believed it was the power of my prayers that had brought my mama back.

She stood there for a moment, suitcases plopped on the grass, just looking up and staring at the house, like she'd been deposited before the home of strangers and wasn't sure whether to walk up the path to our front door or get back in with Mr. Tinsley and drive away. I didn't give her time to make her decision.

Quicker than you could say Sam Hill, I lunged forward, screen slamming behind me. "Mama," I cried, and flung myself in her arms, hugging her so close it made her gasp. What I really wanted was to wrap my legs around her waist and my arms around her neck, the way I used to so she would have to carry me up to the house, but I was way too old for that and—I realized suddenly—now as tall as she. That smashing hug had to suffice.

I didn't see then how tired she looked, just how pretty. Even then, nearing her forties, she was the prettiest woman in all of Eden. And, if you believed some people, Spring Hill and Redden, too.

You see, Mama was the spitting image of Natalie Wood. Not everyone my age knew about the actress who was Queen of the Screen in the 1960s, how they'd charcoaled her skin so she could play a Puerto Rican in *West Side Story*, how the crazy bathtub scene in *Splendor in the Grass* didn't have to be faked. I knew all that. I was raised on Natalie. Mama had even named me Natasha, which was Natalie's pet name, a fact not many people knew.

Mama was five feet tall, exactly like the actress, and had the same dark hair and black velvet eyes and perfect, pouty mouth, so alike they could be twins. People were forever telling her this, and although she made quick to deny it politely in public, her mirror just reflected back the same truth. Which I guess was what started all the trouble. Trouble that began, though I wouldn't know this for years, began back before I was even thought of.

"Did you get it?" I screamed. "Did it happen?"

"Shush, baby," she said, and then she held me out at arm's length and looked me over. "You've grown up." She eyed my bosom. "Up and out."

She'd missed my birthday back in May. I was twelve and, like I said, nearly as tall as she was. For that instant—her commenting on how I'd changed since she left—I wanted to feel as I truly should have felt. Mad at her. For everything. For deserting us, no matter how urgent the cause that took her away. For missing my birthday. For not being there when I'd started my period, and, too embarrassed to ask my daddy for help, had to ask old Mrs. Harewood at the drugstore whatever to buy. Most of all, I wanted to be angry at her for leaving me alone, the only girl in all of Eden without a mama, except Rula Wade, whose mama died birthing her and even she had a step-mama, though one only eleven years older. I wanted to be mad, but I couldn't. All that anger just melted like spring ice off Baldy. It's gospel that no one could stay angry long at Mama. It always was.

"Your daddy inside?" she asked. I couldn't tell if she was hoping he was or wasn't.

"At the mill," I said. For sure, Daddy hadn't the least idea that Mama was coming home today. I sent off a prayer that he wouldn't stop at CC's Bar and Grill—a dive a lot more bar than grill.

Mama drew a deep breath and lifted a hand to shade her eyes as she looked around. "Spring in the Blue Ridge," she said. "It surely shows the Lord's gift with a paint box." Then she said she regretted missing the redbuds in bloom and the dogwood. She said dogwood in blossom looked like "sulfur moths floating over the fields." Like she was telling *me* about the dogwood blossom and redbuds. *I* wasn't the one who had left. What I needed to know was where she'd been and exactly what she'd been doing. I was hungry for details beyond those three-line messages scrawled on the back of postcards.

Before I could say a word, she headed into the house and from that moment on she acted like she hadn't been anywhere more exciting than Lynchburg. While she unpacked and got reacquainted with the house, she asked me a hundred questions about my school and friends and how I had celebrated my birthday. (Which she hadn't forgotten after all. She gave me a little purse covered with beads she said were sewn by hand. Inside was a tube of real lipstick. The six-dollar kind. It made me sick with impatience to think it was summer and I'd have to wait until school to show it off.) Naturally I tried to tell her everything that had happened in the past six months, but when I asked her if she got the part in the movie she just said, "Did you see me riding up here in any Cadillac?" I kept pushing for details, but she deflected my questions with a weary, "Later, sugar." I believed her, believed I'd be learning everything before long, and so let things be. Maybe I shouldn't have, but that day I didn't have a clue four years would pass before I'd learn all the things my mama wasn't telling. By then—by the time I'd unraveled mysteries that took me clear across the country—I'd be bearing secrets of my own.

After lunch, she pleaded exhaustion from the trip (trip from exactly *where?*) and went in to take a nap, not even bothering to change the rumpled sheets, a fact that revealed how tired she was. The linens were gray with grime, and Mama always was finicky about towels, corners, toilet seats, such like. I had tried my best while she was gone, but it was amazing how much work a house required. And I had school, too, which was *supposed* to be a girl's full-time job.

Mama slept through most of the afternoon while I waited outside her door, edgy with unsatisfied curiosity, and fretting about Daddy's maybe stopping at CC's. I plotted about how to get word to him. So he would be prepared. So he would come straight home without detouring for a drink or three. Finally I called the mill, an act so bold it had occurred only once in our family history, when I was knocked out cold by a pitched ball in P.E. But on this of all days, he couldn't be reached.

I could have saved myself the trouble. As if he had some special radar where Mama was concerned, Daddy came directly from work. When he walked through the door she was sitting at the kitchen table, freshly showered and dressed in a becoming pink blouse. The second he saw her he wasted no more time getting mad than I had.

"Welcome home, Dinah Mae," he said.

"Deanie," Mama said.

"Dinah. Deanie. Whatever, darlin'."

It amazed me how a man could welcome his wife back like that without one single word about what she'd been doing since January. Course, Daddy always was a fool for everything about Mama. He thought she hung the moon. His sister Ida said he would carry Mama around on a pillow if it would make her happy. He displayed his love so openly I was embarrassed for him. I thought it was plain silly for a man to act so crazy over any woman. Even Mama. But I guess it's hard to express what there was about Mama. It was as if her even noticing you was a favor, though not in a conceited way. It was just her manner. Long before the phrase ever entered the vernacular, Mama *ruled*.

Daddy's overalls were dirty, and there was flour dust on the back of his neck, creased with a line of sweat. I wished he'd washed up before he'd come home. He was a big man, my daddy, but he always seemed to shrink when he was with Mama. Even though he was capable at the mill and with any kind of machine, around her he was all helpless thumbs.

At last, I thought, we'll find out everything.

To my disappointment, Daddy didn't seem to share my fiery interest in what Mama'd been doing. He was happy to have her back and made it plainer than two sticks. He hadn't been home more than fifteen minutes when they disappeared into their bedroom, not even bothering to glance my way to see if I was watching. At first all you could hear was talking, and once Mama laughed and that set her off in a coughing fit. Then nothing came from that room but silence. They didn't care a whit that they'd left me sitting alone.

I went out to the porch and picked up *Gone With the Wind*, which I was reading for the second time that summer. I loved the first sentence and knew it by heart. *"Scarlett O'Hara was not beautiful, but men seldom realized it when caught by her charm as the Tarleton twins were."* Mama was exactly like that. Loaded with charm. But beautiful, too. Feature by feature. Truly, Mama'd put Scarlett to shame. Whenever I pictured scenes from the book, it wasn't Vivien Leigh I was seeing. It was Mama.

I was at the part where the army was driven back to their winter quarters in Virginia and Christmas was approaching. Ashley Wilkes was on furlough, and Scarlett was frightened by the violence of her feelings for him. She loved Ashley "to desperation," a phrase that thrilled and frightened me every time I considered it. Violence and desperation didn't seem like good things to associate with love. In books, uncontrollable love might sound romantic, but in real life it was sure to be messy. Dangerous. How dangerous, I couldn't imagine, though I was to find out.

I read and reread the paragraph describing how the war had changed Ashley, but I couldn't concentrate. A honeybee kept circling the swing, driving me crazy with its buzzing, but what was really pulling my attention was the silence from behind the bedroom door. I didn't need any road map to tell me what was going on. I picked at a scab on my knee until it bled and was sure to make a scar, then sucked the blood off my finger and made up my mind that I wouldn't even speak to Mama when they reappeared.

When they finally came out—all rumpled and giggly— neither of them had the good grace to look shamefaced. Daddy sat down at the table and drank a Pabst while Mama set about making dinner. Fried ham steak, sweet potatoes, and creamed corn. When I smelled the ham frying, I felt my resolve to stay silent soften, and then the little seed of anger melted into relief. You see, it wasn't that Mama was heartless. She was just carefree, and that could feel like plain not caring.

I sipped a Coke, and felt something clenched loosen inside my chest. Mama was here, cooking dinner and flirting with Daddy. All was well in my world. We were a family again, not just a daddy and his daughter trying to be one, with a mama off somewhere on her way to becoming someone else.

Later, after dinner, we all settled in on the couch and Daddy switched on the TV. Outside, the Bettis twins were cranking by on their dirt bikes. Wiley called for me to join them, but I was staying exactly where I was, snuggled in next to Mama. We watched *Wheel of Fortune* and a rerun of *Moonlighting*. Although she wasn't our type, Mama and I both agreed that Cybill Shepherd knew a thing or two about looking fine. "That girl's got *attitude*," Mama said, like it was a good thing.

Midway through the show, Daddy swung her feet up into his lap, like he had a zillion times. "Size five," he announced to the room, his voice swollen with awe and pride, as if he were both surprised and personally responsible for the miracle of her tiny feet. I swung my own feet up. "Size eight," I said. We all laughed.

Everything was exactly the way it had been before Mama left.

For weeks, I stayed edgy as a kit fox, alert for any sign Mama was unhappy or getting ready to head off again. But she didn't. She stayed on for another six months. Until she left us for good.

1992

*t*he promise of beauty—the kind of real personal beauty that can transform a person's life—arrived in Eden, Virginia, on the fourth Thursday in June.

As usual I arrived through the rear door of the Klip-N-Kurl, and so a few minutes passed before I caught sight of the sign in the front window. I'd been working at the Kurl since school let out. Mostly I did chores: swept the floor, cleaned the sinks and mirrors, refilled the shampoo and conditioner bottles, dumped the ashtrays, straightened out the magazine table, that sort of thing. Because I wasn't licensed, that was supposed to be the extent of it, but once in a while, when she got behind, Raylene let me do a shampoo or a comb out.

I found soaping a head of hair pleasurable. You would be surprised to discover the wide variety of hair. Thin. Coarse. Thick. Wiry. Growing in ways that defy imagination. Hair with three natural parts, or platinum streaks there since birth.

It is not false pride when I tell you that my hair was my best asset, though I'd cut it that spring—a mistake that never would have happened if Mama'd still been with me. I'd started out planning to give myself a little trim, like Elizabeth Talmadge's new do, but getting it so the sides matched wasn't as easy as you might think, and Raylene had to fix up the mess. I'd vowed when it grew out never to cut it again. Just trim the dead ends. I planned on wearing it down over my shoulders, like Kim Basinger, an actress I continue to admire even though that town she bought went bankrupt.

"Morning, Tallie," Raylene said. She was working up a head of suds on Sue Beth Wilkins. An unfortunate mop of hair topped the list of Sue Beth's sorry features. Some of the meaner boys in our class called her LB—short for Lard Bucket—but a kindhearted person like Mama would call her sturdy.

Mrs. Wilkins was sitting over by the dryers flipping through the style magazines. Raylene caught my attention in the mirror and gave a quick eye roll. You had to feel sorry for Sue Beth. Every year in late June—when they held all the practices that led up to tryouts for next year's Flag Corps—her mama dragged her in and, armed with pictures she'd clipped out of some teen magazine, set Raylene to work. Sue Beth wasn't in the least consulted about this and had told me herself she didn't want to be a Corps member—as if that were even a remote possibility. The whole time she sat in Raylene's chair she looked about as happy as a rain-soaked rooster. It was clear as crystal Sue Beth wasn't going to make the Corps or the cheerleaders or the Sparkette twirlers or much of anything else except maybe, *maybe* the chorus. It wasn't just her weight, which certainly wasn't any asset. It was her whole yard dog look, which—having Mrs. Wilkins for a mother—you could understand.

Still, year after year, Mrs. Wilkins persisted. Last fall she'd had a wooden floor installed in their basement and a lumber-yard banister attached to the wall and told anyone who would hold still for a minute that she'd built a dance studio for her Sue Beth. She even hired a private teacher to come in once a week to give lessons. The whole thing about drove Raylene mad.

"Hi, Sue Beth," I said.

"Hi," she said from beneath a cap of foam. She wasn't really so bad. Mama might have found possibilities in her.

"I hear girls' soccer has openings this year," I said. "You thinking about trying out?"

"Sue Beth doesn't go for that sort of thing," Mrs. Wilkins said.

Raylene gave me a warning look like *Don't even get started*. Mrs. Wilkins was a steady customer. Shampoo and set every week, and once a month the whole works—color, cut, and nails. Raylene didn't want me antagonizing her.

"Anything special you want me to do?" I asked.

"Got a load to be folded," Raylene said.

"Right," I said, and headed for the back room. Raylene had installed a new washer and dryer, and my job was to keep up with the laundry. You would be amazed at the number of towels we went through in a day. We never reused them. Like some shops I won't name. Raylene was insistent about that.

"Then you can give the plants a drink."

"Okay," I said. I opened the dryer and lifted out a full load of towels. They smelled sweet from the little sachet sheets Raylene used, something Daddy had forbidden me to buy. I took my time, finding pleasure in folding a neat stack.

On and off since I started working for her, Raylene talked about my going to the cosmetology school over in Lynchburg after I graduated Eden High and then coming back full-time for her, something I can tell you that I had absolutely no intention of doing. Whenever she brought it up, I just nodded, but my resolve remained firm. A person has to take care not to let other people push their dreams on you. I had ideas of my own. They weren't jelled, but they were cooking.

Other than her plans for my future, I liked working for Raylene. For one thing, she was dependable as a ceiling fan. My own life was not so solid, and I liked this about her. The other thing was I liked being in the shop, listening to the sounds of women's voices. Even back when Mama was with us, Daddy had never been much for conversation, and now—with Mama gone and just the two of us—Daddy barely spoke at all. The talk at the Kurl balanced the silence of our home. I listened to the women talk about men and cooking recipes and when to plant bulbs, sorting through the particulars of what they were saying, testing things in my mind and adding the useful items to the book I kept. I'd started the notebook as a way of remembering everything about Mama—so I wouldn't forget—but it had grown into a book about how to be a woman, the kind of stuff a girl usually learned from her mama. You'd be amazed at the things a person could learn just by being attentive.

I was carrying the watering can up front for the ivy when I saw the sign perched on this easel Raylene had set up in the front window. It was a blowup of a blonde all prettied up like a Hollywood star with a feather boa streaming over her bare shoulders like pink lemonade, and Raylene had angled it so it could be seen by anyone in the shop as well as those walking by. On the bottom, *Glamour Day* was spelled out in red letters rimmed with gold.

"Raylene," I called. "What's this?"

"What's what, Tallie?"

"This poster. This *Glamour Day* thing."

Raylene left Sue Beth sitting at the sink with a towel wrapped around her head. Within minutes she was explaining the whole thing, how this company was sending in a team of trained professionals—that's what she called them, a team—to make you over. For twenty dollars you got the complete works—hair, makeup, the whole job—and then a photographer took your picture in five different outfits entirely of your choice. Glamour Pics, the company called it, like you were a Movie Star or heading for center stage at Nashville.

"For the twenty dollars," Raylene continued, "they also let you keep one nine-by-twelve photograph."

I thought about that for a minute, then asked, "Well, how does the company figure on making any money—the glamour makeover and the photo all for twenty dollars?"

"Tallie, honey," Raylene said, "the Glamour Company's lack of business acumen is not our problem." She was as pleased with the whole deal as a cream-fed cat.

Mrs. Wilkins was hanging on every detail. Naturally she'd already signed up for both her and Sue Beth.

Suddenly I was filled with missing Mama. I could just imagine her sporting the pink boa. If she were there she'd probably end up directing *Glamour Day* herself. Mama knew everything about Hollywood. She had direct experience. The fact was that four years ago, when I was in the eighth grade, my mama'd headed off to California. She went there to be in a movie. You may doubt me on this, but it's true.

When Mama left, my daddy and me and her best friend,

Martha Lee Curtis, were the only people in Eden to know why she went off and what her plans were. Tell people I'm off visiting kin and let it go at that, she said. Mama never did care a fig about what others thought. In that way she was unlike most women. So we told people just like she said. When their pointed questions met with no satisfaction, the majority of folks let the subject drop. Town gossip was that she'd left my daddy and run off with another man, which, believe me, was incredible but made sense to just about everyone in Eden. People were always saying my daddy was sweet, but no one pretended to think he deserved my mama. Her included, I suppose.

Of course I was dying to tell the whole county what Mama was up to, but she said no. She made us promise. She had her reasons, she said. I couldn't imagine what they might be. Wasn't it better to have people knowing the truth than thinking she ran out on us? But like I said, Mama didn't care about the good opinion of others. Still, if it were me, I'd want to tell everyone what I was setting off to do. It was the most exciting thing in the world.

Mama's plan for becoming an actress wasn't as impossible as it might seem. First off, she'd been acting for years. In Eden High, she was the star of the annual play every year from freshman to senior. Then later, after she graduated and was at school learning how to type and take dictation, she performed in the theater over in Lynchburg. She had the photo album to prove it. All her life Mama dreamed about being a movie star. She believed it was her true destiny.

Then one day that winter, just after I'd brought in the mail and was sitting on the porch drinking a Coca-Cola, Mama started screaming. By the time I got to the kitchen, she was dancing around the table and waving a magazine in the air. Finally she calmed down enough to tell me how they were going to make a movie about the life of Natalie Wood and how the director still hadn't settled on the actress for the leading role and was, in his words, looking for a fresh face, someone who could capture the essence of Natalie. Mama said this was her big chance. She was as close to the essence of Natalie Wood as anyone. She was practically a twin.

According to my granny Goody, from the time Mama was five years old, people were always commenting on the astonishing likeness, first as the little girl in *A Miracle on 34th Street*, a video we owned and watched every Christmas, then in all the ones that followed. *Rebel Without a Cause. Splendor in the Grass. West Side Story. Gypsy.* It was like Natalie Wood was holding up a beacon for Mama to follow. Final proof was Mama's high school yearbook photo. She looked exactly like Natalie in *Splendor.* That year was when she started insisting on being called Deanie, after the girl in the movie.

"I'm doing it, Luddy," she told my daddy that night. "It's my big chance. It's fate." The way she said *fate*, in a flat, determined voice, refused argument.

Daddy wasn't convinced, though he wanted to agree with Mama—it nearly killed him to disagree with her. At the time, I believed he was afraid she might go off and find another life and was afraid, too, that lying at the other end of her dream was only disappointment. He couldn't bear the thought of Mama being let down any more than he could entertain the thought she would leave him. I myself was torn between wanting Mama to be a star and despairing at the idea of being left without her.

Mama jumped up and tore out of the room. A minute later, she was back holding two pictures that she slapped down on the table in front of my daddy. One was of Mama taken the previous Christmas, and the other was an autographed photograph of Natalie Wood. I'd always believed Mama got that picture from a Natalie Wood fan club or a film studio. It was that kind of glossy up close photo. A person—looking at the two pictures—would be hard pressed to tell which was the real Natalie.

"See," she said. "I'm *supposed* to get this part. It was made for me."

"Oh, baby," Daddy said, "it's not that I don't want you to go. I just don't want you to be disappointed."

Mama's mind didn't hold room for such thoughts. "You know what I believe, Luddy," she said. "The sky's the limit. The sky's the limit and all we have to do is reach for it."

The sky's the limit. Mama always said that. But sometimes—and I do love my daddy—sometimes I wondered if Mama really believed that the sky was the limit, why had she settled on a man like Luddington Brock? Half the men in Eden were in love with her. You could tell this by the way their eyes followed her when she walked down the street. She could have had any man in the county. But she picked my daddy.

Goody had a theory about this. She said in our family women marry down. We marry down, she said, and then spend the rest of our lives trying to elevate our men. Goody had married my granddaddy when he was a clerk at Simpson's Cash Store and then dedicated her days and her daddy's money elevating him until he ended up a doctor for the Southern Railroad. I don't know for sure about Goody's marrying theory, but there is no denying that Luddington Brock was a big step down for the only daughter of Taylor and Jessie Adams.

In spite of Mama's conviction and the two photos on the table staring up at him, Daddy still wasn't persuaded, so Mama just perched herself on his lap, cupped her hands on his cheeks, and made him look straight at her.

"It's something I have to do, Luddy. I have to. If I don't, my life will be filled with regret."

At that time, I truly didn't apprehend the true nature of dreams. I didn't understand they held the power to take hold of you with both hands and pull you along, just sweep you off your feet and turn your entire life on its back. That day, I only recognized my mama's determination. The next day, she was planning it out, showing a lot of grit for someone who'd never been out of Amherst County—and at that time I really did think that Mama had never been outside the county in her life. We rented all the old Natalie Wood movies Mama didn't already own, including *The Last Married Couple in America* and *This Property Is Condemned*, two that most people probably never have heard about. We kept them so long, the video store charged us extra. It was weird, sitting there on the sofa by my mama, her hand in mine, all the time staring at the TV screen and seeing her face reflected back at me. Sometimes I had to tighten my fingers around hers to convince myself she was still there beside me.

Mama didn't just watch. She *memorized*, never taking her eyes off the screen. All the while she'd smoke and drink diet cola. No beer. You have to be careful, she said. On film, the camera adds ten pounds, she said. Between movies, she'd tell me things about Natalie. Mama was a walking, talking Natalie Wood encyclopedia. Where she got this stuff, I didn't know. Like how Natalie had made twenty movies by the time she was sixteen. And how she'd dated Elvis and had even gone to Memphis once, but that Gladys didn't approve of the match and his mama came first with Elvis, before any woman, so that was the end of that.

"Look, Tallie," she'd say. "See how she always wears a bracelet on her left wrist. That's because she had an accident and her wrist has a bump. She always wears a bracelet to cover it up." It was amazing to me that someone as pretty as Natalie Wood would worry about something as insignificant as a bump on her wrist. "How did she hurt it?" I'd ask. "It was back in the late forties," she'd say. "When she was making a movie with Walter Brennan, a bridge on the set collapsed. She broke her wrist and it wasn't set properly." "What movie?" I'd ask, testing her. *"The Green Promise,"* she'd answer, naming a movie even the video store people hadn't heard of.

Mama particularly loved *Splendor in the Grass,* a film I could hardly bear to watch, especially the part where Natalie gets sent off to that place. No matter how many times I saw that part, it always made me cry. That was back when I still could cry and Mama never minded. Sometimes, she'd cry right along with me. Her other favorites were *Gypsy* and *West Side Story* and *Rebel Without a Cause,* but she didn't like *Inside Daisy Clover,* and not just because that creepy Ruth Gordon was in it. "Natalie was going through a hard time when she made that picture," Mama told me. Like I said, Mama knew *everything* about Natalie, so I never thought to question the truth of her knowledge or how she'd gained it.

"She was terrified of water," Mama told me more than once.

"She had nightmares she was going to drown in dark water." Here, Mama's voice would drop and she'd shiver. "That girl had a premonition. Even as a child. She *knew* she was going to drown." Mama used to say that Natalie drowning off Santa Catalina Island was the saddest thing she'd ever heard. Sometimes the way she acted each November 29—the day Natalie died—it was like our family really had lost blood. Mama's sister. Her twin.

Once Daddy gave in, Mama put her plan into action. Before two weeks passed, she'd wangled traveling money out of my Uncle Grayson, bought her ticket and new luggage, and talked the people at the Lynchburg AAA out of a map even though she wasn't a member. Then one night, Daddy drove her to the train. I was asleep when Mama departed, but I always had a clear picture of how she must have looked holding her gray suitcase and a one-track resolve that would not be refused.

I stared at the blonde in the feather boa. I missed my mama so much, it hurt to take a full breath. All the wanting in my heart, all of the missing her was focused on that poster and the possibilities it possessed. The moment I'd seen the sign sitting on the easel and Raylene explained what it was about, I'd known I had to do it, too. As I said, I had plans. Of course, I knew better than to tell anyone in Eden. Not much remained a secret in a small town like ours, and *nothing* was a secret at Raylene's. My plan was this: Like Mama, I was going to be a movie star. Hollywood, for all its falseness, would be more forgiving than acting in New York. For example, you didn't have to know all the lines at the same time. Just the one day's worth.

I recognize the possibility that Mama was the one who had

planted the idea of acting in me, but it was not as unreasonable a dream as you might think. Two years before, when I was only a freshman at Eden, I'd played Emily Webb in the drama club production of *Our Town* and when I delivered Emily's speech on learning about life, people were actually crying. For a fact, Mama would have been proud. She would say I got all my talent from her.

The handicap to my goal was my looks; to tell you the truth, I resemble my daddy a lot more than my mama. For sure, I would never be confused for any famous actress. Except *maybe* Jodie Foster if she were a little plainer and her jaw a little bigger. Talent will take you so far, but Hollywood wants more. To be taken seriously, you must be beautiful. You might argue that there are plenty of actresses out there who aren't Miss America material, or Miss Amherst County for that matter, but—even if they do win an acting award—you'll notice they don't get their picture in *People.* Character actors, they call them, which is about the worst thing you can say. Like they are a cartoon or something. I had no intention of ending up like that.

This is where my mama would have come in handy. I know if she could have taken me in hand, a transformation would be easy. Without Mama, *Glamour Day* was my best shot. It was my ticket out of Eden. My pass to L.A.

I already had my name picked out. (Most actresses change their name, a fact you may not know. According to Mama, Carole Lombard—the actress who married Clark Gable who played Rhett Butler in *Gone With the Wind*—well, she was born Jane Alice Peters. You can see how Carole Lombard was a big improvement.) My movie name was going to be Taylor Skye. Taylor for Mama's daddy. Skye for Mama. On account of her always saying that the sky's the limit, a philosophy she passed on to me. For pure fact, my personal limit was not going to be Eden. Or the Klip-N-Kurl.

Twenty bucks was a dog-cheap price to pay for a dream, and I had two weeks to come up with the cash. The problem was every penny Raylene paid me went to help with groceries or my Daddy's bar bill at CC's. I was determined to find a way. Goody always said I inherited my stubbornness from Mama.

Word about *Glamour Day* spread quickly, and by midafternoon the sign-up sheet was nearly filled. Most of the women who added their names were middle-aged and looked like they could use some glamour. Mary Lou Duval was going through her fourth divorce. Ellie Sue Rucker was six months along with her third. Trashy Bitty Weatherspoon, who drove around town in her new boyfriend's gold Camaro like she was still reigning prom queen, worked nights at the chicken factory. Aubrey Boles, complete with her dyed black hair twirled up in a beehive, added her name to the sheet. My mama believed it was a mistake for a woman to go jet-black. She was fond of pointing out how much improved Priscilla Presley looked after she lightened up her hair. Elizabeth Taylor could get away with it, Mama maintained, because of her pure coloring and those violet eyes.

Willa Jenkins, another regular, signed up, too. She said Raylene was the only white woman she knew who understood black people's hair. She'd talked two of her friends into joining her. Of course, it was a surprise to no one when Ashley Wheeler heard about it and came in. Ashley had an inflated opinion of herself, a view consistently reinforced by her mama and a good share of the male enrollment at UVA. Day or night, Ashley had a smile plastered on her face, looking all sweetness, pure proof that looks do lie.

By five o'clock, there was only one opening left. I'd spent the entire day thinking on how I could earn the twenty dollars and keep it secret from my daddy. I had two weeks to find a way. I just had to keep faith, like Mama was always reminding me. Before we closed up, I added my name to the list. Raylene gave me a little hug when she saw me filling the last slot. Like most people in town, she felt sorry I didn't have a mama. We stood there and stared at the perfect Hollywood blonde with the pink boa all framed in gold.

"Your mama," Raylene said. "Your mama would have loved this."

And she would have. Mama most surely would have.

★ Tallie's Book ★

Don't make Divinity Fudge on rainy days.

Plant spring bulbs in the fall; drop a tablespoon of bonemeal in the hole.

Scald the milk before adding to sponge cake batter.

Take care not to let other people push their dreams on you.

The sky's the limit.

You just have to keep faith.

two

*r*aylene was dead right about how my mama would have
loved *Glamour Day*. I could just picture Mama in the shop
taking charge and bossing everyone around while we got
gussied up to look like movie stars. I missed her so much
then, I could have perished with the wanting. You'd think by
that time I would be used to my mama being gone, but I
wasn't.

My stomach ached with the queer emptiness that came
whenever I thought about her, and I considered heading over
to Simpson's Cash Store and buying a couple of Milky Ways.
Then I thought about how I'd be needing every quarter I could
get my hands on to put toward the twenty dollars for *Glamour
Day*. Besides, by then I knew the big, hollow hole of Mama's ab-
sence wasn't anything a candy bar could fill.

I wanted someone to talk to, someone who would make it
seem as if at least part of Mama were still around. My daddy
couldn't help. Without Mama he was so sad and lonely it was
like I had to take care of both him and me. Finally I settled on

Martha Lee. She wasn't near like Mama, but she was the closest I was going to get.

Martha Lee lived over on the north side of town, a good six miles away. I had no money to be paying Mr. Tinsley for any taxi ride, and with the heat, which had been shooting up steady for a week and now rose off the pavement in waves, I wasn't up to the walk. I had no choice but the Raleigh. Sixteen years old and riding a bike. I might as well have been carting a neon-goddamn-sign saying: *Retard*.

It was four-thirty, the sleepy time of day when there wasn't much traffic, and I was taking up a good share of the road, pedaling hard to get there before anyone witnessed the humiliating sight of me on the Raleigh. I passed the old Tyree house and— predictable as can be—there were the Tyree sisters sitting in a row on the porch. Violet, Myrtle, and Rose. The Flowers, Mama used to call them. They had to be at least ninety. As I rode by, all three waved, their hands rising up in unison, as if connected by one invisible string.

Past the Tyree house, the sidewalk ended and the road got narrower. I continued on past Miss Easter Davis's place and then by the run-down shack where the cripple Charlie McDaniel lived. Before Charlie got polio and had to walk on crutches, my daddy went to school with him and he could remember a time when Charlie walked straight as anyone. I looked directly ahead when I went by. The last thing I needed was to see Charlie. The sight of him always made me sad. But mad, too. Like somehow the two feelings were mixed up together.

I was almost at Martha Lee's, just turning onto High Tower Road, when I heard a car honking on my heels. I pretended to ignore it, but it slowed down and my worst nightmare sprang up in living color. There was Elizabeth Talmadge in the yellow soft-top Jeep her daddy'd bought for her. An early graduation present, she said. A whole year early. Seemed like everything came early to Elizabeth. Early and easy. She was the lead twirler for the Sparkettes and acted like that made her Queen of the World. The car was filled with kids dressed in swimsuits, heading out to Elders Pond no doubt.

"Hey, Tallie," Elizabeth yelled. She slowed down like we were best friends or something but really to take pleasure in my humiliation. I was probably the only sixteen-year-old in the entire Commonwealth of Virginia who didn't have a license, let alone a car. If the universe were fair, Elizabeth would get a serious case of acne. Or eczema. Ringworm. But if I knew one thing for sure it was that the universe didn't bother itself about being fair, so pure-skinned girls like Elizabeth Talmadge got to drive around in Jeep soft-tops while I rode a rusty Raleigh, sweaty as a hard-broke horse. Still, I had legs like a lifeguard, while the Queen of the World's were soft as Wonder Bread.

I looked straight ahead, like it was a good thing to be riding a bike, like I was riding it by choice, like I was in training for that important bike race over in France, like maybe I was going to escape with the least amount of humiliation.

"Hey, Tallie," a boy called.

My ears would have recognized Spaulding (everybody called him Spy) Reynolds's voice if he'd been speaking out in a crowd in the center of Washington, D.C. I felt heat flood my chest and rise up in patches to my throat and cheeks.

I stood on the pedals, ignoring him, and pumped furiously.

"What's the matter, Bullwinkle? Cat got your tongue?"

I was pumping so hard, I pulled right ahead of the stupid
Jeep.

"Nice ass," someone said. Not Spy. I didn't *think* it was Spy.

"Shit heels," I said aloud. I pictured the way I must have
looked, all red-faced and sweaty in ripped jeans, looking like
the poor trash they all thought I was. I wished my mama was
around. Mama'd see to it that I had *style*. If my mama were
there, Elizabeth Talmadge would freeze in her tracks, just
struck dumb with my style. Then I remembered the *Glamour
Day* photo. My ticket out of Eden. I swore that before I headed
for Hollywood I was going to make sure that Elizabeth got a
look at it. And Spy Reynolds, too. I wanted him to see me looking like a movie star. For once—just once—looking prettier
than any girl in town, even Miss Sparkette, the Queen of the
Universe herself.

Elizabeth punched the gas pedal and left me in a patch of
dust. "Shit heels," I yelled after her.

Martha Lee's house wasn't exactly a trailer, but as near as a place
could be without actually having wheels. Mama'd said she lived
there to spite her daddy. Samuel Curtis owned half of Eden, but
you wouldn't have a clue to that by anything Martha Lee did.

Her pickup wasn't in the drive, so I fished the key out from
under the cracked slab of black stone by the front steps and let
myself in. The place was in its normal state, which is to say pure
mess. I'm not the world's greatest housekeeper, but you'd need
a front-end loader to make a serious dent at Martha Lee's.

It wasn't because she was lazy. She was an LPN and didn't
mind taking on the dirty jobs. Anyone who would change an
old lady's diaper and bathe old men wasn't shirking work.

Mama always used to say Martha Lee was a saint. And maybe she was, though my piddling knowledge of saints made it hard to picture a holy person drinking and smoking and leaving a week's worth of laundry heaped on the floor.

While I was waiting, I put a load of wash in the machine, wiped down the counters, then swiped myself a beer and went to sit on the steps. Most of the yard was as run-down as the house, but off to one side was just the prettiest patch you could imagine, where Martha Lee had planted hydrangeas and zinnias and hibiscus with blossoms as big as a meat platter. There were tomato plants I had to look up to, and bush beans with marigolds laced between each plant. Nothing was neat or in rows like most people's gardens, but it was so pretty and rich it looked like the Garden of Eden. Lush is what Mama used to call Martha Lee's garden, and the word set exactly right.

Whatever Martha Lee did with her yard would have been perfectly fine with Mama. They had been best friends since second grade, although no one in Eden could figure how two girls so different could be tighter than the knot on a noose. Daddy called them the original odd couple, and I had to agree with him there.

Martha Lee Curtis was, Jesus forgive me, the plainest woman in Eden. The kind of homely that was hard not to stare at, even if you've seen her all your life, which I had.

Mama was nothing if not delicate. She was the kind of woman who could put a gardenia in her hair and not look foolish. The flower sat there like it had spent every moment of its short but flawless life just waiting to be pinned in that bed of dark curls. For a fact, no one on earth would even consider fixing flowers in Martha Lee's hair. A flower would just up and shrivel at the prospect of landing anywhere near her head. I think men felt pretty much the same. Even Mama, who had a kind word for every drunk and fool in Eden, even Mama didn't protest very long when Daddy said Martha Lee's face would stop a blind mule dead in its tracks.

Martha Lee was a big woman. And she didn't hold much truck with personal grooming. Half a block away you could tell she cut her own hair. And she didn't know about things like using the juice of a lemon to bring out the shine. Mama used to encourage her to pluck her eyebrows and give lipstick a shot, but Martha Lee couldn't be bothered. My personal theory—which I've given a lot of thought to—is that if you look like she does, early on you give up even trying.

I was maybe seven or eight when my mama began her earnest campaign to get Martha Lee to pluck. She used her own eyebrows as the example to which Martha Lee should aspire. I would sit in the corner of my mama's bedroom and watch her working till the brows of her arches were as neat and perfect as Greta Garbo's, an old actress Mama greatly admired, along with Carole Lombard, who died eight years before Mama was born and, like Garbo, had pencil-line brows.

When Mama attended to her own, it was a precise and perfect ritual. Her eyes would narrow against the stream of smoke curling up from the ashtray on her dresser and she would lean in close to her reflection, smooth a fingertip over the patch of skin beneath her brow and then, with a sharp jerk, yank out a stray hair. She never so much as winced, although I know for a fact that it had to hurt. I myself tried it once, and I want to tell you it made my eyes water something fierce. I can see why Mariel Hemingway chose not to pluck, although I know Mama would have believed it would advance her career if she thinned them just the littlest bit. This was a theory she employed to explain the acting career of Joan Crawford, who, Mama said, was beautiful early on when she waxed her brows, but as soon as she let them grow out thick as a man, all she got was those creepy roles. This was pure fact. I don't think Mama could even bear to watch Brooke Shields.

So for years Mama had been dying to get her hands on Martha Lee. Mama maintained thin brows would be the start of a big improvement—a *transformation*—but Martha Lee would pop the tab on another can of Pabst, light two more Salems for herself and Mama, and laugh her big laugh. "You can't transform the hound dog into the flea," she'd say. In most things, I stood firmly on Mama's side, but I was glad Martha Lee held her ground. I couldn't picture her with nervous Garbo brows.

I took another sip of my beer and watched while a hawk circled over a stand of white ash to the left of Martha Lee's house. I knew he was only searching for his dinner, but I started thinking about how that bird had a big picture of everything on the ground, a *context* for things, and I had to wonder how my life would look if I could see it from a distance instead of always being stuck in the middle. I wondered if things somehow would settle easier in our hearts if we could see the whole picture of our life while we were living it, like the hawk's view of the ground, instead of jangly bits and pieces that didn't seem to fit.

I was still drinking the beer, enjoying the prickly feeling it brought to my forehead, and staring at Martha Lee's garden and reminding myself that things didn't always have to be laid out straight as string to make sense, when her truck pulled in the yard.

"Hey, there, Cookie," she said, like she expected to find me there.

"Hi," I said, stashing the beer below the steps.

"How's things going at the Flip-N-Furl?" Martha Lee had a deep disdain for Raylene's shop. Then and there I decided to keep the facts about *Glamour Day* to myself. Telling Martha Lee wouldn't be one bit like telling Mama.

She kicked off her shoes, then—right in the front yard—stripped off her nurse's uniform, which sported some kind of stain on the front that was gross-gross-gross, an orange splotch that made me queasy just to look at it. I didn't even want to *think* about where that might have come from. I went in the house and grabbed a clean T-shirt and cutoff jeans for her to cover herself with. Martha Lee in bra and panties was not a sight you'd want to be spending much time looking at. Not like Mama, who could have modeled for Victoria's Secret if she'd wanted to.

"How's your daddy faring?" she asked as she got dressed. You didn't need a translator to know she was really trying to determine if he'd been drinking.

"He's okay." Course he was drinking, but without Mama, my daddy was so lost, it was hard to stay mad at him. And he still kept his job at the mill. In our town, a drinker who held his job wasn't an alcoholic, just a man enduring a streak of bad luck.

"What about you?"

It was so good to have someone listening to me, I reeled off my list of complaints, starting with the scene with stuck-up Elizabeth Talmadge, who was *so* obvious, it was pathetic. Then I told her how I was the only one in my class who couldn't drive and how my daddy said he'd teach me but never had the time when he was sober and after he stopped at CC's you wouldn't want to go with him unless you planned on ending up in some culvert counting broken bones. Finally, despite myself, I told her the whole thing about the Glamour Company coming to Raylene's and how there was a team of trained professionals who did your makeup and how you got to pick out five outfits and how they took your picture and you got to keep one. "Raylene says they make you look like a star," I told her, but she didn't seem the least interested or say anything like Mama would have.

"I miss Mama," I finally said.

"I miss her, too, Cookie," she said. She went in to get herself a beer and then rejoined me on the steps.

Back that summer, when Mama returned home from Hollywood, a full day hadn't passed when Martha Lee showed up. Though I wanted to keep Mama to myself, I wasn't completely sorry to see Martha Lee's pickup turn into the yard. I'd been impatient for facts, and Martha Lee would see to it that Mama'd start talking. You could count on it. They didn't have a secret between them.

The second Martha Lee hit the ground, Mama was out the door and across the yard. They'd grabbed each other and started twirling in circles, squealing like baby pigs. I'd had to bite back a taste I knew was jealousy—Mama hadn't acted half so happy to see me—and trailed after them as they headed for the house. With the two of them sitting in the kitchen, it was just like old times. Although it wasn't yet ten A.M., Mama opened the refrigerator and got out a couple of bottles of beer.

She set them on the table, not even bothering with glasses. Martha Lee took out a pack of Salems, lit two, then handed one to Mama. I hung around the door, trying to look invisible. This was my best chance to find out the precise details of what Mama had been doing for those months and whether she had come close to accomplishing what she'd set out for. Of course, Mama spotted me right off. "Tallie, sugar, be a good girl and go play. Martha Lee and me got some catching up to do. Girl talk."

"But I'm a girl."

Mama took a long drag on her Salem and gave me her *I'm not fooling here* look. "Go on with you."

"But, Mama," I'd wailed. This was my chance, and I couldn't pass it up without a fight.

"Go on, now. I mean it."

I'd slammed the screen door in protest, and sat on the glider, pretending to read about Scarlett and trying to overhear the conversation in the kitchen. By then I'd decided that, despite all the postcards with the hurried messages about her life at Paramount Pictures, Mama hadn't gotten the part in the movie. Like she said, there sure wasn't any Cadillac sitting in our drive. But if she hadn't snagged the role, what had kept her out there for six months? And why wasn't she telling me?

I slid off the swing and crept closer to the door, taking care to step over the board that squeaked.

"Tallie's grown," Mama said. "She's nearly a woman. Lord, it nearly broke my heart to look at her."

I felt a flash of satisfaction and crept even closer, though it meant risking discovery.

"She was the one I was nervous about. After her, I knew Luddy would be easy."

"Luddy will always be easy where you're concerned, Deanie," Martha Lee said. Something in her voice almost made my daddy's love for Mama sound like a failing.

Mama gave a sigh. I heard the scratch of a match, and a minute later cigarette smoke came through the screen onto the porch. "Lord, it's weird to be back," Mama said. "Like swimming under water with your eyes open."

I heard her inhale deeply, then expel a lungful of smoke. "I mean, things seem the same, yet changed. Not just Tallie growing up. Little things, too. Dishes stacked in different cupboards. Chairs moved. Like it's not my house anymore."

"What did you expect?" Martha Lee said.

"I don't know," Mama said.

"It's been six months. Things change."

I looked around. Not one thing about our house seemed changed to me.

"Maybe it's like that writer said," Mama said. "Maybe we really can't go home again."

My heart stopped beating.

"Or maybe," Mama continued, "maybe that poet got it right. Maybe home is the place where when you go there, they have to take you in."

Have to take you in? Didn't Mama think we wanted her here? Was she mad because I'd changed a few dishes around? Was she going to leave again? If she did, would it be my fault?

"Maybe both are true," Martha Lee said.

"Sometimes," Mama said, "sometimes I think all opposites are true." She gave a little laugh and started to sing "I'm just a walking contradiction" in her Kristofferson imitation. Off-key, as usual.

After that, things were quiet for a while, then Mama asked, "Do you think I was selfish? Going off the way I did?"

"It's done, Cookie," Martha Lee said. "You did what you had to do."

"That's not what Goody'd say," Mama said. "My mama'd surely say I was selfish. She's called me selfish since I could walk, and I guess I can't rightly argue with her. 'You're the center of your own universe, Dinah Mae,' she'd say."

"What child isn't?" Martha Lee said.

"I guess I just didn't outgrow it," Mama said.

"We seldom outgrow our foolishnesses, Cookie."

"Goody would say that's dressing it up, calling it foolishness. She'd call it plain sin, what I did."

Sin? A mosquito landed on my arm, but I didn't flinch him off. I didn't even breathe.

"Lord, it's confusing," Mama said. "We're given one life, and what we do with it—foolishness or glory or a mix of the two—is what we've got to answer for in the end."

"According to some," Martha Lee said.

I listened hard while Mama went right on. "And it doesn't seem to matter if life is marked by days or weeks or years. It's too little, whatever the measure. It's a hard thing to figure, how to live life—the one life we've been given—and how to be true to yourself and to those you love. I just don't know how to figure it out."

"Who does?" Martha Lee said.

"I hope I have time left to do it in," Mama said, and then added something more, but her voice was too soft to hear. When I stepped in closer, the porch floor creaked underfoot.

"Little pitcher," Mama called out. "Your ears will burn up, you go listening to what isn't meant for you."

I backed away, back to the glider, and picked up my book. "What, Mama?" I called in my most innocent voice.

I'd been glad to stop listening. My brain hurt with all Mama said about sin, and not being able to go home again, and the puzzle of attempting to be true to yourself. I retreated to the safe distance of life at Tara. I'd reached the part where Scarlett was thinking how Rhett knew exactly what she was thinking and how odious it was for a man to know what was in a woman's mind.

I sat on the glider and considered that idea. What if we could read minds? Then I would know everything my mama had been doing and what she was planning next. The snippets of conversation I heard about drove me mad. "Can you be sure?" . . . "see her again" . . . "give up hope" . . . "another big mistake."

If we could read minds, I thought, I'd have some warning if Mama was planning on leaving us again, which had been my big fear ever since she climbed out of Mr. Tinsley's taxi, though I'd tried to erase the idea. I pictured us the night before, eating the dinner Mama had prepared and watching TV. I consoled myself with this image and the way things seemed to have returned to the way they were before Mama got the Holly-wood dream stuck in her head.

Much later, the sound of the refrigerator door closing brought me back. Then I thought I heard someone crying, but I must have been mistaken, because not one second later I heard the unmistakable sound of Mama's laughter.

The sun was straight overhead, and I was hungry.

"Hi, darlin'," Mama said when I went in. The tabletop was littered with empty Pabst bottles.

Martha Lee was staring off through the window, avoiding my gaze. I got a can of tuna out of the cupboard. Mama reached for another Salem.

"You sure you should?" Martha Lee said.

A little late to be asking, I thought. The whole kitchen stank of smoke.

"Don't start," Mama said, lighting up.

"I mean that with my heart," Martha Lee said. "Not as criticism."

"I know. I know."

When I turned to ask Mama if she wanted a sandwich, I caught the way they were looking at each other. I was mistaken about everything being like it used to be. Something had changed, but I didn't know what.

Weeks would pass and the tomatoes in Martha Lee's garden would turn from green to red before I would learn that Mama's coming home had nothing to do with movies and not getting the part.

I was trying to decide if I dared reach for the beer I'd hidden under the steps, when Martha Lee offered me a swig from hers, but all I could picture were the germs sitting on the can top, and that stopped me cold. That was one thing I was particular about. You would be amazed at the number of germs in the average person's mouth. Dogs are even worse. "No, thanks," I said.

If Mama were around, this would be the time they'd start telling tales, the "Remember" stories I called them 'cause they always started out with "Remember when we . . ."

"Martha Lee?" I said after a minute.

"Yeah?"

"Tell me a 'Remember' story." I sounded like a baby. I didn't care.

She stared off into the woods that ringed her property.

"A Duane one," I said.

When they were girls, every Halloween, Mama and Martha Lee would fashion a dummy out of straw and dress it up in my granddaddy's old clothes. Then they would dream up a prank using the dummy. They named every dummy Duane, after this boy who had such a crush on Mama in the fifth grade that he told her he'd shoot himself if she didn't go to the movies with him. Sometimes, at night in bed, I'd imagine Spy Reynolds telling me he'd kill himself if I didn't go out with him. I'll have to think about it, I always said, before I conceded, not wanting his death on my conscience. "Did Duane really die?" I asked Mama once. "Better," Martha Lee said. "He ended up marrying Effie Webb." And naturally this would set them off.

Sometimes, when they started telling these stories, they would laugh so hard—scream with laughter, actually—that Mama had to beg Martha Lee to stop or she'd pee her pants. They must have told these stories a hundred times, but each time they'd laugh like it was something they'd done only the week before.

One Halloween they took one of the Duanes to the overpass south of town and then waited for the ten o'clock that went from Washington to New Orleans. When they saw the lights making the curve, they lifted Duane and tossed him over the fence and onto the rails. Even knowing it was a straw-filled sack of my granddaddy's clothes, they gasped at how it looked like a real man lying down there on the rail bed. Then, to hear them tell it, all hell broke loose. Mama maintained you could hear the squeal of the engineer laying on the brakes all the way to Memphis. Next, in what looked like slow motion, the train derailed. It just folded up like a child's toy and bucked off the track. Mama and Martha Lee took off, heading for the woods by Elders Pond. They stayed there half the night, listening to the sound of sirens crying in the distance.

"We could go to jail for that," Martha Lee kept whispering to Mama, "it's a felony or something," and Mama kept telling her to shut up. The story was front page for a week. By some miracle no one was seriously injured, but even so, the state police were called in to investigate. Mama and Martha Lee made whispered phone calls every day all that week, agreeing they'd confess if Duane's clothes were traced to my granddaddy, even if it meant they'd go to jail.

The Doberman story was my favorite. That Halloween they were sixteen and had heard about a monastery just over the border in Kentucky where the monks raised Dobermans. They borrowed Samuel Curtis's car, the one papered with *God Is the Answer* and *Jesus Cares About You* stickers on it—which, in the telling, only made the whole thing funnier—and headed for Kentucky with Duane the Dummy sitting up front with them, riding shotgun. They got lost twice before they finally found the place and got to toss Duane over the chain-link fence. Within minutes, those old Dobermans went crazy, barking and yapping and spitting drool. "They went ape shit," Mama used to say. Then the whole place lit up, and all these bald monks came running out of the house dressed in their underwear. They would repeat this part to each other over and over, crying with laughter.

Once, Goody was there when they were telling the Doberman

story and she got up and stomped out. "That's a fine good example you two are setting for Natasha," she sniffed, which only set Mama and Martha Lee off again, doubled over and peeing their pants.

"Tell me a Duane story," I said again.

Martha Lee lit a cigarette and stared off in the distance.

"The one about the monks and the Dobermans," I prodded.

She reached over and ruffled my hair. We sat there listening to the catbirds. She never said a word.

I know what she meant. It wasn't the same.

We sat awhile longer, then I got on my bike and knocked back the kickstand.

I was pedaling down the drive when Martha Lee called after me. "Hey, Tallie."

"Yeah?"

"The Furl is closed on Monday, right?"

"Right."

"Come over Monday morning."

"What for?" I didn't even turn around. It wasn't her fault Mama was gone, but the heaviness was setting so hard in my chest that I had to punish someone.

"Well, do you want to learn to drive or don't you?"

Daddy wasn't home when I got there.

I'd forgotten to stop at the Cash Store, so there wasn't much in the house to eat. Sometimes I got so tired of cooking and keeping house, I'd pray that Daddy'd get married again. Rula Wade said after she got used to her step-mama, it wasn't half bad.

But I didn't really want another mama. What I wanted was my own mama back. I would have given anything for her to be standing at the stove preparing supper. Pan-fried catfish and butter beans. Or her potato pancakes with applesauce. Or her salmon patties with white sauce. Blackberry cobbler for dessert.

I heated up some canned spaghetti. Fried with some chopped bacon and onions, it wasn't so bad. After supper I went to my room and got my notebook. Sometimes, when I was missing Mama fierce, I'd read over the list I'd made of everything I remembered about her, starting with the easy things, like when she was born and stuff about her parents and her brother, Grayson, and where she went to school, and how she met and married my daddy.

They met at a dance in Lynchburg. You wouldn't think it to look at my daddy, but that man can really dance. Mama said that was what first attracted her to him, but what made her fall in love was his smile. "He had the most beautiful smile," Mama used to tell me. "The first time I saw that smile I just fell ass over bandbox in love."

At first I liked the story about my daddy's smile and how it had the power to win my mama, but after a while, when I really thought about it, it made me nervous. It was unsettling to think of a simple thing like a smile having the power to change a person's life. I was too young to know a person could want that kind of thing, could give herself over to it, regardless of consequences. As it turned out, losing yourself over something as simple as a smile was what the women in our family did. Like marrying down.

When I first started making the lists about my mama, I'd put on her red cashmere sweater and breathe in a mixture of My Sin and cigarette smoke. I did this until the smell wore out. I'd write down all the things she used to do. Like how when I was

real little she'd pretend her eye pencils were little kings and
queens and would make up stories, putting on and taking off
their sharpener-top crowns. And how sometimes she made
hand puppets out of rolled-up socks. And how she could walk
with a book on her head, could even go up and down stairs
without it sliding off. And, if she and Daddy had been out late
the night before, how she'd lie on the rug and put cucumber
slices over her eyes and make me do it, too. I'd write about how
she loved to dance. She could do the Twist and the Chicken and
all sorts of dances with weird names that she taught me. She
could boogie like a backup singer, shaking till you'd think her
tits might fall off. Mama was the only adult woman I knew who
could stand on her head.

At school they made me go to a therapist for a while. "How
are you doing?" he asked me the first time I went, which was
such a stupid question, I didn't even bother to answer. I mean,
duh. How did he think I was doing? Then he asked me to talk
to him about Mama, so I told him some of the things on my
list. He listened like he really cared and then he asked me if I
thought it was possible that maybe I was "idolizing" her, and
after that I didn't say a word to him. They'd pull me out of P.E.,
and I'd go sit in his dumb office and stare at him and not say one
thing and finally they stopped making me go.

Another thing. Mama loved birds. And butterflies, which
she said were bugs with birds' souls. She was plumb crazy about
butterflies. She got chickadees to come and eat seed from the
palm of her hand. And she knew the Indian names for all the
full moons. Names like Snow Moon, and Feather Shedding
Moon, Strawberry Moon, and Travel in Canoes Moon. And she
could recite by heart all the lyrics of songs from the '40s to the

'80s. Even the sad old ones like "Isle of Capri" and "Streets of Laredo," and she'd sing them loud. Pat Boone. Little Richard. Elvis. The Platters. Patsy Cline. Barbra Streisand. Reba. She knew them all. The other thing was she had this really bad voice. She couldn't hold a tune in a ten-gallon pail.

Mama taught me things that I kept written down in a book I called my rules for living. Forks go on the left. Always stand tall. Everything tastes better with a little salt. Everything. And if you really, truly want something, you can have it.

Which wasn't true.

All the wanting in the world wasn't going to bring my mama back.

★ Tallie's Book ★

Forks go on the left.

Everything tastes better with salt.

Always stand tall.

Things don't always require a pattern to make sense.

Use the juice of a lemon to bring out the shine in your hair.

three

*W*anting hasn't one blessed thing to do with the way things turn out. Or with what ends up coming our way. During the winter of 1988, when Mama was off pursuing her dream, I'd spent every waking moment wanting her back. But when she came home that June, I still wasn't satisfied. I wore discontent like a second skin. I wanted *more*. I wanted everything to turn back exactly the way it used to be, as if she'd never gone away.

I wanted Mama to restore order to our lives. Instead, she acted like every rule ever made was designed for other people. Later I wondered how I could have missed this neon clue that something was wrong. Nobody changed overnight like that. Not without a reason.

Before she went to Hollywood, Mama used to take pride in her housekeeping even though our house wasn't much, nothing like Mama's childhood home. "You deserve better," Goody used to tell her, which was her common theme. By "better" we all knew she meant better than my daddy. According to

Goody, Mama's marriage to my daddy was the biggest disappointment in her life.

"It killed your daddy," she'd tell Mama. "Just killed him."

"The thing that killed my daddy was living with you," Mama'd shoot back. "If anything gave Daddy a heart attack it was living with you." Mama was the sweetest thing in three counties; Goody alone could make her take off like that.

Anyway, after Mama came home from L.A., all the rules went out the window. She left dishes in the sink and the beds unmade. She drank soda for breakfast and didn't check to see if I'd brushed my teeth at night. She didn't make me wait an hour to go swimming after I ate. "An old wives' tale," she said, although the summer before, if I'd taken so much as one bite of a soda cracker, I would have to sit on the blanket and wait for a full sixty minutes to be marked off on her watch.

That summer, I spent a lot of time swimming at the creek, working to get in shape for the swim team and outdo Sarah Reynolds, my biggest competition. Sarah was small, like Mama, but she was tough. A good swimmer. We were school friends. She was a rich girl, but not a bitch girl like the others who lived up on the hill in two-story houses. Back then, my biggest secret, the one I even kept from Mama, was the crush I had on Sarah's older brother, Spaulding. If I married Spy, I'd be marrying up for damn sure.

All the other kids went over to Elders Pond to swim, so Mama and me would have the creek to ourselves. While I practiced the breaststroke and crawl, Mama'd lie stretched out on the blanket, smoking and calling out instructions. "Head down, Tallie," she'd yell. "Legs straight. Keep your legs straight."

Buoyed by the water and Mama's attention, I would lock my knees and flutter kick, knifing through the creek, growing stronger every day. Florence Griffith Joyner was setting records in the U.S. Olympic Trials that summer, and Mama cut out pictures of her and pasted them on my mirror. For inspiration, she said. For a role model. Mama said Flo-Jo proved a woman could be loaded with glamour and win medals, too. It was a useful thing to know, she said.

On the way home from the creek, we usually stopped at the Dairy Queen. Mama drove a used Dodge with rusted-out rocker panels, but she'd pull right up to the drive-thru like she was driving a new Buick. One afternoon she unfolded a twenty that my Uncle Grayson had sent her. "Get whatever you want," she said. This wild permission so unhinged me, I settled for a single cone, no dip. "You sure that's all?" she asked, then ordered a butterscotch sundae for herself. With whipped cream and extra nuts. And she didn't jiggle her knee, her tip-off sign that she was nervous about something like spending too much. Mama told me that whenever Daddy was feeling bad about something he did, he'd whistle an old Bo Diddley tune called "I'm A Man." He didn't know he did it, and Mama didn't tell him. And I never told Mama about her knee jiggling.

Nothing was predictable about Mama that summer. Some nights we'd have cereal for dinner. Other times she'd fry up a chicken. One day she spent the whole week's food budget on a leg of lamb. "For a barbecue," she'd announced. I watched while she sliced an entire bulb of garlic into little slivers and stuck them in the meat. Then she put it on a platter and coated it with oil. A marinade, she called it, which sounded like something she must have learned about in California. Then she made a little tent for it out of aluminum foil and set it over coals on our old charcoal grill. All afternoon, while she napped and I rested on the glider and read, the smell of cooking meat filled my throat and drew the Bettises' yard dog. Later, when Mama took the lamb off the grill, it was lumpy and black, charred beyond recognition, but instead of being upset—all that work, all that money—she just laughed and tossed it to Old Straw.

Nights after supper, she took the food left on the table and, instead of wrapping it for another meal, tossed it outside for the birds. "I don't plan on eating one more sorry leftover ever again," she told us. Raccoons took up residence beneath our back stoop. I expected Daddy to complain and talk about how money didn't grow in a garden, but he didn't say one word.

As if to make up for the reckless wastefulness of Mama, I hoarded things. Silver foil I'd peel off gum wrappers. Pieces of string. Elastic bands. Anything I could get my hands on. I would have saved the songs coming out of the radio if I could have figured a way to draw them from the air. I picked up soda cans in roadside ditches and biked over to the Cash Store to turn them in for the deposit. Every morning I counted the pile of change.

"What're you saving for?" Mama asked me one day.

"Nothing," I said. I was rolling nickels into a coin wrapper I'd picked up at First Federal. "Just saving." She watched while I counted out fifty pennies and slid them into their paper cylinder.

"Oh, baby," Mama said. "Forget saving. Use it up." She flung her arms wide and tossed back her head. "Spend it. All of it. Squander it."

Squander. The word gave me chills. I wanted to yell at my

mama that one of us had to be responsible. I was a miser that summer, holding on to everything, not yet knowing that no matter how tight we held on to things, they'd still slip away and there was no way on God's earth we could prevent it.

On Saturday, when I got to the shop, Raylene had Etta Bird under the dryer and was giving Miss Tilly Pettijohn a shampoo and a roll-up. On the house. Miss Tilly's husband, Lloyd, died back in the '50s, and except for a grown son who left town and never came back, she had no relatives. She and Raylene went way back, back to when Lloyd was alive and the Pettijohns had money. Now Miss Tilly went from month to month waiting for Mr. Rollins to deliver her Social Security check. According to Raylene, by the end of the month Miss Tilly reused tea bags so many times that if she asked you to sit and have a cup you had to figure out the date or you'd end up drinking tea so pale and watery it looked like pee.

Lenora was there. She had owned the shop before Raylene and was older than Moses, with fingers bent sideways from arthritis and eyes all filmy. Once or twice a month she liked to come in and do a few perms. "To keep my hand in," she said, but Raylene said it was because she got lonely and needed to feel useful. "Every living soul needs to feel useful," Raylene said.

Lenora was giving Pearl Summers a permanent, and the whole place stunk from the solution, one of the worst odors on God's green earth. With all the dumb inventions people come up with, you'd think someone could figure out a way to make the permanent wave solution smell better. Cinnamon would be good.

The place was abuzz with the comforting hum of women's voices. Usually I could pick up some information for my book. All I had to do was listen. Like the time Mary Lou Duval said a woman should never get hitched up with a man who wore more jewelry than she did, which made sense to me, so I copied it down. Cora Giles and Effie Bailey were talking about whether or not Bitty Weatherspoon was knocked up by her new boyfriend, but that was nothing I wanted to add to my notebook.

I got out the broom and swept up the clippings from Etta Bird's cut. Etta was stuck under a dryer revealing her latest revelation to Miss Tilly. Etta was about ninety-two, but she was real peppy and still got around good. And she was always having a *revelation* of one kind or another. It could run from big things like Jesus appearing in a dream to minor stuff like rain on the way. I swept around the chairs and the edges of the rubber floor mat, taking care to get every gray snip from Etta's cut so we wouldn't be tracking them around all day. Then I used the excuse of straightening out the magazines to go out front by the *Glamour Day* photo. By now I knew every detail: the attractive way the blonde's hair curled over one cheek and, on the other side, swept back behind an ear to reveal a crystal earring; the way her lipstick matched the feather boa; the precise way in which she held her hand beneath her chin, fingers slightly curled, a pose I had perfected in front of my mirror. I knew every particular by heart. There was nothing about that blonde even Mama could have thought to improve on.

Saturdays were always busy, and I got to shampoo Effie and Cora, which meant the possibility of two more tips to add to the two dollars and thirty-five cents I had managed to hide in

Mama's silver syrup pitcher. The pitcher once belonged to Goody, and before that to her mama. It was real silver and used to be just about my mama's favorite thing. She'd polished it every Saturday night and showed me how to use a toothbrush to get the engraved part clean. When Mama made us griddle cakes on Sundays, she'd set it out like we were eating in some fancy dining room instead of on a picnic table in the kitchen. Sometimes she used it to hide the money my Uncle Grayson sent her, which was where I got the idea to stash my *Glamour Day* money there. Two dollars and thirty-five cents. Seventeen and change to go. With luck, Cora would tip me fifty cents. Effie wasn't any sure bet. She was the kind of demanding customer who drove us crazy and didn't pay for the privilege.

"I want it *big*," she'd tell Raylene during the comb out. "Make it look big."

"I ain't no magician," Raylene complained about Effie. "That woman ain't got but three hairs on her head and two of them is damaged."

I rinsed Cora and worked in another dab of shampoo. (Wash, rinse, wash, rinse, then conditioner was how we did it.) I was lost in the pleasure of shampooing and half dreaming—thinking about Spy Reynolds was what I was doing—when Cora interrupted my thoughts.

"Tallie," she said. "Call Lenora over here. I need her to take a look."

I sighed, thinking, *This is all I need.*

The peculiar thing about Lenora was that she knew how to read soap bubbles. She said her mama had done it, too, that the gift ran in her family. Sometimes she'd be shampooing a head of hair and chatting on about how her son, Earl, was thinking of buying a place down at Virginia Beach or about how Earl's wife, Sophine, a woman Lenora couldn't abide, had aspirations beyond her place, or about how young Earl was doing up in Charlottesville, where he worked maintenance for the University and fathered such a brood of kids a person'd think they were Catholic, and she would pause right in the middle of a sentence and get this vague look on her face. Her hands would freeze and she'd fix her filmy old eyes on a patch of soap foam in the sink, like she was seeing it and not seeing it at the same time. "You're having a visitor this weekend," she'd announce to the woman tilted back under the faucet, who would say why, yes, that was right, she was expecting a second cousin from Richmond.

Lenora saw a whole world in those suds. Women with moles on their faces. Someone crying. People who walked with a limp. Weddings and funerals and money being spent too freely. Once she saw a rabbit in Mrs. Harewood's soap and told her to slow down, she was taking on too much. "Can't," Mrs. Harewood said. "Got too much to do." And then the next week she'd had a heart attack, which had slowed her down for good.

"Surprised I didn't see a dove," Lenora said when she heard the news. Death usually came in the shape of a dove, unless it was violent or tragic and then it was a horse. A heart meant a new friend. Or a bride. Flowers could mean a funeral or wedding; but usually they signified a celebration. Lenora said everyone had the gift—especially women—you just had to be open to it, to pay attention.

"Lenora," Cora yelled. "Come over here."

Lenora left off the permanent wave rollers she was putting in Pearl's hair and walked her arthritic shuffle over to the sink. Just watching her made your knees ache.

"My ruby ring," Cora said, "the one that belonged to Boyce's mama. It's lost."

Lenora sunk her hands into the helmet of suds and wrung up a handful that she flung into the basin. She stared at it like she was watching TV. I looked, too, but no matter what Lenora said about everyone having the ability, the gift, I just saw ordinary soapsuds.

"It's on the bedside table in your spare bedroom," Lenora declared after a minute.

"I remember now," Cora said. "I left it there when I was washing windows."

As if she'd done nothing more amazing than read the lunch menu at Wayland's Diner, Lenora dried off her hands and went back to rolling Pearl's hair. I *never* let Lenora shampoo me. Anything she could see in my hair, I wasn't wanting to know. It was better not to know. People liked to think it would help, but it wouldn't. I already knew the past, and there was no preparing for the future. For sure it wouldn't have made one bit of difference to me if I'd known back during that summer what was waiting ahead for Mama.

All that first month after Mama came back to us, I was edgy. I'd wake up at two or three in the morning, the heat of summer mixing in with the heft of waiting and soaking me through. Some nights I'd go out on the porch, hoping to catch a breeze. I'd open my shirt and let the air bathe me. Like Mama'd noticed, I had grown out. In the past few months I'd developed distinct breasts, and I was starting to have feelings about my body. I'd wrap the night around me and stare into the darkness while some unknown thing hung in the air like a promise, as

real as the fireflies that danced and sparked above the grass. I'd
never seen a firefly in daylight, but I pictured them like minia-
ture dragonflies. Delicate and nearly transparent.

One morning when she'd been back about three weeks,
Mama and I sat on the porch, drinking iced tea and playing gin
rummy. A pair of beetles settled on the railing, rear ends
hitched. "They're mating," Mama said.

"For real?" I said. I must have seen them hitched up like that
a hundred times, but I'd never known what they were up to.
"What are they?"

"Fireflies."

Well, that stopped me in my tracks. I couldn't have been
more surprised if she'd told me they were buffalo. It didn't
seem possible that those ordinary brown bugs were what pro-
duced the flickering light or that something so common, so
utilitarian was capable of producing magic. Mama said we see
what we want to see and that most beauty was an illusion anyway. She'd been staring at the beetles when she told me this.
"Change," she said suddenly. "Fireflies signify change."

I didn't like the sound of that one bit. "They do?"

"Absolutely. Beetles signify change." Mama knew all kinds of
things like that. Way back, there was Indian blood in Goody's
side of the family and whenever Mama wanted to get Goody's
goat, she'd bring that up. I was hoping this time she'd mistaken
the sign. I'd had about as much change as I could handle. But
even when I was given a clear indication of what lay ahead, I
turned my gaze and looked the other way. Back then I believed
it was possible to erase something if you pretended hard enough
that it wasn't happening. In that way, Mama and I were alike.

Some days, Martha Lee came with Mama and me to the

creek. While I swam, they'd spread out a blanket and play two-handed canasta and drink gin tonics from a Thermos. The mix of their laughter and cigarette smoke and Coppertone would float out to me.

When I finished swimming, I'd flop on a towel near them and pretend to be asleep, hoping they would forget I was there. I liked to eavesdrop, especially when they talked about men and sex. They'd argue about who was good-looking. Although Martha Lee thought he was overrated, Mama plain adored Elvis. She said that she'd let him put his boots under her bed anytime. Martha Lee said when she found a man whose boots were bigger than hers, then she'd let him stow them under her bed. Goody would have had a heart attack if she could have heard them carrying on. Between them they knew the secrets of womanhood, everything a girl could want to know. Mama knew how to dance, dress pretty, and flirt without looking foolish, and how to stuff a chicken and make biscuits, how to put on makeup and make everyone fall in love with her. Martha Lee knew practical stuff, like how to raise vegetables, drive a stick shift, and care for sick people. I wanted to learn it all.

One afternoon, after I'd practiced the crawl until my legs were limp, I spread my towel near them and fought not to drift off to sleep. The buzz of their words circled me. " . . . come so close . . . the punishing weight of secrets . . . only regret I didn't get to see Natalie's grave . . . thought there'd be plenty of time." Just before I fell asleep, I heard my name.

Some time later, I woke to their conversation. I kept my breathing steady, feigning sleep.

" . . . going to tell them?" Martha Lee was saying.

Mama was quiet.

"They'll have to know sooner or later."

Mama gave a thin, wispy sigh. "They'll find out soon enough."

I forgot how to breathe. *They'll find out soon enough.* Find out what? Then I realized it must mean that Mama was going to leave us again. I must have made a noise, because they stopped talking.

After that, I kept watch for the first sign betraying Mama's intent to leave. I stopped hanging out with the Bettis twins and stayed right at her side. I checked to make sure the gray suitcase stayed empty. Most nights, when everyone was sleeping, I continued to sit on the porch watching homely brown beetles night-altered into something special. Change, they flickered in the dark. *Change.* I'd concentrate on erasing their message and pray for things to stay the same.

When Raylene closed up at five, I had another dollar to add to my savings. Effie hadn't tipped me a penny, but Cora was so happy knowing where to find her ring, she slipped me four quarters.

On the way home, I stopped by Simpson's Cash Store and picked up a couple of pork chops. My plan was to get supper ready, to make something really good. I figured maybe it'd get Daddy back on track. Although I generally stayed away from Halley's Mill, I even considered riding out to tell him I'd be fixing something special.

The mill was older than any person in town, built back before the Civil War, and it was one of only three working water-powered mills in all of Virginia, a fact my daddy liked to repeat with pride, as if he owned it instead of just working there.

When I was younger, I'd go out back in the warehouse and play hide-and-seek between the rows of full sacks, stacked nearly to the ceiling. Or I'd make out the letters on the blackboard that swung overhead by the cash register, listing the things available: laying mash and hog meal. Barley and oats. Cottonseed and peanut hulls. All kinds of flour: corn and wheat and bran. I'd stand on one of the big iron scales—the one with raised letters declaring *July 3, 1894, Moydyke & Marmon Co., Indianapolis*—until someone came along to weigh me. I loved the sound of the mill, all the whirling of the belts and pulleys and elevators and the chatter of corn falling in the hopper. I liked the way every bit of wood in that place was worn smooth and how you could leave reverse footprints in the flour dust. Sometimes I'd climb up to the second story and stand at the window by the steel waterwheel, listening to the hollow sound of water coming through the run and then the soft, liquid *splish, splish, splish* of it hitting the cups. And I'd stare at the sparkle of water flicking off in the air like real rhinestones.

Just like Mama knew everything about Natalie Wood and movie-making, my daddy knew everything about that mill. He said milling by water was becoming a lost art. He showed me how to tell which grain was being milled just by the feel of it. Wheat grain was small and smooth. Corn was flat and round and bigger than wheat. Barley was easy: coarse husk. Buckwheat was a three-sided grain. Oats was a husk type. I'd try and try, eyes squeezed tight with concentration while I rolled the meal between my fingers, but no matter how I tried, I could never tell them all apart. My daddy, he'd just rub his thumb over a few grains and tell you right off, never missing.

Used to be I couldn't get enough of the mill, but about the

time I turned twelve and Mama was off chasing her dream, my feelings changed. Once, one of the farmers from out of town found me in the back feeding one of the mill cats and, quicker than you can imagine, he opened the front of his overalls and exposed his pale, wrinkled thing that made me want to puke-puke-puke. Sure wasn't nothing to be so proud of, is what I wished I'd told him. And a few days after that, I saw a rat as big as a small-sized dog. After that I stopped spending time at the mill. And Daddy began spending more time at CC's.

For a long time, when Mama first came back from L.A., he stayed clear of CC's and I had hopes this good habit would stick, but after she left us, he started up again. At first I felt alone, like a real orphan. The only thing worse would have been to live with Goody in Florida. After my granddaddy died, Goody sold the house that had been in her family for three generations, moved south, and took up golf. She announced to anyone who'd listen that she lived in a "gated community," like this was a place to be proud of instead of sounding like some sort of prison. And wouldn't you know, the year Mama left us for good, Goody started her campaign to have me move there with her.

"We can't have Natasha staying here with you," I heard her tell my daddy. "She'll be running wild in no time and turn up pregnant." She said this like she was privy to special knowledge, like one of Etta Bird's revelations, but the only thing it proved was how little she knew about me.

My daddy stood right up to her and said I'd be staying with him right where I belonged thank you anyway. He made it sound like we were a team. Even if it didn't exactly work out that way, staying with him was better than any gated community in Florida with Goody, who played golf and wore gardening gloves all the time to protect her hands and spent the rest of her time warning people not to be getting too big for their britches or go getting a swelled head, which pretty much took care of both ends.

I picked out four pork chops, some fresh green beans, and a jar of applesauce. Mr. Simpson hesitated when I told him to add the total to my daddy's bill, then lowered his voice so everyone in the universe wouldn't hear. "Okay this time, Miss Tallie," he said. "But you tell your daddy to come see me."

I felt my face heat up. I knew this meant Daddy hadn't settled up. Mama used to say Daddy was a hardworking man but no darn good with money. I felt the weight of the quarters from Cora Giles in my pocket and considered putting them toward our account. But with the Kurl closed Sundays and Mondays, I only had eight more workdays until the Glamour Company people came.

"Okay," I said to Mr. Simpson, and grabbed the bag off the counter before he could reconsider. Just as I was settling the bag into the basket on the Raleigh, wouldn't you know, Spy Reynolds pulled up to the gas pump in his souped-up, T-top Camaro. I felt my heart contract under my ribs.

"Hey there, Tallie," he said. His hair was wet, like he'd just been swimming, and I was close enough to see the way the teeth of his comb had separated the strands into neat stripes. He was dressed in clean chinos and a white shirt, the sleeves rolled back revealing muscular arms. When he smiled, he looked pirate handsome, like the hero in one of Mama's old black-and-white movies. "How's it going?"

"Just fine," I said, hugging the package to my chest and

pretending I was pretty as my mama and thinking *shitfuckpiss*. He *never* saw me when I was looking good.

"Hot day to be riding a bike."

"Sure is." I never acted right around Spy. Sometimes, alone at night, I'd practice conversing with him, but whenever I saw him, all the things I'd rehearsed just stayed locked on my tongue, leaving me struck dumb and looking stupid.

"Want a ride home?"

"No, thanks," I said. Course I wanted more than anything in the world to be sitting in Spy's Camaro, but I wasn't going to do it looking common as dirt. I held this picture in my mind of the first time I sat in his car: I'd be wearing a skirt and blouse—store new—and smelling of the strawberry shampoo I'd bought especially at Winn-Dixie four months before so I'd be prepared.

"Be no trouble."

I knocked back the kickstand and straddled the bike. My head was so full of things I wanted to tell him that I turned dizzy with the weight of them.

"You could leave your bike here and pick it up later."

"Can't," I said. "I got to build my legs up for swim team."

He took a long look at me, staring directly at my legs. "You sure are building them something fierce," he said.

I didn't know how to take that. Could he mean my legs were getting too big? "See ya," I said and left him standing there, pump nozzle in hand.

At quarter past five by the kitchen clock, I prepared the chops for pan-frying and cooked up some potatoes the way Mama used to, with plenty of bacon grease and onions. I set the table and waited, passing time by practicing my *Glamour Day* poses in front of the bathroom mirror, using a dish towel for the feather boa.

By six it was clear as clean glass Daddy wasn't coming home. Sometimes I thought he forgot he even had a daughter. I finished cooking the chops, opened a beer, sat down, and ate. Occasionally, when I was alone like this, I pretended Mama was there with me. I imagined her sitting right across the table in the place I'd set for Daddy.

"Mama," I said, "the *Glamour Day* people are coming pretty soon."

I told her how everybody'd signed up. Even old Miss Tilly Pettijohn. I told her how I'd saved up more than three dollars and had it in the silver pitcher. I told her how Martha Lee was going to give me my first driving lesson on Monday. Then I told her a little about Spy. I asked her what she thought Spy meant when he'd said my legs looked fierce. It didn't sound exactly like a compliment.

Finally I stopped. Having a one-way conversation with an empty plate was about the loneliest thing in the world. Lonelier than silence. Worse than not talking at all. That was when I decided to become a wild girl. Shit, I thought, I might as well have some fun before I die.

★ Tallie's Book ★

Never marry a man who wears more
jewelry than you do.

A woman can be pretty _and_ strong.

Everyone has a need to feel needed.

Beetles signify change.

i woke up with the Christmas feeling—that unexpected happy way you feel when you know something good is about to happen but you can't recall exactly what—then I remembered it was finally Monday. I didn't stop for breakfast, just grabbed the last doughnut from the box on the counter and pedaled over to Martha Lee's, not even bothering to brush my hair. Sometimes it was a good thing Martha Lee didn't care a lick about a person's appearance.

Although it wasn't yet eight, it was already hotter than Satan on his best day, and by the time I reached High Tower Road I was sweat-sticky and slightly nauseated from the heat. Mama would have cautioned me about heatstroke. She would have seen to it that I'd had breakfast and took water with me. But then if Mama'd been there, I wouldn't be needing to have Martha Lee teach me to drive. I'd have had Mama. I could actually picture it. She'd make an occasion of it. She'd switch on the radio while I settled myself behind the steering wheel of her Dodge and we'd start off, her sitting next to me, telling me not to worry I'd get the hang of it, just have fun. And she wouldn't press her foot against the floorboards to signal I needed to brake. Or reach out to correct my steering if I veered close to the centerline. She'd be singing in her off-key voice, belting it out with Buddy Holly or Sam Cooke. *You-oo-oo-oo send me.*

But Mama wasn't there, so Martha Lee would have to do. Which was a damn sight better than taking driver's ed with Mr. Harold-goddamn-Nelson who carried a squirt bottle of breath freshener in his pocket and drove around in the bright yellow Chevy with a *Student Driver* sign on the roof like a pizza delivery car. Even my Raleigh beat that. As soon as I wheeled into the yard, I could see a yellow slip of paper flapping on the front door. No sign of Martha Lee's pickup.

The scrawled note said she'd been called in unexpectedly on a case—old Temple Fallon over in Mission Wales had fallen and broken her hip. *Shitpissfuck.* I ripped the note off the door and scattered the pieces in the yard. In recent years, I'd trained myself not to plan on much, which take it from me was the best way to avoid disappointment, but I'd been *counting* on this driving lesson. At this rate I'd be as old as Temple Fallon before I learned to drive. Didn't they have nurses in Mission Wales? Was Martha Lee the only LPN in Amherst County or what?

The thing was, sick people always wanted Martha Lee taking care of them, especially dying people, although you'd think that if a person was about to die, she'd want to be looking at some sweet-faced angel type instead of someone like Martha Lee. I know when Mama fell ill, she wouldn't let another nurse near her. Martha Lee was angel enough for her.

It wasn't true, of course, but Mama seemed to get sick overnight. One week she was swimming with me at the creek and dancing up a storm with Daddy, and the next week she was too tired to fix cake batter. She was always slim—she used to buy her clothes in the girls' section at Shucks Discount—but by the time school started in September, she was downright bony. She took to wearing my daddy's long-sleeve mill shirts, thinking, I guess, that we wouldn't notice, but instead of hiding her thinness, Daddy's shirts emphasized it. Often, when I came home after school, I'd find her sleeping. Not on the couch or the porch glider, but in her bed, which was scarier. One day I found her puking in the bathroom. When she reached out to flush, her sleeve fell back revealing an arm so thin, it looked like it would snap if you sneezed.

"Don't tell your daddy," she said.

"Okay," I said. It shamed me to think a part of me was glad Mama was sick. For sure, she wouldn't be leaving us if she was feeling poorly.

"Promise," she said. "Promise you won't tell him."

The weight of conspiracy settled on my shoulders, but I agreed to it without hesitation. Like most people in her life, I couldn't deny Mama anything. Still, I wondered how she thought she could keep this from him. Course now I understand you can always keep from people things they are determined not to see. You can even keep things from yourself if you've a mind to.

The next day, when Martha Lee showed up with a pot of chicken necks and dumplings, I heard them arguing in Mama's room. They never, ever fought, and this scared me more than finding Mama on the bathroom floor.

"Well, I'm not standing by," Martha Lee said. When she came out of that room her lips were all tight, like her mouth was full of the vinegar milk Mama used to make corn bread. I didn't even pretend not to listen while she phoned a doctor over in Lynchburg.

"He'll see you tomorrow," she told Mama.

The next day, Daddy stayed home from the mill to drive her. When I insisted on skipping school to go along, I got set for an argument, but they caved without a word. I sat between them on the bench seat of the Dodge as we headed toward Lynchburg. Usually I felt protected sitting there, the three of us tight as June bugs, but that day, wedged in between the heft of my daddy and the unbearable weightlessness of Mama, nothing felt safe at all. We drove past the Ford dealership, the video store, past the run-down house with a sign that said inside a lady would read your palms, past the converted service station where they sold silver jewelry and cowboy boots, past the whole sorry strip of fast-food places pushing tacos and barbecue and fries. All the way to Lynchburg no one even turned on the radio. Once, Mama reached over and took my hand in hers. It was lighter than smoke, like holding Pick Up sticks encased in skin, or something dead, and I pushed it away. "Oh, sugar," she said, and reached up and brushed the hair out of my eyes, but I refused to look at her. I wished I'd gone to school after all.

That night they argued about what the doctor had said and what Mama should do.

"We've got to make some decisions here," Daddy began.

"Oh, Luddy," Mama said. Even from my bedroom I could hear her deep sigh. "There's no use thinking about all that."

"Don't you worry about the cost," Daddy said. "None of that matters."

"It's not the cost."

"What is it, then?"

Mama spoke so soft that I couldn't hear her and I guess Daddy couldn't, either, because I heard him ask her what she'd said.

"It's too late," Mama said.

"Too late? What're you talking about?" Daddy said. "You heard the doctor. There's things can be done."

"Things," Mama said in a flat voice. I heard the creak of the kitchen chair as she sat down and then the answering creak as he sat next to her.

"That's right," Daddy said.

"Like chemo?" Mama said. "Like all that poison?"

"Yes."

"The average person with stage four lives three days longer if she has chemo. Did you know that? Three days. And for what? Losing my hair. I'm not doing it."

"Maybe they could operate?" Daddy said.

"You mean cut me open? No, Luddy. I'm not doing it."

"Do it, Mama," I whispered. "Do it. Let them cut you open."

"For God's sake, Dinah Mae." My daddy was a big man. I'd seen him heft two sacks of flour on his shoulders like they weighed no more than air. And he was smart about certain things. Once, he nursed a cowbird back to health, ignoring folks who said a bird with a broken wing was as good as dead. I waited for him to tell Mama she had to do what the doctor said. "Hair grows back," he said.

"Forget it, Luddy."

"Jesus, Dinah Mae."

"It's too late," Mama said, not shouting, not even reminding him to call her Deanie.

"How do you know? The doctor didn't say anything like that."

"It's been too late for a long time."

"How long?" It sounded like he was speaking with a mouth full of broken glass.

"What does it matter?"

"How long, Dinah Mae?"

"Easter," Mama said.

That's how I found out Mama'd been sick for five months.

Still, I thought she'd give in. I believed that after she got used to the idea of the treatments and losing her hair, she'd decide to do whatever she had to to get well. I thought with Goody and Daddy and Martha Lee all working on her, she'd let them give her poisons or operations or whatever it took. I thought she'd do it for me, though that was the last thing I wanted.

The whole day stretched before me. I supposed I could hang around and wait for Martha Lee, but there was no telling when she'd return. For all I knew, Temple-goddamn-Fallon and her broken hip would require twenty-four-hour nursing. I thought about helping myself to a beer, but I'd made a rule about not drinking before noon. I knew alcoholism could run in families, and Mama always said drinking in the morning was the first sign of a person heading directly for trouble. Naturally I'd put that in my rule book.

Finally I got the key out from under the black stone and went inside. A mess, as usual, but I wasn't about to pick up. As far as I was concerned, old Temple Fallon could hobble all the way over from Mission Falls and clean up after Martha Lee. I got myself a glass of orange juice and after a while I began to snoop around. It was like Martha Lee breaking her promise gave me permission. I started in the bedroom. Naturally, the bed was unmade.

There was no mirror hanging over the dresser. No makeup in sight. Not even an old tube of lipstick or bottle of dime store perfume. The only things on the dresser were a dirty ashtray, a half-empty can of Pringles, and a balled-up tissue. It was probably the ugliest bedroom in three counties.

I headed for the bathroom next and checked out the medicine cabinet. Toothbrush, toothpaste, stick deodorant, aspirin—the cheap, no-name brand—a ratty box of Band-Aids, disposable razor, and an aerosol can of shaving cream. The stuff could have belonged to a man.

I returned to the bedroom, still looking for something worth the trouble of the hunt. I opened the top drawer of the dresser, prepared to find soiled underwear stuffed there but everything was folded in neat little piles. A stack of panties and another of bras, all practical and businesslike, white cotton, nothing pink or silky like Mama's. I checked every drawer and each one was like that, as if all the mess was on the surface of Martha Lee's life but underneath she kept things orderly.

I found the pictures in the bottom drawer. There were tons of them, some so old, they were black and white. They were of Mama, going back to the time when she was a little girl. Baby pictures of her and my Uncle Grayson, school pictures, and a bunch of snapshots taken of Mama and Martha Lee lying on a blanket at a beach and several of the two of them in front of a Christmas tree. There was a Halloween picture: Mama in a flapper dress, sporting a headband and cigarette holder, Martha Lee as a gangster, with a dummy propped between them wearing a hat with a wide brim and holding a fake machine gun. Duane. Just looking at it, my chest got full of stones.

Toward the bottom there was a picture of the three of them: my mama, daddy, and Martha Lee. I didn't know when it was taken—shortly after I was born, I guessed, because there was a baby carriage in the corner of the photo. They were all holding hands, my mama in the middle. Daddy and Martha Lee were staring straight out at the photographer and looking like this was not their idea. I wondered how they got Daddy in the shot anyway. He always said he'd rather face the business end of a shotgun than have his picture taken. Mama looked so happy. Sometimes I almost forgot just how beautiful she was.

After a while, I put the photos back, just like I'd found them, and headed to the kitchen to refill my orange juice. I drank it slow so I wouldn't get sick pedaling home, then rinsed the glass. I wasn't even mad at Martha Lee anymore, just lonely and sick in my heart from looking at the pictures.

I was setting the glass in the strainer when I saw the First Federal envelope lying on an open shelf by the refrigerator. There was a wad of cash sticking out in plain sight, right there where any thief could walk right in and take it. I intended to walk away but I was sick with wanting for that money. It drew me to it, like I was hypnotized the way I'd once seen someone at a carnival I'd begged and begged my mama to take me to. The main show was in a tent, and there was a magician dressed in a shiny black suit with a red silk lining to the jacket and a narrow string tie like a cowboy might wear. After he did some dumb card tricks any four-year-old could figure out, he asked for a volunteer from the audience. When no one moved he chose Nell Mosley and kept at her until she climbed up on the stage, half laughing and making little brushing motions in the air with her hand. He got her to sit up on a tall stool, then he swung a watch in front of her face and told her she was getting sleepy, sleepy, sleepy, repeating this until she closed her eyes. He told her to stick her tongue out, and she did. Then he told her to get up and quack and waddle like a duck, which she did, too, right there in front of everyone, waddling around the stage in her ugly yellow dress, not even stopping when everyone screamed with laughter. I almost peed my pants I was so relieved it wasn't my mama up there quacking.

I had nightmares for a week after that, each one about a man turning all of us into animals. Mama was a cat, my daddy a mule, and I'd been turned into a cow, which was the worst thing of all.

Now, just like Nell Mosley watching the magician's watch, I stared at that money. *Glamour Day* was less than a week away. You can ask her for it, a voice told me. She'll give it to you, if you ask her. That was absolute fact. Martha Lee would have given me about anything. But the money was all mixed up with disappointment over the driving lesson and seeing all those pictures of Mama.

There must have been a hundred bills in that envelope. I only took two. A ten and a five. Just what I needed and not one dime more. After, I pedaled straight home and put the money in the syrup pitcher. I thought I'd feel relieved that I had almost enough money, but I didn't. Taking from Martha Lee was different from lifting penny candy down at the Cash Store. Martha Lee was kin. Or close to.

Daddy wasn't home, and I was far too edgy to settle down. I spent a little time cleaning up the kitchen. After a while, I decided to bike over to the creek. All the other kids would be at the lake, the girls lying around in new bathing suits and oiling themselves up, the guys showing off, swimming out to the raft and diving in, making a big deal out of it. There'd be music playing on every blanket. I didn't belong. Being without a mama made me different. Half the time, people acted like I was a special case, and the rest of the time, they acted like I should be used to having a mama who was gone, like that was something a person could get accustomed to. No one ever talked about her, or asked me one thing about her.

When I felt lonely like that, I tried to imagine the future and the day I would come home from Hollywood. It'd be in the summer, maybe, and I'd be on a short break from filming a movie that was opening at Christmas. The *Eden Times* would do a story about me and take a picture that they'd feature on page one. People would ask for my autograph and I'd sign one for everyone. *Taylor Skye.* I'd write it out in serious blue ink, not something tacky like purple. And I'd be extra nice to everyone, even Elizabeth Talmadge, who'd have grown fat by then, have a head full of split ends, and no longer be queen of anything except the cash register at Winn-Dixie.

I pulled on my old swimsuit from last year, which was too small and rode up my butt. There wasn't much in the cupboard so I made myself a PB&J and grabbed a can of Coke. I considered taking a beer, but by the time I got around to drinking it, it would be warm. Warm soda tasted a sight better than warm beer. I was flipping up the kickstand on my Raleigh when a blue DeSoto pulled up. Wiley Bettis. For once without Will.

"Hey, Tallie," he said. He opened the door and got out.

"Hey, yourself." It was strange to see him without his twin, like half of him was missing. "Where's Will?"

"At the pond."

"Why aren't you there?"

"Didn't feel like it. Where you off to?"

"Swimming. The creek."

"Come on, I'll give you a ride."

Wiley had this decrepit '57 DeSoto someone had stripped the plates off and left for dead in the Winn-Dixie parking lot. He'd towed it home and spent the entire previous summer rebuilding the engine. Wiley'd gone through grammar school in the slow reading group, but he was some kind of genius when it came to engines.

"I'll bring you home, too," he said, staring at the ground where his toe was busy working a hole in the grass.

For heavens sake, Wiley Bettis, I wanted to say. Straighten up and look at me. One thing I knew I would demand in a boyfriend—not that I ever *considered* Wiley boyfriend material— was that he be able to look me straight in the eye. Mama said you couldn't trust someone who didn't, and I put that in my notebook, too.

"Okay," I said. A girl didn't have to worry about how she was dressed when she rode in an old DeSoto with a front seat patched with duct tape.

When we got to the creek, we headed straight for the water, both of us grateful to be getting cool. Wiley didn't do any of the dumb things boys usually did, like splash you, or dive under water and try to lift you on their shoulders or swim between your legs, their hands brushing against your tits like being in water gave them permission to touch you in a way they would never try on dry land. After a while we got tired of swimming and we spread out my blanket and sat down. Then I split my sandwich with him. He refused the Coke, to my great relief, since I didn't know how I'd drink it after his germy lips touched the rim. Then we swam again. We'd been coming to the creek every summer since we were old enough to go without our mamas. Will and Wiley were our only neighbors, and the three of us had played together as long as I could remember, mostly riding bikes or building forts in the field behind their house. Being without Will changed everything, like Wiley was some-one new. Course, any fool could see he liked me. I wished there was a way I could switch his deep affection for me with Spy Reynolds's apparent indifference. It was a mystery to me why things like love couldn't be equal. Why, when someone loved you, you couldn't just accept that love and return it in equal measure. My theory was that one person always loved the other more. Even if they were both in love, one person was more the lovee and the other the lover. Like my daddy and my mama.

I was lying on the towel, conscious of the way my bathing suit was riding up my butt and wondering if I should pull it down or if that would only serve to draw Wiley's attention, when he started talking.

"What're you doing after high school?"

"Haven't decided," I said. "We still have another year of high school." Of course, I knew all right. Like I said, I was running off to Hollywood. I planned on leaving the day after gradua-tion, not that anyone would be missing me. Certainly not a daddy who'd clean forgotten I was alive. "What about you?" I asked, like I didn't already know he'd end up working at Chaney's Garage, fixing cars for his uncle. Just like Will would continue on at Winn-Dixie, where he bagged groceries on weekends. Spy Reynolds and Elizabeth Talmadge and all the others who lived over by Carlton's Way in two-story houses with screened-in porches would go off to college. Someone like Ashley Wheeler might have the gumption to open a little bed-and-breakfast and hope to get the business of the tourists on their way across to the Blue Ridge. The rest—even the smart ones—would be teachers and accountants, bank tellers and store clerks, and would get married and have children and start the cycle of life in our town all over again.

People in Eden didn't have one stick of imagination. They couldn't picture a life beyond the present circumstance or geography. Mama was the only one I knew who had the capacity to dream. *A person's as big as her dreams*, she used to say. Her scrapbook was full of actresses who'd come from humble beginnings and transformed themselves into famous stars. Joan Crawford was born poor in San Antonio, Texas, and was once a telephone operator before she became an actress. Her real name was Lucille Le Sueur, which Mama thought sounded like the name of a stripper. Mama said we could learn a lot from the glamorous stars of the thirties and forties. She said those women knew how to invent themselves before people like Cher or that awful Madonna were even born.

No one I knew had the imagination to dream. Or to even think of reaching for the sky. A perfect example of this was the school play. Just before school closed for the summer, we held a big meeting to decide what next year's play would be, which was a complete waste of time as far as I was concerned since we all knew it would be *You Can't Take It with You.* As long as anyone could remember, there were only two plays ever done at the high school. That one and *Our Town*, which we had just performed. This year Mr. Nelson, who taught driver's ed and civics, was the Drama Club adviser because Mrs. Franklin, our English teacher, was pregnant. So he held this meeting and made us have this big vote for something already set in stone. Which shows you what happens when you're a civics teacher. Like you have to prove "democracy in action," which was his favorite phrase.

I guess that was what made me raise my hand. "Why don't we do something else?" I asked. "Do you have a suggestion, Tallie?" Mr. Nelson said, as if he were going to actually consider it, even though it came from me. He made a big show of pretending to be fair—*democratic*—but he had his favorites and he made it clear I wasn't on that list. Every time I got an A on a test— which was most of the time, truth be told—he handed me back my paper and said, "Tallie Brock, an A," with this great surprise in his voice, like *How did that happen?* He was the only one who didn't treat me special 'cause I didn't have a mama.

As a matter of fact I did have a suggestion. I wanted us to do *Spoon River Anthology*, this really great play about all these dead people in a cemetery who get to talk and tell their stories. The character I liked the most was this old woman who talked about dancing in Chandlerville and raising children and living a full life. "It takes life to love life," she said. I just loved that line. It sounded exactly like Mama. I decided it would be my motto forever. I was thinking about that when I offered my suggestion to Mr. Democracy in Action.

"What's it about?" said Elizabeth Talmadge, who, wouldn't you know, was the president of the Drama Club as well as Queen of the Universe. When I explained, someone said, "Dead people. How creepy," and Elizabeth said, "Morbid," and then the whole room got quiet. "Let's put it to a vote," Mr. Nelson said. He made a big show of counting hands and then announced that next year's play would be *You Can't Take It with You*.

Wiley had stopped talking and the sun was directly overhead and I thought about dragging the blanket over beneath a willow to get some relief, but it seemed like too much trouble so I lay back and closed my eyes. It was funny being there without Will. Wiley stretched out on his stomach on the other side of the blanket, and I inched way over on my side so we wouldn't touch by accident. Even quiet, men take up more space. Not just on things like blankets and chairs. It was like they required more air.

I lay there considering this and after a while—in that dreamy space where you're not quite asleep and not totally awake—I started pretending it was Spy Reynolds lying there. It's funny how the power of wanting something can slip right over into believing that it is. Once, I heard Mama tell Martha Lee that it was the things we were denied that we wanted the most. And, judging from the way I wanted Spy, that was surely true. After a while I could picture him being there so clear that when I felt a shadow block out the sun, when I felt a hand touch my arm, I believed it actually *was* Spy. As his fingers traced down to my hand and then interlinked with mine, my stomach got that nervous feeling like before a swim meet or when I had a big test in school. But not exactly like that. Then, still holding my hand, Spy reached over with his other hand and turned my face toward his. I knew he was going to kiss me, and at that moment—stuck in my dream—I knew I'd let him. Judging from the talk in the girls' locker room, I was the only one in the class who'd never been kissed. Practicing on your own hand isn't the same. Then I smelled peanut butter and heard Wiley's asthmatic breathing and knew it wasn't Spy at all. I sat up and pulled away.

"I got to be getting home."

"Okay," Wiley said, not looking at me.

Neither of us said a word all the way to my house.

Martha Lee called after supper. When I heard her voice the receiver turned slick in my hand. I opened my mouth to tell her how I was sorry about taking the money and how I really had planned on telling her about it and how I'd pay her back before the end of the summer, but before I could open my mouth she was saying how bad she felt about not being there for my driving lesson and asking how about next Monday, would I like to do it then, and so I said yes and we hung up before I could even mention the fifteen dollars.

That night I had trouble falling asleep. All mixed up with the funny feeling I had about taking the money from Martha Lee and my disappointment about not learning how to drive was how I'd felt lying on the blanket at the creek, expectant and, I don't know, open in a way, and believing that it was Spy with me and then the disappointment of Wiley, the peanut butter smell of him. Being a wild girl wasn't as easy as I'd expected.

When I finally fell asleep, I had the old dream about the carnival magician. Except it was Spy Reynolds, and he was holding out a deck of cards for me to choose from and when I did, it turned out it wasn't cards he was holding but all the photos of Mama and Martha Lee. And Daddy was there, too, pointing me out to Wiley Bettis, who had a badge on his chest and a pistol on his belt and had come to arrest me for stealing.

★ Tallie's Book ★

Drinking alcohol before twelve noon is a sign of trouble.

You can't trust a man who won't look you in the eye.

Alcoholism runs in families.

It takes life to love life.

A person's as big as her dreams.

It's the things we're denied that we want the most.

five

*i*t was "Seniors' Day" at the Klip-N-Kurl. Back in January, when things were slow, Raylene decided to offer a 5 percent discount on Tuesdays to customers over seventy. The shop filled every week, crowded with old ladies like Miss Easter Davis, who barely had enough hair to fiddle with in the first place but who believed growing old was no excuse for letting yourself go. The main topic of conversation was disease and digestion. Brittle bones. Plumbing problems. Incontinence. Hattie Jones, who was usually first in line waiting at the door for Raylene to open, was an expert on that problem. "I always peed my pants when I got to laughing," she'd say, "but now all it takes is one good sneeze." It gave me the creeps.

Raylene didn't mind Tuesdays. She preferred them to lice season, when half the kids in the grammar school came in for treatment and she'd have to get all armored up with gloves and a full-length plastic gown like she was in some sci-fi movie. "You can't be too careful," she'd tell me. She said lice could jump amazing distances. She said they actually preferred clean

hair 'cause they lay nits on the hair shaft. Raylene knew everything about lice, but it made me itch just watching her go to
work on some kid's head. De-licing was almost as bad as doing
perms. She hated the tediousness of rolling all of those tiny
curlers, but more than perms or lice season, Raylene hated re-
pairing the damage customers did at home. "Kitchen beauti-
cian," she'd say when someone called in wanting her to fix a
home cut or color. Once she got a panicky call from Ruth
Evans, whose head was smoking. I'm not kidding. Smoke was
actually rolling off in waves. "Serves her right," Raylene said before she calmed Ruth down, explaining how the chemicals in
the drugstore coloring kit had mixed with the minerals in the
Evanses' well water and that was what caused the smoke.

At least the pace was slow on Tuesdays. None of them
wanted their hair blown dry. They wanted to sit under the
dryer and talk. They were there for conversation as much as
anything. For sure they weren't there for speed. One thing
about old people, they weren't in any hurry. Not like Saturdays, when everyone was in a rush and we'd have to grab a
sandwich and eat it in five minutes flat, swallowing without al-
lowing time to chew.

Old people acted like they had all the time in the world instead of like their sand was almost through the glass. Slow as
snails, most of them. And *small*. People shrink when they get
old, have you noticed? As if life were leaking out of them inch
by inch.

I couldn't picture Mama old. Not Mama who brought music
with her wherever she went and could stand on her head and
turn cartwheels like a cheerleader. Couldn't picture it any more
than she could picture herself losing her beautiful hair to chemo.

*   *   *

When it was clear she wasn't going to do anything the doctor or Daddy wanted, everybody accepted the fact that Mama wasn't going to fight. That's when I knew I'd have to battle for her. First thing, I went to the Eden library and read every book they had on the subject of cancer, which wasn't much. Then I talked Martha Lee into driving to Lynchburg and buying bottles of vitamins. A multi and all the antioxidants. One thousand milligram capsules of C. Smaller ones of A and E. I mixed up so much juice for Mama it was amazing she didn't turn orange. And I cooked up all the food Goody said Mama'd craved in childhood—things like grits and whipped potatoes, sweet potato pie and milk toast—made them even though she couldn't eat much anymore. "That looks so good, sugar," she'd say when I carried in a plate of cheese grits. "Just put it down and I'll try it later."

One of the books I read said prayers held the power to cure, so I started going to the Baptist Church, the one out on the back hill, thinking maybe that was what was needed. Elijah Baptist was so different from the Methodist Church, it was like going to Disneyland. To begin with, everyone dressed up. The little girls wore party dresses with frilled lace on their socks, and the boys wore ties, every one of them from the youngest to high school seniors. The ladies wore hats and sang loud, like each one thought she was Aretha Franklin. They called each other "brother" and "sister" and all through the sermon shouted out things like, "That's right," and, "Thank you, Jesus." There was a large choir, too, and when they sang, you just wanted to rise right up out of your seat and dance, even if you were in church. One man played the drums and another blew a trumpet. The preacher's name was Reverend Tillett and he was tall as a tree and sounded exactly like Jesse Jackson. Sometimes, right in the middle of the sermon, he'd march straight from the pulpit and parade down the aisles like he was the drum major of the Eden High School Band. I was the only white person there. They were all nice to me, though, and when the Reverend Tillett found out about Mama, he included her in the healing prayer, calling her "sister" and asking the Lord to cure her. The ladies hugged me. Real hugs, too. Not fake. They held me close like I was kin.

None of it made a g.d. bit of difference. Not Mama's comfort food or the vitamins or the prayers of the Reverend Tillett and the people at Elijah Baptist. Mama kept fading right before my eyes. I was desperate by the time I thought of going to see Allie Rucker.

Allie lived outside of town, and everyone in Eden knew she was a witch. Once, Wiley dared us into riding our bikes out to her cabin, where people said she made moonshine in a genuine copper still. We planned on shouting things about her being a witch and throwing eggs at her house, but when we got there we were so spooked that we just turned around and came back. According to what folks said, Allie knew everything. She could tell whether a pregnant woman was carrying a boy or a girl. She knew how to get rid of a baby you didn't want, or how to get a baby if you wanted one and weren't having any luck in that department. She knew spells and how to put the hex on a person. How to make a man crazy with loving you, if that's what you wanted. Maybe Allie Rucker was a witch, like people said, but with everything else failing, a witch was exactly what was required.

A move this bold required backup, so after school I found the Bettis twins and made them swear on spit not to tell what I was about to reveal. Then I told them about Mama's sickness and how she wouldn't take medicine because she didn't want to lose her hair and how I needed to go out to Allie Rucker's. Wiley, reliable as rain, agreed at once to help, but Will said, "Jeez, Tallie, I don't know."

"You don't have to go," I told him, but before we'd gone ten feet, he was right there with us, pedaling off to see the witch before we all got cold feet. It took us close to a half hour to reach the woods west of town out by the holler where Allie Rucker lived.

"Jeez," Will said when we got there, like that was the only word he knew.

Allie's shack made Martha Lee's place look like Buckingham Palace. It was worn gray, like it had never held even passing acquaintance with a coat of paint. Out front there was no path, just hip-high grass that looked like it could be hiding *anything* and nearly stopped me in my tracks. "It's for Mama," I whispered to summon my courage. "Wait here," I told the twins, and gave my Raleigh to Wiley, who immediately turned it facing out in case we needed a quick getaway. As I walked toward the shack, I felt them watching me. I hoped I could count on them.

I climbed the steps, my palms all sweaty on the tree branch Allie had fashioned into a railing. Before I could even raise my hand to knock, the door swung open. I expected Allie Rucker to be short, about my mama's size, and all bent over like most old folk, but she was about ten feet tall, with this colored rag wrapped around her head that made her look even taller. She looked strong, too, like—old or not—she could swat you down like a flea if she had half a mind to.

"Hello," I stammered. "I'm Tallie Brock."

"I knows who you be," she said, causing my insides to jump halfway to my mouth. *She knew who I was?* Like she'd been keeping an eye on me for years. I didn't like the idea of that one bit. Part of me was saying, *Get the hell out of here,* and the other part was saying, *Maybe this will work.*

"You be the spittin' image of your daddy," she said. She knew my daddy, too? "What you be wantin' here?"

"Mama's sick," I said, stammering out the whole story, how she had lung cancer and wouldn't take chemo or have an operation. She motioned for me to come in. I looked back at the twins.

"Those be the Bettis boys?" she said, squinting out to where the twins sat on the bikes, ready to take off. "Twins, they got powers."

Did she know about all of us? The idea was so creepy, I couldn't think about it. I paused for a minute, trying to remember when I'd had my last tetanus shot. Then I remembered Mama and went on in. The door slammed shut behind me.

"How long your mama be sick?" she asked.

"Since spring." Inside was one big room with these giant plants growing everywhere, like I'd fallen into a jungle. She didn't ask me to sit, and I couldn't have even if she had. Every chair was piled with junk. Broken things: cooking pots with no handles; magazines you wouldn't want to even consider holding in your hands; stuff most people would throw away. It smelled of mildew and some other, slightly sweet, odor. I held my arms close to my sides to keep from touching anything. If the twins left me here, I was going to kill them.

"Last year," Allie repeated to herself.

"That's right," I said. I wished I knew more about witch stuff. Should I have brought along something of my mama's? Some of her hair? I wouldn't have to cut it. Just take a few strands from her brush.

"Your mama, she be puffing up or turning to bones?"

I thought of Mama's thin arms, the weightless heft of her Pick Up—stick hands. "She's lost a lot of weight," I said.

Allie crossed to a cupboard that, I swear to God, had cobwebs hanging from the top. Inside, the shelves were crammed with old jars and discolored plastic containers, each one filled with things that even from across the room I could see looked like nothing you'd ever want to be putting inside you in a million years. It made the idea of chemo look like a grammar school picnic.

She took down about ten of the jars and opened each one. Once, she put back one jar and selected another. She crossed to a chair and dug around until she came up with an old plastic bag, the kind store bread comes in, and started filling it with stuff from the jars.

Eye of newt, said this scratchy voice inside my head from this play in our English class text, and I had to bite my cheeks to hold back from laughing, the nervous kind of laughing I'd do when we still went to the Methodist Church and Mrs. Duval sang in that thin old crackly voice of hers. I used to get to giggling so that my mama'd have to squeeze my hand to make me stop.

"Here," she said, holding out the bag.

I didn't take it right away.

"For your mama," she said.

"What is it?"

"This here be the Queen of Cures."

"What's that?"

"The Queen of Cures. That's all you be needing to know." Then she told me to dump the stuff in the bag into a big pot and stir in five cups of water. Boil it up good, she instructed, and after ten minutes, strain it off. Then I was supposed to boil it again with another five cups of water. "This time you be putting a lid on it and letting it cook for two hours," she said. Then she told me to strain it again and put the two batches of liquid together. She made me repeat her directions twice. *Eye of newt*, sang the crazy voice inside my head.

"You be givin' your mama a full cup," she said. "Every night. Right before she be goin' to sleep."

Believe me, I didn't even want to *touch* that bag, but I grabbed it and got out of there. I was so glad to escape, I didn't even say thanks. I ran all the way to where the twins were waiting.

We rode like the devil himself was at our back. I gripped the plastic bag against the handlebar, and it swung back and forth madly like some creature inside was trying to break free.

We got so out of breath, we had to stop after we'd gone no more than a mile.

"What was she like?" Will asked.

"A witch," I said. "And tall. And she knew who I was. And you, too. She knew who you were. She said twins have *powers*."

"Jesus Sweet Christ," Wiley said.

I knew exactly what he meant.

Will was looking at the plastic bag. "What the hell is that?"

"Stuff I'm supposed to cook up and give to my mama."

"I don't know about that," Wiley said.

"She said it's the Queen of Cures," I said.

"Jeez," Will said. "That sounds like a curse." He made his voice all spooky and thin like the Wicked Witch in *The Wizard of Oz*. "The Queen of Cures, my pretty."

"It's probably poison," Wiley said.

Well, poison was what Mama said they gave you to get rid of cancer. Maybe one poison was as good as another, though I hoped it wouldn't make her hair fall out. I couldn't picture Mama without her black hair curling round her face.

When I got home, Mama was sleeping, so I got right down to boiling up the cure, emptying the bag into the stew pot she used for making soup, measuring out the water, precisely as Allie Rucker had instructed. Mostly the stuff looked like dried grasses and some chunks that resembled wood or mushrooms, but I didn't look too close. If there was something in there that had ever swum, walked, or flown, I didn't want to know.

The stuff hadn't even come to a full boil when it started to smell. A sour stink that clouded the kitchen. *Eye of newt.* I shut the door before it could escape to the rest of the house and opened the back door and the windows. It smelled like something that would do a lot worse than make a person's hair fall out. It smelled evil. I grabbed the pot holders I'd made Mama when I was nine and snatched that kettle right off the stove. I carted it out some distance behind the house to a spot where the grass grew in patches and dumped it. Then I got Mama's garden spade and buried the whole mess. When I got back to the house, the kitchen still reeked, so I flipped a dish towel around in the air, then put a pot of water on with some cinnamon in it. By the time Mama woke up, the evil smell was almost gone.

That night I couldn't sleep. I lay in bed, thinking about the stuff I'd buried in the backyard and wondering if it would have helped Mama. Wondering if it was just what she needed. Wondering if I had gotten rid of the very thing that would have healed my mama. Wondering if I really had thrown away the Queen of Cures.

★ Tallie's Book ★

Twins have powers.

It's hard to figure out what will kill you
and what will cure you and how to
know the difference.

People shrink when they get old.

a t noon, the temperature hit one hundred on the First Federal thermometer, and by five, when we finished up with the last Seniors' Day discount customer—not *one* of them tipping, like "discount" meant "permission to be cheap"—it only dropped to eighty. Raylene got real bossy and said it was too hot for me to be riding my bike. Even when I said I wasn't a baby, she insisted on tying the Raleigh to her car bumper and driving me home.

There was a note on the table from Daddy saying he was taking a truckload of grain over to Redden with one of the Halley brothers and he'd be home after dark. Well, what else was new? I might as well have been living alone.

There was nothing on TV except reruns, so I got out my rule book and put in a couple of things I'd heard from the ladies at the Kurl, like what Hattie Jones'd said about nylon panties and Easter Davis'd said about raspberry tea. Stuff like that. Then I got myself a beer and went out and sat on the glider. It was too hot to eat or read or do much of anything and there was no telling when my daddy'd be coming home. Finally I finished up the beer, grabbed my bathing suit—which was way too small and probably doing damage to my woman parts—and rode over to Baldy, pumping easy and walking the uphill parts so I wouldn't get a stroke. That time of day, it was quiet at the creek. No one was there but me. I left my bike leaning against a tree. It must have been the heat or the beer or something, because the next thing—without even thinking about it—I stripped to the skin, tossed my bathing suit on the ground, and dove right in the creek, inhaling sharp at the first touch of water on my belly, then stretching out and enjoying the absolute freedom of it. If Goody could have seen me she'd have said I was cheap, cheap, cheap. It was continually amazing to me that someone as fun loving as Mama had been birthed by Goody, who, before she moved to Florida and took up golf, was hard as dirt. Goody wouldn't know a good time if it walked up and bit her. She maintained you were sinning if you so much as held a deck of cards. Not Mama, though. If Mama'd been there, she would have been skinny-dipping right along with me, shouting and laughing at the pure joy and freedom of it. Mama just loved swimming. She said she was in her element when she was in water. That was about the only way she differed from Natalie. For a while I swam laps (breaststroke and crawl), then I flipped over on my back and floated faceup, just staring at the sky, enjoying the slippery sensation of the water against my skin. It reminded me of how I felt nights when I'd sit on the porch glider and open my pajama top so the evening air could cool me down.

Off in the distance I heard the whistle of the six o'clock heading toward Roanoke. Train whistles always made me think of my granddaddy. He'd been a physician for the Southern Railroad. A railroad man head to toe, Mama said, even after he'd had to quit because he'd developed a weak heart. Granddaddy used to have a model train set up in his living room and he'd play this cassette recording of train sounds that about drove Goody mad. When I was little I'd sit on his knee and listen to him talk about the days when trains ruled. He had a whole head full of train stories and loved to tell them all. Especially the one about how once an entire train got buried in a tunnel cave-in under Richmond. That train was probably there to this day, he'd said, with everyone still in it, a piece of information that gave me nightmares for a week. Were the people still sitting in their seats or were they crowded against the windows, trying to get out? How long had it taken for them to die?

The other thing Granddaddy knew about was trees. He could tell a white oak from a red. He could look at a stump and tell you how old it'd been when it was chopped down, and its dry years from the wet ones. I thought everything in the world would be different if Granddaddy were still alive. Just like it would be different if Mama hadn't gotten sick.

By October, Mama was spending most of her days watching the soaps and reruns of *Roseanne* and *The Golden Girls.* Martha Lee had arranged for County Health to bring over one of those mechanical beds with a button you could push to raise the head or the feet. Daddy hated it, but Mama called it her throne. Sometimes, I'd lie there with her. After a while, she'd send me to get the hairbrush off her dresser. I was a fool for Mama brushing my hair. She'd start with her fingers, lacing them through my hair, pulling it back from my face and lifting it off my neck. Then she'd take the brush and begin, nothing impatient or snappy—not even if there were snarls—just long, gentle strokes that calmed us both. Later, on nights when I couldn't sleep, I'd pretend she was making those even, slow strokes and just the thought could lull me off.

By then the house was a mess. I could imagine what Goody would say if she got a look, but Mama didn't care. "Housekeeping's an overrated occupation, sugar," she'd say. "There're more important things in the world than a clean floor." Like what? I wanted to ask. Tell me, Mama, tell me all the things that are important. Tell me everything I need to know. I longed to turn off the TV and climb up on that narrow throne next to Mama, adjusting it so the foot part was high, and ask her everything I wanted to know. Things I needed to know then and things I'd need to know for the future.

First I'd ask her kitchen questions, like how long to cook butter beans and how to make cobbler so it doesn't sit heavy after you eat it. And I'd ask how a person would know for certain when another person likes her, and then I'd start on love questions. How did you know when you were in love, and was sex love different from marrying love? Did you need to know exactly what to do when a boy kissed you, or did instincts take over? I'd ask her if you could trust instincts when it comes to love, or did they just land you in a hog pile of trouble. Should you really marry a man because his smile made you crazy?

Then I'd ask her to tell me everything about those months she spent in L.A. I'd ask her where she lived out there and what it was like to work at a real Hollywood studio. I'd listen with both ears so I'd have a head start when I landed out there. I'd start with the pile of postcards she'd sent home and I kept in a cigar box under my bed. There was one of the big *Hollywood* sign, which was not actually a real sign, but giant white block

letters sitting on the side of a hill. On the back, Mama'd written that it used to spell *Hollywoodland,* and before the last
four letters had rotted away a starlet had committed suicide
by jumping off the final "D." And back in the '30s, another
actress had jumped off the "H." It gave me the chills just looking at that card. There was another postcard of the Walk of
Fame, which was this sidewalk outside a theater in Hollywood
where famous actors got to put their handprints and footprints in the cement. The card she sent had the prints of Jane
Wyman and Henry Fonda and Jack Nicholson, and—believe it
or not—Natalie Wood. The date *12-5-61* was etched in the con-
crete next to Natalie's little handprints, along with the imprint
of a pair of high heels, so small they looked like they belonged
to a child. Course, now they have big stars outlined with brass
and the actor's name set in the middle. The person doesn't
even have to be real. It can be a cartoon. Like Mickey Mouse,
which doesn't seem right to me.

Mama sent me a picture card of the arched gates in front
of Paramount—"my studio," she wrote on the back. Another
time I got a picture of Mann's Chinese Theatre with a message
that said she'd had lunch in the commissary the day before and
Kelly McGillis had sat at the next table. As lonely as I'd been for
her, it made me smile to think of Mama in Hollywood having
lunch with a real star. I'd asked her about the lunch with Kelly
McGillis once, figuring I'd start there and work into what she'd
been doing the entire time she was there, but all she said was,
"Oh, sugar, that's all water past the dam." Maybe to Mama it
was, but not to me. I had things I was needing to know. Another time I asked Mama for her foolproof cobbler recipe, but
all she said was that it wasn't always necessary to have precise

directions. Often as not things turned out just as good without them, she said, and that was as true of life as it was of cooking.

I never got to ask Mama all the questions I had in mind. I'd just be getting started—warming up with the household things, like the secrets for making a good cake—when it seemed something always stopped me. She'd fall asleep. Someone would stop by. One day, we were sitting there and I was all set to begin, but before I could even ask my first question, the back door opened and Martha Lee came in. She looked at my mama with a steady, appraising gaze before she caught my eye. Then she smiled and switched from being a nurse back to being Mama's friend.

"Hey, Cookie," she said right off to Mama. "You up for a Dairy Queen?" Which meant I wasn't invited. Going to the Dairy Queen was their special code for getting high. Before she'd given up on getting Mama well, Martha Lee would bring over weird stuff from the health store in Lynchburg, like an industrial type juicer that must have cost a fortune. She'd make these gross drinks with carrot juice and parsley and wheat grass and protein powder and other stuff that reminded me of Allie Rucker's cure I'd buried in the backyard. Mama wouldn't touch it. She'd just laugh and say she'd prefer a beer. Martha Lee had long ago let go of trying to talk Mama into what she should or shouldn't be doing. And if Mama wanted to get high, Martha Lee'd bundle her up and carry her to her truck, which she'd outfitted with a quilt and so many pillows that there wouldn't have been room for me even if they'd wanted me along. An hour or two later, they'd return, glassy-eyed, silly, and stinking of pot. Like I couldn't figure it out.

I watched while Martha Lee carried Mama outside and got

her settled in the pickup. Martha Lee had the radio cranking. Bobby McFerrin was singing "Don't Worry, Be Happy," which was about the dumbest song in the universe, as if it were possible for a person to *decide* not to worry.

"We'll bring you back a milk shake," Mama promised.

Okay, Mama, I should have said, *have fun,* or anything nice, but all I could say was, "Don't want one," in my coolest voice, knowing she'd bring one anyway. And when she smiled and asked for a kiss, I pretended not to hear. Everything inside me loved Mama, loved her to distraction, but since she'd gotten sick there were days when I couldn't help being mean-hearted. Once, I told her I was planning on going to Florida and moving in with Goody, but Mama just grinned wickedly and said to go ahead if that's what I wanted. One day Martha Lee found me crying out by the willow 'cause of something mean I'd said to Mama. I felt like a baby, but she told me to go on and cry all I wanted. She said salt cured everything, whether it came from tears or sweat. She said I wasn't mean, just hurting, and that's why I said the things I did. She said my mama understood. I wanted to believe her.

When the two of them headed off, Mama waved. I didn't wave back. A pair of Spring Azures the size of small moths fluttered around my ankles. *Bugs with birds' souls,* according to Mama. October was late to be seeing butterflies, even in Virginia. In science, Mr. Brown told us they flew thousands of miles each year. *Thousands.* I thought that was as close to a miracle as it was possible to conceive. If you smudged the dust off their wings, butterflies couldn't fly, yet they migrated through thunderstorms and windstorms on those translucent wings, flying till they reached Mexico and places like that, flying all that distance for no apparent reason except to end up where they started in the first place. How was it that something so delicate could stand so much, and someone like my mama, who used to be able to swim more than a mile and boogie all through the night and still be ready for more, got sick? Why was that so?

Once, Mama told me in Mexico or Africa or someplace like that there were women who made pictures out of pieces of butterfly wings. Imagine. The Spring Azures were circling my feet, and I could see how their wings would make a beautiful painting. Without thinking about it or planning it, still mad because Mama and Martha Lee had left me behind, I stomped on them. Right away I lifted my foot, but it was too late to take it back. Was that how it felt to be God? Did he ever regret making someone die? And who was he, anyway, to be sitting up there deciding things like who got to live and who got the shaft?

Thinking about the butterflies and Mama and all the times I'd been mean to her made me too sad to stay in the creek, no matter how good the water felt against my skin. I waded to the bank and padded ashore. That was when I realized I'd left my towel hanging on the line at home. I was reaching for my T-shirt, figuring I'd use that to dry off, when I got this creepy feeling, this *knowing* I was being watched. Someone was standing off in the trees. For a second, I was scared. Goody was always warning me about men lurking about looking for girls like me, men involved in white slavery, though when I asked her to name one girl who'd ever been kidnapped, she couldn't. I was remembering Goody's warnings when I suddenly *knew* who was watching me. Like overnight I had developed special radar, the kind of radar Daddy used to have for my mama that let him know where she was without anybody having to tell him. Or like I'd developed Etta Bird's ability for revelations. *Spy.* It was Spy hiding in the trees. Spy watching me for sure.

My heart contracted under my ribs. Course, I should have yelled at him or held the T-shirt tight around me, but I didn't. I stood up straight—back to him—and shook my hair out, just like I was home alone in my room. I could feel his eyes on me, his gaze heating my legs, shoulders, hips, and ass, warming all the places the creek had just cooled. I shook my hair again. Then I turned full to him. *Cheap, cheap, cheap,* Goody shouted in my head, but I didn't feel one bit of shame. The skin on my belly and tits grew tight, like my body was growing beneath its skin, swelling up like I'd been stung by bees. I was heating in secret places. Goody'd say I was turning into trash. No better than Bitty Weatherspoon, she'd say. Like she'd predicted all along. I didn't care. I was heating up and could have stood by Bald Creek forever, stood there and taken in the peculiar feeling that was a cross between ache and pleasure. I was turning into a wild girl, all right. I moved like a motion picture in slow motion, letting Spy have a real good look. Then I thought of Mama and imagined her watching me. Heat scalded my face, and pleasure flowed clean off my body. Too late, I turned and covered myself. I was the most shameless girl in all Virginia and I didn't need Goody to tell me that.

Still, for those moments when Spy was taking in my body, I felt—I felt almost beautiful.

★ Tallie's Book ★

Raspberry tea soothes cramps.

Sour milk is better than sweet for cake batter.

Nylon panties cause yeast infections.

Salt cures everything.

It isn't always necessary to follow directions—for cooking or for life.

A boy's gaze can make a girl feel almost beautiful. Truly.

seven

i figured by the morning, if Spy was like most Eden boys, it'd be public knowledge in five counties he'd seen me strutting around buck naked. For sure everybody'd be commenting on what a slut that Tallie Brock was and wasn't it a blessing her mama wasn't there to see it. Goody'd have said I should have thought of that before I'd displayed myself so openly. I dreaded facing Raylene. I figured the best thing was to march straight into the Kurl and deny-deny-deny the whole thing.

When I got there, Raylene was pissing quarters. "Don't let me near a gun," she said. I could tell it was going to be one of those days. Aubrey Boles had showed up late and that set the whole damn schedule off. Aubrey made a regular habit of waltzing in a half hour past her appointment time, then she'd make excuses and ask for extras. A manicure. A cut in addition to color. She'd make this giant point that she only wanted a trim, just a little off the top or a half inch off the ends, hoping a trim would be cheaper than a cut, though Raylene'd told her a zillion times that one costs the same as the other. Then

Ashley Wheeler came in asking for a bikini wax. Everyone knew Raylene never did below the neck. Brows, mustache, and chin, that's all. Anything else you had to go to Lynchburg.

"You'd look ten years younger if you'd let me cut your hair," Raylene said to Ellie Sue Rucker. She was wielding her blow dryer like a pistol, and I knew enough to stay clear.

"Hell," Ellie Sue said. "I'd look ten years younger if I put on makeup."

Raylene was always telling customers what they should do, not that anyone paid the least attention. Everyone thought they knew what fit them best, like Effie Webb who insisted on bangs, no matter what Raylene told her. "If you have a fat face, I don't care what you do," Raylene said. "Bangs ain't going to look good." But the fatter the face, the more they wanted bangs. Just like short women wanted big hair. "Rat it up good," Mrs. Gilbert would say. "So I'll look tall." And Raylene would grumble that she'd just end up looking like a short woman with tall hair. Raylene said all kinds of things, but the customers never took offense. She maintained she never said anything about anyone she wouldn't say to her face. And she never did.

The radio was blaring, driving me bughouse. It was set on 88.9, all Christian preaching and church music instead of the oldies or the hot stomping guitar I was wanting. As if the women in the shop needed gospel. Probably no one in there had tasted sin in two decades. They probably wouldn't be up to it if sin came knocking on their front door with a fistful of lupine. Unlike me, who was developing a personal acquaintance. Wasn't it sinful to stand shameless and let a man lay his eyes on anything he wanted?

No matter how busy I got that morning, or how much I

tried to forget, I couldn't stop recalling how it felt to have Spy's eyes fixed on my body. I'd get tight-skinned all over and my body'd start to frizzle in all its secret places and I'd start to speculate about where he was at that very minute and what he might be doing. I'd picture him in his T-top Camaro and daydream about what it would be like to be sitting next to him, his hand setting on my leg. I'd wonder what his hair smelled like up close, 'cause everyone's got a smell that's theirs alone and I was hungry to know the smell of him. The next thing I'd be thinking about the creek and wondering if he'd be there later that day. I'd get to daydreaming about the two of us swimming in the creek and I found myself coming to an understanding of why boys thought they could touch you when you were swimming, touch you like they wouldn't dream of on land. It was like the water really did give a person special permission. Then my hands would fumble at whatever I was doing, which was how I happened to knock over the shampoo, the gallon size we used for refills. It was a mess to clean up and that was when I was afraid I was going to cry, even though I hadn't shed one tear in four years. Raylene thought I was upset because of the shambles I'd made, or maybe because I was in my moon, which was what Mama'd told me to call it instead of all the dumb names the girls at school had for the monthly time. Next, Raylene turned all sweet, which is what people always did around me when I was upset, like being without a mama meant people should fix everything else for you, even dumb things like spilt shampoo, things that they'd get mad about if anyone else had done.

"Oh, honey," Raylene said. "Don't you fret. Everything will be all right."

*   *   *

Everything will be all right. That's what everyone said when
Mama was sick. Once news of her illness got out, half of Eden
came to see her. Even The Flowers stopped by, toting their
famous burnt-sugar cake. Women would fuss around the
kitchen or have Mama move to a chair while they spread fresh
linens on her bed. Men, the same ones who'd envied my daddy
'cause he was married to Mama, stood back by the door and
found the floor an object of great fascination. If Martha Lee was
there when they came, she'd stomp out and drive off in her
pickup. "Jesus," she'd say when they'd cleared out and it was safe
to return, "why don't you tell them to leave you alone." "They
mean well," Mama'd say. And I suppose they did, but they drove
Martha Lee crazy and me, too. When they were leaving—man,
woman, didn't matter which—they'd take me aside. "Don't
you worry about a thing," they'd say. "Your mama's going to be
just fine." I knew they said things like that because they
thought it was a consolation, but it wasn't. It scared me. Like my
eyes were lying and I couldn't trust the truth of what was playing out right in front of me. For sure if I knew a girl whose
mama was sick like that I wouldn't tell her things were going to
be goddamned-fine. I'd say straight out that I was sorry to hear
her mama was sick and maybe I'd offer to take her for pizza
some night. Or the movies. Or, if I knew her well and thought
she'd let me, I'd just give her a hug, like the ladies at Elijah Baptist hugged me. For sure I'd keep my fat mouth shut. The truth
was there was a lot to worry about. And things weren't fine, not
by a long shot. Mama was fading right before our eyes and there
wasn't a blessed thing we could do about it.

I liked it best when no one was there, not even Daddy or Martha Lee, just me alone with Mama. I'd make her mint tea and if her feet were cold I'd put her socks on, which was harder than you might think. They always went on crooked, and it took me a while to get them right. Sometimes I'd sit on the floor by her mechanical bed and do the homework she was so insistent I keep up with. She'd ask me what I was learning about in school. She'd tell me that even if it made the teachers mad I should always ask questions in class if I didn't understand something or, even more important, if I disagreed. "The only dumb questions are the ones you don't ask," she'd say, which was definitely not the opinion held by the majority of teachers at Eden High, who pretty much liked us to keep our traps shut.

Sometimes, especially before it got too hard for her to talk much or she got using the morphine drip, she'd talk about the importance of having dreams. Once, she asked if I understood about her going off to L.A. for the Natalie Wood movie. I told her I guessed I did, but recalling the months she'd been gone, I could feel the ugliness start to come on me and I'd had to tighten my jaw to keep from saying something full of spite.

"Come here, sugar baby," she said, and made me lie next to her. I pretended like I didn't want to, but she'd move over, patting the place by her side until I gave in. "I'm sorry I had to leave, sugar—I know it was hard, hard on you and hard on your daddy—but I'm not sorry I went. I'd be lying if I said I was."

"Even if you never got to make the movie?" I asked.

"Sugar," she said, "it wasn't the movie that was important. It was the dream." Mama believed in the possibility of achieving a champagne dream even if you only had a Budweiser budget. She told me what counted was conceiving of possibilities that stretched beyond us. It was knowing the sky was the limit, of having aspirations in spite of your geography or circumstance, and then reaching for them with all your might. That's what mattered, she said. That and not letting fear of anything or anyone else stop you. If your dreams were true and your heart was big enough, Mama said, you could make them happen. You just couldn't wait too long.

I didn't believe her. How could failing to grab on to the dream you'd believed in and reached for with all your heart, even if it meant deserting a girl and her daddy, how could that not matter? I thought inside she must have been real sad that she didn't get to be Natalie. At that time I thought I believed I knew everything that had ever happened to my mama.

One other thing she said that day. I was lying on the floor arguing with algebra when she whispered something. "What, Mama?" I said, hardly listening. I was thinking that of everything we were supposed to be learning, the one subject I could pretty much be certain of never using in my natural life was anything to do with finding out the value of x and z.

"You're beautiful," Mama said.

"No, I'm not."

"If I'm lying, I'm dying," she said, ignoring the obvious. "You're beautiful, Tallie Brock, and don't let no one ever tell you different."

I didn't believe it, any more than I believed her when she said it was having the dream that mattered, not attaining it.

Finally I finished cleaning up the shampoo. I put in a load of towels and wiped out the sinks. Pearl Summers was sitting in the styling chair and Raylene was applying color and they were both listening to Easter Davis go on about the birthday party she was planning for herself.

"Same as last year?" Raylene shouted. Like half of Raylene's customers, Easter was getting hard-of-hearing.

"Yep," Easter said. "Ain't inviting nothing but men." If Easter wasn't edging into ninety, I'd eat her shoes.

"Do they bring you presents?" Pearl said.

"Well, last year one of them took me to bed."

Everyone laughed, but this didn't seem funny to me. It seemed pure amazing. I tried to imagine a man who would find this chicken-necked old woman worthy of desire. I didn't want to even consider the image of them actually doing it. Desire— the heat of it, like Scarlett wanting Rhett, or Mama falling ass over bandbox for my daddy, or how I felt about Spy—that kind of burning want seemed to rightly belong to the young. I finished cleaning the sink and started on the mirror. I made sure no one was looking and stared full at myself. I wondered if it was me, Tallie Brock, who Spy desired when he'd watched me at the creek, or if he'd have enjoyed the sight of any girl's naked body. I wasn't beautiful. Or even pretty. Not like Elizabeth Talmadge. Or the blonde on the *Glamour Day* poster. Still, I had to admit that in spite of all proof to the contrary staring straight at me from the mirror, the nearest I'd ever come to believing there might be more to Mama's words than the wishful thinking of a mama looking at her daughter, the closest I'd come to believing I was beautiful, was when I'd been standing tall and buck naked in the late-day sun with Spy Reynolds looking on.

The rest of the day we ran late and it was nearly six by the time the last customer left and we'd cleaned up. Raylene told me I could leave at five, but I stayed on. I was feeling good because Easter Davis had surprised me with a whole dollar. At last I had the full twenty I'd be needing for *Glamour Day*. Besides, there was nothing for me to hurry home to except the possibility of getting myself into trouble again. I figured if I stayed busy, there was less chance I'd take myself over to the creek.

Well, surprise, surprise, surprise, when I got home, Daddy was there. He was standing in the kitchen, cooking up greens and pork. Far as I could tell he hadn't been drinking. The only explanation I could figure was that someone had told him about me and Spy, and he'd decided to act like a daddy for once and keep his eye on me. I decided I'd stick with the tactic I'd set out with that morning and deny, deny, deny. Still, I was so nervous, I couldn't sit quiet and got chattering on, trying to make him laugh by telling him about Easter Davis and her men-only birthday party. After a while, when he didn't mention a word about Spy Reynolds, I began to relax. It was almost like it used to be.

My daddy wasn't always the disappearing man. When I was a little girl, he'd take me to Halley's Mill, set me on the counter, and tell everyone I was his little girl. Like I said, he'd explain about the different grains. In early spring, he'd let me go in the room where they kept the chickens. There were hundreds of them, shipped one day old from McMurray Hatchery in Iowa. They arrived at the mill in March and by the end of a month, every one of them would be sold. When they were only days old, Daddy'd lift one out and place it in my hands. It would still be warm from the heat lamp and so soft and light, it was possible to believe it didn't yet have bones. Then Daddy'd take it back and put it in with the others, handling it gentle, like he was afraid it might break. My daddy was probably the only man in all of Amherst County who didn't hunt. Not for sport and not for food, though he'd eat three bowls of venison stew if you put it in front of him.

Before Mama went to L.A., and then when she came home again, Daddy wasn't a drinker. He used to come home regular, every night, without a detour by CC's. Sundays he'd make us barbecue. His pulled pork was better than hers, though she'd make a show of pretending it wasn't. Sometimes he'd turn up the music Mama was playing and make her dance with him, holding her close and dipping her back on the slow ones, even in front of Goody, who'd leave the room sniffing like she smelled something bad. Daddy stood up to Goody's scorn. He said he never pretended to be anything he wasn't.

Even a fool could see he loved Mama more than life. If my daddy was weak, like Goody was always saying, it was the kind of weakness that comes from loving too much, of giving himself away, and I figure there are worse kinds of failings.

Mama loved him back, even if not as hard or deep. "Your daddy has his feet planted solid on the ground," she told me once, "and that allows me to fly." When she was sick, Mama told me, "Anything happens to me, you take care of your daddy," and I promised I would, even when I was wondering who was supposed to be taking care of me.

★ Tallie's Book ★

The only dumb questions are the ones
you don't ask.

Women with fat faces shouldn't wear
bangs.

Conceiving of possibilities is as important
as attaining them.

i stayed in bed late Monday morning. No sense in getting all excited about the prospect of a driving lesson since there'd probably be another broken hip or heart attack calling Martha Lee away. Before I ever learned to drive I figured I'd be courting brittle bones myself. I'd probably be so ancient, I'd present a danger to oncoming traffic, like half the Tuesday customers at the Kurl. I swear their cars looked like rejects from the demolition races over in Spring Hill. Fenders scraped. Doors dented in so far, they hardly opened. Those old ladies were always backing into something. Only thing that kept most of them alive was they drove about as fast as a milk cow standing in the rain. It made Daddy mad enough to suck spit when he got stuck behind them. Except for Easter Davis. She was so tiny, she had to sit on four cushions to see over the steering wheel, but that didn't stop her. Even with every dryer in the Kurl going full blast, you could hear the squeal of brakes every time she pulled into the lot. "Glad to see no radar coming up the road," she'd tell Raylene, testy as usual. One time she lost it on a curve and then walked away and left her car in a ditch somewhere. Daddy said Easter was a hellcat when she was younger, and nothing I could see indicated anything had slowed her down.

It remained a mystery to me why someone like Easter Davis or the Tyree sisters went on living and someone like Mama died. No sense asking questions like that, Goody told me before the funeral, it's just the Lord's way. Which is where I thought He was wrong. It didn't make bit of sense. If He was so powerful, then I hated Him for taking Mama. And if He wasn't and things like people dying had nothing to do with Him, then what was the point of praying? All that talk about the mysterious ways in which He worked was what people like the Reverend Tillett said when they couldn't find meaning in it, either.

Sometimes I wondered how Spy sorted it out after Sarah died. Nights when I used to practice how I'd talk to him if we ever got alone, that's one of the things I worked on. I also wanted to explain why I didn't go to the funeral, how I just couldn't. I wanted to tell him how nice Sarah was, not stuck-up like her friends. I wanted him to know that I never believed the mean-hearted things some of the other girls said about how Sarah died and that I for one truly believed it was possible for a person to drown in Elders Pond, even if she was the best swimmer in the school.

Sarah died the summer we were twelve. The same summer Mama came back from L.A. Mama was the one who told me about Sarah. "Com' here, sugar," she said. "I got something to tell you." I knew it was bad, 'cause all the music was gone from her voice. I thought something had happened to Goody. Or maybe even Daddy. Accidents and fire were the big dangers of working at the mill. When Mama told me Sarah'd drowned, I thought it was a mistake. I didn't think kids like us could die.

The Reynolds had Sarah's funeral at the Episcopal Church, and everyone in town went, but I took myself out to the creek instead and that's where Mama found me. She didn't scold me for not going to the church, or try to make me talk. Mama always knew when it was time for words and when it wasn't. She sat with me until it got dark and didn't say dumb things like it was all right to cry if I wanted to.

"Do you think it hurt to drown?" I finally said.

"I don't know, sugar," she said. "Maybe it's like falling asleep. Maybe after the first—I don't know, panic, I guess—maybe when that goes, you just drift off. Maybe it's like being a baby inside a mama's belly, taking water into your lungs. In that way, maybe it's like returning home."

Talking like that, Mama made it sound almost comforting, but I didn't think it was that way at all. Not close. One time I'd swum too far out in the same pond where Sarah drowned and I was taken by a cramp. Before Wiley and Will could get me, I went under twice, thrashing my arms like a crazy person, screaming for my mama and choking till it burned. All the things I knew about swimming just went flying clear out of my brain. When Wiley got me to shore, I nearly puked. Then I made both of them swear not to tell Mama. From this personal experience, I didn't think drowning was some kind of drifting off at all. I was fixing to tell Mama that, but something stopped me. Maybe she was needing to think it'd be peaceful. Maybe she was thinking of Natalie Wood. Mama had nightmares about Natalie drowning. She knew all the details by heart—how Natalie'd been all alone and maybe crying out for help while that awful

Robert Wagner, who always looked like he had makeup on, was getting drunk with that other creep Christopher Walken. I wondered if Sarah had cried out. I wondered if she'd screamed for her mama. I wondered why she was swimming alone in Elders Pond, something she'd told me her mama forbid.

Rula Wade told me about the funeral. She said Sarah was wearing the white dress she'd worn for the awards assembly, the one with the lavender sash, and was laid out in a white coffin covered with flowers, thick and complete as a blanket. She said someone put a teddy bear in with Sarah, which was a baby thing to do, 'cause she was twelve, but later all the girls agreed it was okay because when they closed the lid and put her in the ground, it would be nice to think of her not being alone. Rula said at the visiting hours every table in Wesler's Funeral Home was covered with flowers except the ones holding photos of Sarah. There were about a thousand photos, she said, starting from the time Sarah was a baby, all the way to her class pictures. Her trophy from the spelling bee was there, too. And all her ribbons from swim meets. Rula said the kids from school were crying, even the boys. Even Spy? I asked, and she said yes, everybody. She said Sarah's mama was talking crazy and grabbing on to everyone and saying what a beautiful girl her Sarah was, what an angel, and how her angel was with God now, but Rula said she wouldn't let go of your arm and you had to kind of jerk it away, and the adults were whispering she was acting that way because she'd taken too many of the pills that were supposed to calm her down but didn't. Hearing about it, I determined funerals were spooky and I vowed I was never going to one. Not even when Goody passed.

Mama's funeral came that November.

*   *   *

A horn blasting outside interrupted my thinking. Not the dum-da-da-dum-dum honk that Mama used to sound when she was impatient to get moving. This was serious blasting, someone lying on the horn, not about to give up. "Okay, okay," I shouted. "Keep your damn pants on." I stripped off my pajamas and struggled into a pair of too tight cutoffs. Daddy never noticed things like my needing clothes. Pretty soon I'd have to talk to him about getting things that fit, a prospect that was none too pleasing. He'd take me to Shucks Discount or one of the outlets on the way to Lynchburg and wait in the truck while I shopped for something my size, which was better than the first time when he went inside with me and made me so nervous, I shoved this dumb pair of purple and blue striped pants in the cart just so we could get out of there. "That all you need?" he kept asking and, desperate to escape, I'd said yes.

Martha Lee was waiting outside. "Come on, Cookie," she said. "We've got places to go and people to see. Where've you been, anyway? I thought you'd be waking me up instead of the other way around. I thought you wanted to learn how to drive."

"So stop talking and let's go," I said, and slid into the cab without looking at her.

"You okay?"

"Sure," I said. It was hard to look directly at Martha Lee. The money I stole kept getting in the way.

"You had breakfast?"

"Not hungry," I said.

She pretended to push a buzzer on the dashboard. "*Bzzzzz.*

Wrong answer." She swung into the drive-thru of the doughnut shop and ordered two jumbo coffees, with double cream, and a box of chocolate-covered. "Got to fuel up, girl. We got serious business at hand." For a nurse she wasn't overly concerned about nutrition. Diet wasn't even in her vocabulary. Once on the road, we headed west, out toward the Blue Ridge. She downed two doughnuts before I got the lid off my coffee. A blind man could see how she got to be so big. But then she didn't have to worry about the extra ten pounds the camera added to your figure.

The whole cab smelled of grease. "Where're we going?" I asked. I reached for a doughnut. One wouldn't hurt, even if the sweetness of it so early in the day might make me a little sick.

"Someplace where you can get behind the wheel without smashing into anyone so I won't have to be getting a loan to pay for insurance." She licked her fingers clean, then fished around in the box for another chocolate-covered.

"I'm not going to hit someone," I said. Jeez, if Elizabeth Talmadge could learn to drive, or Rula Wade, for God's sake, how hard could it be?

Finally we got to this stretch of dirt road so overgrown, it looked like it hadn't been used since the Baby Jesus was teething. She pulled over and switched the engine off so we could change seats. Then we went through all the stuff about the clutch and brake and accelerator, the business about shifting gears, which she made me practice. The first time, I ground those gears like hamburger 'cause I didn't depress the clutch all the way in, but pretty soon I could do it smooth as milk and she said I was going to be a natural. At last she told me to turn the key and set the gear in first. I pushed the clutch in so hard, it almost went through the floorboard, then stepped on the gas, letting up the clutch at the same time like she told me, but the old pickup started to buck and jump and the box of chocolate-covereds went flying off the seat, and then we stalled. Martha Lee didn't get mad, she just said real patient-like, "Ease up on the clutch. That's the secret. Let it up real easy. Okay. Let's try again." I could just imagine how Mr. Nelson would be acting if this were driver's ed. He'd be having a double coronary.

I tried again, but I was getting pretty nervous and the damn truck was jumping so much, you'd think I was riding a bronco. Pretty soon the cab was such a mess with spilled coffee and smashed doughnuts, it'd take a washing with a hose to clean it out, but Martha Lee was laughing like crazy, like that was the least of her worries, and that set me off, too. We got screaming so hard, I had to concentrate not to pee my pants and it didn't even matter if I was going to learn to drive or not. All the laughter erased all the bad feelings in my heart about stealing the money, and I could look Martha Lee straight in the face, but each time I did, we'd just start up again. The last time I'd heard her laugh like that—the screaming laughter that ended with you crying or peeing your pants—was when Mama was alive.

By the end of October, Mama pretty much stayed in bed, and Martha Lee had all but moved in. Goody even came up from Florida, and for once she was in the house more than ten minutes without getting in a spat with everyone. She kept calling Mama her baby and fixing little bowls of vanilla custard for her. She'd make cups of peppermint tea, which she said always soothed a sour stomach. Even after a couple of days passed and she'd returned to being her usual bossy self and kept telling

Daddy that Mama should be in a hospital or someplace where there were real nurses to take care of her and not an LPN, my mama stayed calm. That's enough, she told Goody in this real quiet voice, and wonder of wonders, Goody just shut up.

After that, Goody started cleaning the house like dirt was her enemy. She scoured everything but the inside of the toilet tank and probably would have done that if she'd thought of it. She grumbled on about how Mama was born stubborn and if she didn't change her ways her pigheadedness would be the death of us all, and the trouble with Mama was that no one stood up to her, least of all my daddy, that in the eyes of most people Mama could do no wrong, and any sane person could see she should be in a hospital where she'd get sufficient care. She was careful to say these things when Mama couldn't hear. She'd save most of it up until night, when we were in bed, then she'd start in, like I was at fault. The whole bed smelled of her dental adhesive and the sour smell of old skin, and I'd think, God, if you're listening, if you're even *there*, why can't you take this mean old woman instead of Mama? In spite of everything, I don't think any of us—Goody or me or Daddy—really believed Mama was going to die. How could someone that beautiful and alive die?

At Halloween, Mama asked me what costume I was going to wear, just like this was an ordinary year, but I told her I was too old to go off with the Bettis twins. I said I'd stay home and hand out Tootsie Rolls. The next day, when I came home, Martha Lee was there as usual and there was a dummy sitting on the mechanical bed with Mama. He was dressed all in black, both the suit and hat, and was wearing sunglasses, just like the ones of the Blues Brothers. For the face, Martha Lee had used a mask of Bill Clinton. It drove Goody crazy. She was sputtering

and slamming things around in the kitchen. Every time she
came in the front room where Mama's bed was, she'd give
Martha Lee an evil look.

"Is it Duane?" I asked Mama. It drove Goody bughouse
when they started in on the Duane stories. Usually she'd get up
and leave the room, dragging her sniffy disapproval with her.

"Nope."

"It's not?" As far as I knew, they'd never made a dummy
that wasn't named Duane.

"Nope."

"Then who?" In spite of herself, Goody was getting interested.

"G. R.," Mama said.

"G. R.?"

"Yep."

In my head, I ran through the list of everyone we knew.
"Mr. Rollins?" I asked, though I had no idea what his first name
was.

"Nope," Mama said.

Then I thought of George Reynolds, Spy and Sarah's daddy.
He always wore a suit and tie, even at the annual school picnic
when even the teachers knew enough not to dress up.

"No," Mama said.

"Give me a hint," I begged.

"One hint," Mama said. "It isn't anyone from Eden." She
and Martha Lee couldn't stop grinning.

I studied the dummy, looking for some clue. "A movie
star?" I said. "Or someone on TV?"

"Nope."

"I know," Goody said.

"You do?" I said.

She smiled, pleased with herself. "It's the Great Redeemer."

"Nope," Mama said. "But you're close." She and Martha Lee giggled harder, until the coughing started up.

"Well, who then?" I said. "I give up."

"The Grim Reaper," Mama said.

Goody stood up so fast, her chair fell over. Her chin started shaking like she'd got palsy. "You go too far," she said to Martha Lee. "You go too damn far."

For once I had to agree with her.

The next day Goody told Mama the dummy went or she did, and when Mama wouldn't cave, Goody went back to Florida. Everyone thought she was spitting mad, but the night before she left, she was quiet in bed, not one complaining word about Mama or Daddy or Martha Lee. Later that night, I woke up to her crying. I just lay there pretending to sleep and listening to the scary sound of her little hiccuping sobs. "Oh, my baby," she said once in a low, ragged voice, like she had pains in her belly.

The next day, when Daddy and I drove her to Lynchburg, she gave me a kiss on the lips and before she got on the plane, she handed me a ten-dollar bill. I almost fainted from shock. And even though I was relieved that I wouldn't have to be sharing my bed anymore and listening to her complaining, I was suddenly sad she was going.

The Grim Reaper stayed in a chair next to Mama's bed and pretty soon it seemed like he belonged there. Martha Lee took to dressing up his outfit. She jammed a cigarette in the mouth of the Clinton mask and set a bottle of Pabst in his hand. Once, she hung an *Out to Lunch* sign around his neck and set the hands on the little fake clock to read eight P.M. Mama pulled a rose from the bouquet my Uncle Grayson sent and stuck it in his lapel. After that, the dummy got a flower from every bunch that came into the house for Mama. Roses, carnations, and daisies covered his suit coat like some kind of badges. They stayed there even after they wilted. Before long, when people came to visit, they brought things to give to Duane, which was what Mama and Martha Lee had gone back to calling the dummy. When the preacher from Elijah Baptist came by, surprising Mama, who didn't know about my attending there regular, he asked to be introduced and then patted his pockets until he found a stick of Juicy Fruit. Raylene brought a comb from the Kurl, one of the pink ones with *Klip-N-Kurl* in gold letters on the spine that she handed out at Christmastime. "With a head of hair like that, he'll be needing it," she said. Daddy was the only one who never brought anything for Duane. Then one night, he slipped a crow feather in the brim of the black hat; when he did that, Mama smiled at him like he was handing her a gift. After that, there was no stopping him. He brought a pumpkin and a little pack of cigars and a feedbag from the mill that he fashioned into a sling, like Duane had a broken arm. Later, when Mama went on the morphine drip, he made one for him, too. Mama said it was the best Duane ever.

After a while I wanted to give up on the driving, but Martha Lee told me to try it one more time, and maybe it was because I was relaxed from laughing so hard and didn't have room for nerves, but this time it was perfect. I cranked the shift from first straight through second to third without jerking at all, easing up on the clutch like I'd always known how. The rest was easy.

I didn't even swerve all over the road like you might think I would. Martha Lee said I had a natural aptitude for steering. She promised she'd get me a book of driving rules and said we could practice again the next week. Then she took me out for pizza and ice cream.

"Don't tell your daddy about the driving," she said when she dropped me off. "We'll just surprise him." Which was fine with me. There would be less chance that he'd say I couldn't do it. If he even remembered I was alive.

I was fixing dinner when I realized I hadn't had the empty-hole-feeling in my belly for hours. For a fact I'd have to say it was the best day I'd spent since Mama passed on.

★ Tallie's Book ★

Peppermint tea will soothe a sour stomach.

Even if people act like they're mad, underneath they can be really feeling sad.

Like most things in life, driving isn't hard once you get the knack of it. Getting the knack is the hard part.

for the next three days I rode over to the creek straight from the Kurl, and it had nothing to do with the record high temperatures we were experiencing or my need to get cooled down. Truth was, I didn't want cooling down. I wanted to feel the heat in my belly again, the way I had when Spy was looking at me. For sure, I knew I should be staying away from Baldy and this shameful temptation to display myself, but you couldn't have kept me away if you tied me to a kitchen chair and double locked the door. Some mighty force inside was pulling me, like in science class when we watched the little black filings swoop across the lab table to the horseshoe magnet. "Magnetic attraction," Mr. Brown told the class. He said it was an irresistible force of nature. That's how I felt. Like I had this urgent force building inside me, and the lodestone drawing it was Spy.

Just thinking about the possibility of him being there made my thighs feel heavy and my belly get warm, but he never came. Not once. Wiley was there the second day I went there, but Will was nowhere to be seen. He acted like such a goof that I finally asked him what the hell was the matter, was he having the curse, which was one of the things the girls in school call being in your moon. He turned red and said what was the matter with *me*, I was the one acting like she was on the rag, which is one of the gross things the boys call your moon. Goody said sometimes men could be crude-crude-crude, and Wiley was proving her right.

When Spy didn't appear on the third day, it occurred to me that he might have gone to Virginia Beach and that was why he hadn't come back to the creek. Va Beach was what the popular kids all called it, like it was their private oh-so-cool name. Their special code. But if one of the regular kids said it, they'd look at them like there was snot running down their chin. Going to Va Beach was a summer tradition for kids going off to college in the fall. They'd rent a house for a weekend and would party-party-party, then they'd spend the rest of the summer bragging about how wasted they got. I wouldn't go if they asked me, and not only because Elizabeth Talmadge would have wrangled herself an invitation even if she hadn't graduated yet, and I'd have to spend the weekend listening to her make fun of my clothes. During lunch period, she always made a big deal about how there was a clothing sale at the church thrift shop in town and maybe I should check it out. She did that even before Mama took sick.

The Queen of the World was the one who started calling me Bullwinkle, after that stupid cartoon with the moose, because my real name is Natasha like one of the characters on the show. I told her I was named for Natalie Wood, and she said, Oh, really, how droll, which is the phony way she talked sometimes. Mama said Elizabeth teased me because she was jealous, which is the kind of thing mamas have to say to their kids.

"Right, Mama," I said. "Elizabeth Talmadge, who is the most popular of all the popular girls, who lives the perfect life in a perfect house and wears perfect clothes, Elizabeth Talmadge who is Queen of the Universe, who is probably Queen of the Whole Solar System, yeah, Elizabeth Talmadge has plenty of cause to be jealous of Tallie Brock. She probably cries herself to sleep every night, she's so envious of me."

Mama told me that sarcasm wasn't becoming, and then she said there wasn't a soul alive who lived a perfect life or was perfect, least of all a girl who tried to humiliate others.

Anyway, when Spy didn't show up at the creek, I was feeling that irresistible attraction so strong that before I could stop myself, I phoned his house just so I could hear his voice. The first time I called, his mama answered. She sounded so whispery, I could barely hear her. The second time, I swear she said, "Sarah, is that you?" I remembered what Rula had said about Sarah's funeral and I hung up while she was still asking who's there and was it Sarah. I tried one last time, at night, when I thought for sure Spy'd answer, but this time I got Mr. Reynolds and he threatened to call the police if whoever it was didn't stop harassing them. I knew you could get these things to attach to your phone that'd show who was calling and that would be all I needed, so I stopped.

Finally I decided the best thing to get Spy interested was to wait until I had the nine by twelve Glamour Pic of me transformed into a star. I'd find a way for Spy to see that picture if I had to mail it to him. Everything depended on the photo. Both getting to Hollywood and getting Spy.

Just because I was preoccupied with Spy didn't mean I'd given up my idea of going to L.A. I figured it out at night when

I couldn't sleep. When Spy was at UVA working toward becoming a lawyer, I'd be developing my career. We'd come back to Eden to be married. Ours would be the biggest, most important wedding Amherst County had ever seen.

My mama and daddy never had a wedding, which was another thing Goody used to rant on about. I must have heard a thousand times how she'd been cheated of seeing Mama dressed in white and going down the aisle. They had this argument so many times, I could recite it by heart.

"That's why we eloped, Mama," my mama told her. "Luddy and I couldn't face the prospect of the circus you were hell-bent on providing."

"What's wrong with wanting to see your only daughter married in style?" Goody said. "Just tell me, what's the sin in that?"

"Don't pull that 'only daughter' crap on me," Mama said right back. "It's not my fault you didn't have more kids."

"Perhaps I should have," Goody said, straightening her wrinkled neck. "Then I might have had a daughter with a bone or two of gratitude in her body, a daughter who *appreciated* all the sacrifices her mama made instead of throwing it away on some bit of mill-hand trash."

Mama got the dangerous look she wore whenever Goody was mean about Daddy. "If you're so all-fired hot to have a wedding in the family," she said, going for the place that would hurt Goody most, "then you should tell your precious Grayson to get married."

"You leave Grayson out of this," Goody said.

My Uncle Grayson lived in Atlanta, where he was an accountant for some big company. He lived with another man, his housemate, according to Goody, who told people Grayson was waiting to find the right woman, a woman good enough for him, not the first piece of trash to swing her skirt across his path. Goody said that, but it was common knowledge Uncle Grayson wouldn't ever be getting married. At least not in any wedding that Goody'd want to be within a million miles of.

Mama loved him, though. "You ever need anything, sugar, you call your Uncle Grayson," she said when she was real sick. She told me lots of things I should do when she was gone, like finish school and follow my dream and not let anyone get in my way or tell me I couldn't have the life I wanted. I couldn't bear to listen at first, and at the end, with the morphine and all, what she said didn't make sense. She'd say things like, "Listen to the bark of trees," and, "Bite the vein of life," and other stuff that sounded crazy. Sometimes she'd look straight at me and smile and call me Sasha. At first I thought she was having trouble with my name, but then she'd say it again. Clear as can be. *Sasha.* "It's me, Mama," I'd say. "Tallie." "I know, dear," she'd say, and call me Sasha again.

The shame of life is we're only given one chance at everything as it passes by. If I could do it over again, I'd take back every mean-hearted thing I ever said to Mama. And I'd concentrate on everything she said and I'd write it all down careful, word for word. Then I wouldn't have to try to recall it all from memory. And I wouldn't have to be always listening to the women at the Kurl and conversations in the girls' room at school for things to be putting in my rule book, things a girl needed to know to become a woman. I'd get it straight from Mama.

*   *   *

By that November, Mama wasn't eating enough to keep a bee alive. She stopped listening to TV because the noise hurt her. She didn't even want music, music that'd been like blood in her veins—country and Elvis and all the oldies. She asked us to turn it off. She wanted peace, she said. She needed quiet. During the day, she lay drowning in the folds of her blue robe, her lips chapped and cracked. Sometimes she'd ask for little pieces of ice that she'd hold in her mouth till they melted. In the night, I'd hear her moaning. "I'm here, darlin'," Daddy'd say. "Right here." He'd taken to sleeping on the floor beside her mechanical bed.

"She'd be better off in the hospital," the doctor told Daddy one day.

"She wants to stay right here," Daddy told him. "In her home."

"Can't you make her go?" the doctor asked. "Can't you make her see the sense in being there where we can regulate things?"

Daddy kind of smiled. "Not a person alive can make Dinah Mae do something when she's got her mind set."

Then the doctor said something about "lungs to bone to brain," and I ran out of the house before I could hear any more. It made me worse than sad to see Mama like that, but I didn't cry. I was afraid if I started I'd never stop, and I think that was when the hard black thing first took root in my chest, a thing that hurt, like a rib was broken or missing.

It made my heart about break to look at Mama's feet. Her perfect, size-five feet, feet that had danced the boogie and enraptured my daddy, had turned ugly, swelling nearly double and fatter than Effie Webb's and hers spilled over the tops of her shoes. When she was on morphine, Mama kept telling us her feet were cold but when we covered them with a blanket, she got fussy and told us to get rid of it. "Take off my shoes," she said and, no matter how many times we told her she wasn't wearing any, she kept after us to take them off. "Okay, Cookie," Martha Lee'd finally say, "we'll take them off," and that would calm Mama down.

It made me jealous sometimes, the way Martha Lee did everything for Mama, but I was glad, too, relieved that I didn't have to do things like change the diapers she had to wear or clean up the snot that ran out of her nose when she was out cold from the morphine, stuff that I couldn't do no matter how much I loved Mama. But Martha Lee didn't mind a bit. "Come on, Cookie," she'd say in this straight voice that wasn't the phony kind people sometimes used, like they were talking to a retard instead of a sick person. Her voice was soft and made the back of my throat ache just to listen to it. "Let's get you cleaned up and in a new outfit and then I'll put some lotion on your back." Then she'd bring in a basin and cloth and wash Mama all over and put on a clean gown, one of those ugly things that tie in back like they make you wear in hospitals. She'd brush Mama's hair and tie it back with a ribbon, and put a little blush on her cheeks, and while she was at it, she put some on Duane's Clinton-mask cheeks, too. That always made Mama smile. Martha Lee'd tell Mama she looked as pretty as a carnival doll. "You, too," Mama'd say back. There was not a cold chance in hell anyone would ever be mistaking Martha Lee for a carnival doll, but watching her with Mama I could understand why sick folk might believe she was an angel.

*   *   *

Anyway, with *Glamour Day* a key part of my plan to get Spy to
love me, I was so het up, I couldn't sleep the night before the
team of trained professionals was finally set to arrive. I'd close
my eyes and picture the blonde in the poster, then I'd put myself in her place, the pink boa draped around my neck. Then I'd
open my eyes and check the bedside clock to see how much
longer I had to wait. It felt like morning would never arrive.
Daddy rolled in after one. Last call at CC's, I thought, and stared
up at the ceiling, at the stars Mama'd stuck there. She'd put
them there when I was ten. A whole constellation that glowed
faintly in the dark, with moons and planets complete with little
rings. I didn't see them at first and when I finally noticed them,
she said they'd been there for a week. "Why didn't I see them?" I
asked her. "You weren't expecting them," she said. "Sugar," she
said, "you got to keep your eyes open for the unexpected. Especially when it's been right in front of you all the time."

I could tell right away it was one of Daddy's noisy nights.
Sometimes when he came home from CC's, he wasn't too bad,
but that night I followed his progress through the kitchen,
falling over every chair, then into the bathroom. I prayed he
wasn't too drunk to aim true, because I was so g.d. sick of
wiping his pee drops off the floor, I could puke. I'm not the
maid, I wanted to tell him. Finally I heard him fall into bed and
pretty soon he was snoring. My daddy was the champion
snorer. If they had medals for it, he'd have gotten the gold.
"Your Daddy's not a bad man," Raylene told me once. "He just
needs someone to take him in hand."

*   *   *

He woke up before I did. When I walked into the kitchen, he had the coffee made and was frying up some eggs, although you had to marvel that he could walk straight, never mind handle a fry pan. "Early bird gets the breakfast," he said, and poured me a mug, then—surprise-surprise-surprise—he gave me the eggs he'd been cooking for himself. He was happy as a pig in shit, whistling like crazy while he fried up more eggs for himself. I'd eaten half my breakfast when I really tuned in, and that was when it hit me. He was whistling that old blues song, "I'm a Man," the one Mama knew meant he was working himself up to apologize for some harm done.

I shoved the eggs around the plate, my appetite flown straight out the window. It's nothing, I told myself. He's probably only feeling bad for staying out half the night and drinking up the bill money while the Cash Store cuts off our credit and I go around in midget's clothes. It's nothing. But in my belly, it didn't feel like nothing. When he sat down to eat, he stopped whistling, but guilt lay on his face, plain as white on rice. On the pretense of getting more coffee, I took a look out the window to check on the truck, see if it was smashed up, but it was the same as usual, just the one fender bashed in. It's nothing, I told myself again, searching for reassurance. Then I remembered Rula Wade and how her daddy'd married a woman half his age. I knew women hung around CC's. I looked across the table and stared at him, trying to picture him with anyone but Mama. The closed place deep inside my chest got a little tighter. He'd finished his eggs and was taking up the tune again.

When he left for the mill, he mussed up my hair, like I was five. He was still whistling when he went out the door. To erase the notes from my head, I cranked up the radio. They were playing an Elvis tune. "Blue Hawaii." Which of course made me think of my mama. Mama never was convinced Elvis had actually died. His name was misspelled on the tombstone at Graceland, she said, and that was a sign intended to show it wasn't really him buried there. Lord, but she pure adored Elvis. I remembered the time by the creek when she'd told Martha Lee that Elvis could put his boots under her bed any night. He and Sam Shepard, even if Sam wasn't handsome in the traditional way. Mama said Sam Shepard looked like he could carry on a conversation without having to circle around to repeat himself. I thought this revealed Mama's imagination. Then I wondered how you could have feelings of desire for more than one person. I thought that would get complicated.

After I finished with the dishes, I took a shower. Even though they wouldn't show in the picture, I shaved my legs and coated them with lotion. From time to time, in spite of the radio blasting from the kitchen, Daddy's old blues tune took up residence in my head, making me edgy, but then the excitement about the *Glamour Day* pushed it aside.

I hadn't said one word to Daddy about the picture. I wanted to surprise him. I could imagine how proud he'd be when he saw me *transformed*. I was thinking, too, that when he saw I could be pretty, like Mama, maybe he'd want to pay more attention to me.

When I was finally ready, I was so excited, I could have run the whole way to the Kurl. Last thing before I left, I went to the kitchen, switched off the radio, and reached up for Mama's silver syrup pitcher. Before I even lifted the lid, I knew the money was gone, and then I understood why Daddy'd been whistling and looking so guilty. I didn't waste one minute attempting to deny the hard proof that lay right before my eyes. Of all the bad times in my life, all the disappointments and losses, this about matched the day they buried Mama. But, just like then, I didn't cry.

It took a while to get settled. I had to sit down and close my eyes and rock. Back and forth, back and forth, holding tight to the dark place, holding tight till I could get steady.

★ Tallie's Book ★

Not one person alive lives a perfect life.

Keep your eyes open for the unexpected.

Never count on anything.

t e n

*m*aybe you'd think I would be mad at my daddy, that it would be what that head doctor called *proper affect*, but I didn't waste the time. It made about as much sense getting mad at him as at Old Straw for chasing squirrels. He stole from me, but nothing but three dollars of that money was ever mine anyway. Him taking the money was no worse than me stealing it from Martha Lee. We both were just going after something we desired. Seems like that was what everyone was doing. Everyone, Daddy and me included, was just going around trying to satisfy cravings held inside. It explained why Martha Lee ate chocolate dough-nuts and Goody went to Florida. It was why Mama married Daddy. It was why she went off to Hollywood. It was why I stood naked as a newborn and let Spy travel his eyes all over my body.

Besides, I had too much on my mind to be occupied with being mad. All the time I was riding the Raleigh to the Kurl, I was busy asking for a miracle. Even when she was real sick, Mama said it never hurt to ask for one. She said documentation existed proving miracles happened all the time. Blind people regaining their sight. Crippled people walking. Wishes being granted. Mama believed that life was full of miracles. She said when you thought about it, a baby being born should be proof enough for anyone. I wasn't asking for something big, like curing cancer. I was asking to be able to be transformed.

Raylene wasn't open when I got to the Kurl, but there were ladies already standing outside, crowding at the door like it was half-price sale at the Dollar Days. Inside, the *Glamour Day* people were already setting up. The team of trained professionals were actually two women, both bottle blondes and wearing identical pink suits with *Glamour Day* spelled out in purple stitching on the pocket, and high-heeled shoes that Mama would say were killer. I thought the company could have taken more care with the people they sent out if they wanted us to believe they were capable of causing transformations. The large one—Mama always said never to call someone fat; she said "large" is a good word to use for a big lady—the large one was setting up her equipment at one of the comb-out chairs. She unloaded this square purple suitcase that was full of makeup and held about a hundred lipsticks and jars and jars of other stuff and a big bag full of throwaway sponges.

The skinny one was out front rearranging the chairs and magazine table to make room for the camera. She had this black folding screen set up with a chair placed in front of it, where she'd take the pictures. Off to the side was this full-sized, chrome coatrack, the kind you see at restaurants, and it was jammed with so many clothes, there wasn't room to fit one more item. Feather boas in every bold color you could imagine. Dozens of sequined halters in red and green and purple and gold, hanging like racing silks at the Derby. Velvet tube tops and stretchy tight ones. Satin blouses with low necks. (The picture only showed you from the neck up.) Leather jackets in a dozen shades, some with fringe attached to the sleeves. On the shelf over the rack there were hats. Cowboy hats and berets and a couple with wide brims and veils. There were elbow-length gloves in a variety of colors, and a compartmentalized container that looked like an oversized tackle box that was crammed with jewelry. Big rings with fake stones and rhinestone bracelets, wide slave bracelets, and dangling earrings that fell near to your shoulders. I saw a pearl choker. And some flapper girl headbands. Even a tiara.

Finally everything was ready. When Raylene unlocked the door, the ladies pushed in, shoving like the first one got a prize. As I said, there was usually a lot of talk in the Kurl, but I swear you could hear the babble of voices clear down to the old depot. They were acting like high school girls crowding around the girls' room mirror at a school dance. They were making jokes about men and sex. I couldn't remember seeing grown-up women act this way, except for Mama and Martha Lee.

Even though she wasn't the top name on the list, everyone insisted that Miss Tilly was first. While Raylene was doing her hair, the others started pawing through the clothes, talking about what they were going to choose when it was their turn, until the skinny woman had to calm them down. When Raylene had Miss Tilly washed and was doing the roll-up, I began on Ellie Sue Rucker, whose stomach was sticking out so far, I was just hoping she didn't give birth while I was shampooing. The miracle of birth wasn't what I'd had in mind when I'd been praying. Lorena was shampooing at the other sink, and we were so busy, she didn't have time to even think of looking at suds and telling fortunes. We had an assembly line going. Pretty soon every station had a lady sitting in the chair. One got shampooed, another got a set, or a blow-dry with a touch of the curling wand. One lady sat in front of the mirror and let the large blonde pile on the makeup, while another one was posing in front of the camera, dressed from the waist up in the most beguiling getup she could conceive. The rhinestones and elbow-length gloves were proving popular.

Miss Tilly was the first one to get done. At her age, she had more pink scalp than hair, but Raylene ratted every strand of what she did have and arranged it in little curls around her face, then lacquered the whole job, spraying on so much, you'd need a chisel to set it free. At the makeup table, the large woman was wielding a fat brush just like the highly trained professional the company said she was. "We want everything going up," she said while she flicked blusher on Miss Tilly's cheeks. "Gravity drags us down." By the time Miss Tilly was ready for the photo part, everyone wanted to help her pick out the clothes. I still couldn't imagine why she wanted her photo taken, but she was acting as silly as the rest. Everyone had an opinion, but she finally decided on a deep blue velvet blouse. Someone, I think it was Bitty Weatherspoon, fastened this band of blue velvet at her neck and pretty soon every inch of her crepey skin was covered in velvet. She sat carefully in front of that black screen, like she'd suddenly become glass, and I had to admit she looked sort of regal. You got to pick five outfits and the skinny blonde took your picture in every one, but Miss Tilly was so pleased with the velvet, she only changed jewelry.

Pretty soon it was so noisy, you couldn't hear the radio if it'd been cranked on full. Willa Jenkins arrived, dragging her two friends along, and the three of them were all gussied up, calling each other *sistah*, and acting like they were the Pointer Sisters. They were naturals at this glamour business, and people began asking their advice. Like should they wear the satin or the sequins for the last shot. Even Mary Lou acted like they were regulars at the Kurl. The Glamour ladies had long since stripped off their pink jackets. Their faces wore pinched looks, like their feet hurt. I could have told them they should have brought other shoes. By noon, the place was packed with overly made-up women, glittering and giggly. It looked like outside the Dorothy Chandler Pavilion before the Academy Awards. Even the ones who'd already had their picture taken weren't leaving. They were crowding around the clothes rack and making suggestions for the next person in line. You could almost touch the excitement. Like in school the last day before vacation. Or on the Fourth of July, that exact moment you heard the tubas, just before the Sparkettes came into view, leading the Eden Marching Band.

Raylene was outdoing herself in the coiffeur department, ratting and lacquering up a storm. I was running my feet off, shampooing and throwing in load after load of laundry, and all the while hoping for a miracle. Hoping someone would come along and hand me a twenty-dollar bill.

I was finishing up on Aubrey Boles, rinsing conditioner out of her too-black hair, and Raylene was working on Etta Bird's hair, right in the middle of swirling it into an updo, an early Grace Kelly style that to this day remains popular in Eden, when the door opened and everyone stopped talking. The sound *whished* right out of the Kurl like air from a punctured Goodyear. I looked up and although I believed my lifetime

capacity for surprise had long been exhausted, I was so astonished at what was right in front of my eyes, I stopped dead in
the middle of Aubrey's rinse. Martha Lee was standing at the
door, feet rooted on the pink and black linoleum.

"Why, Martha Lee, honey," Raylene said, polite and com-
posed as if Martha Lee showed up every day. "You come right in
and grab yourself a seat. We're kind of busy here, but I'll be with
you in a sec."

For a minute, standing on the foreign territory of the Kurl,
Martha Lee got this panicky look on her face, then she bucked
up, as Daddy would say, and stood her ground. She didn't once
look my way. "I came for that," she said, and pointed to the
easel holding the framed photo of the blonde. Raylene finished
spraying lacquer on Etta's French twist, then crossed to the
desk and made a show of checking the sign-up sheet.

"I'm sorry, honey," she said to Martha Lee. "The schedule is
jam-packed full. You needed to sign up before this."

Martha Lee swallowed so hard, I swear I could hear it over
the sound of the dryers, which were the only things making
noise. For once, everyone's mouth was shut tighter than a tick.
"Please," she said. "Isn't there something? I'll wait."

This was not Martha Lee talking. The Martha Lee I knew
would be hightailing it out of there the first time Raylene called
her honey. The Martha Lee I knew wouldn't be caught dead at
the Kurl in the first place. This was a person acting like she'd
been taken over by ETs. Oh, Mama, I was thinking, if you could
only see this. Martha Lee was still trying to talk Raylene into
adding her to the list and Raylene was saying, sorry, honey, but
the schedule is filled and there's not one thing I can do about it,
and Martha Lee was persisting and I couldn't understand her

determination or what reason she had for coming in. I wished she'd just get out of there before she saw Ashley Wheeler smirking behind her back, and it was all I could do to keep from slapping Ashley 'cause she hadn't had to spend one day in her entire life wondering what it would be like to be born plain. Then I thought about Martha Lee teaching me to drive and I heard Mama in my head telling me what to do, and going along with Mama's voice was my own, and it was telling me I wasn't getting any miracle, but Martha Lee could have hers since that was what—for whatever reason—she was determined to have. I left Aubrey Boles dripping in the sink and marched over to the front desk.

"Raylene," I said. "Martha Lee can have my spot."

Raylene gave me a hard look. "You sure about that, Tallie?"

"I'm sure," I said, though a part of me was half counting on Martha Lee refusing my offer. But Martha Lee, who had been listening to me steady for two weeks going on about nothing but the *Glamour Day*, Martha Lee who didn't know I'd lost the money for it, Martha Lee didn't even pretend I should keep my appointment. She took my spot like it was possible for me to have a *Glamour Day* every week of my life, like it was nothing special for me even though she'd have to have gone deaf as a post not to have heard me say I was counting on it. She went over to the waiting chairs and buried her face in an old copy of *Hair Style*. She was still wearing her goddamn gardening boots and looked as out of place as it was possible for a person to look and still manage to take a breath. Still, mad as I was at Martha Lee, I knew if Ashley said one mean thing or rolled her eyes one more time, I'd slap her.

"You're a good girl," Raylene said. Even though I knew she

believed that because she couldn't see the truth of my trashy, stealing self, I liked hearing it. "Your mama'd be proud," she said.

Soon everything got back to normal. We hadn't stopped for lunch, and around two, Raylene surprised everyone by taking money out of the cash box and sending for pizza. When it was time for Martha Lee's shampoo, I was busy with Sue Beth Wilkins and Lenora got to do her, which made me just as glad. It would feel funny to have my hands on Martha Lee's head. Lenora had to show Martha Lee how to sit in the shampoo chair, and I could tell my mama's best friend was embarrassed, but she'd gotten herself into this, and I wasn't doing anything to get her out. I was rinsing Sue Beth, when Lenora made this funny noise. I looked over and she was staring in the sink where the soap from Martha Lee's shampoo was sitting. Jesus, God, I prayed, don't let it be the dove of death or worse, the violent-death horse, 'cause I don't think I can take another funeral. When Lenora looked up she stared at me just like she'd been staring at Martha Lee's suds, and she got this real peculiar look on her face. She looked at Martha Lee and then at me, like she was seeing something that connected us. Next thing, she started laughing.

"What's so funny," Martha Lee said, and I could tell by the knife in her voice that she'd about used up everything she had that had gotten her to the Kurl.

"Nothing," Lenora said, but she was still looking at me, her eyes all crinkling, and I wanted to break every bone in that old arthritic body. I guessed she knew about the money I took from Martha Lee. But at least she wasn't seeing any old dove in the sink.

Raylene didn't set Martha Lee's hair. She combed it flat and gave the ends a little trimming, then blew it dry, turning under the ends with the styling brush. It wasn't any prizewinner, but at least she didn't make the mistake of putting Martha Lee's hair in curls. The large lady doing the makeup bit her lip when Martha Lee settled in her chair, but she didn't hesitate. I took a break, 'cause this I wanted to see. I pretended to be eating a slice of pizza, but I kept my eyes fixed on Martha Lee. First the lady applied Pan-Cake makeup with a sponge. She smeared another, lighter foundation on under the eyes, and then she took a pot of powdered rouge and flicked it on Martha Lee's cheeks, wielding that brush like a wand. Martha Lee looked like she was sitting at the dentist. Next, the makeup lady applied eye shadow in an arresting shade of blue, and then a dark gray liner, all the time scolding Martha Lee to for heavens' sake keep her eyes closed. With each layer, Martha Lee looked less like herself. Next the lady pulled out a chart with little squares of color that she showed to Martha Lee. "What shade lipstick do you normally use?" she asked, causing me to almost choke on the pizza. I thought about Martha Lee's sorry medicine cabinet with nothing in it to show it belonged to a woman. "That one," Martha Lee said, making a blind stab. Her finger landed on a medium pink, which wasn't bad considering she could have hit the one that looked like dried blood.

You might think that all the makeup would improve her looks, but to me she looked like a man trying to look like a woman. As if she knew this, Martha Lee picked out a simple cream-colored blouse for the photo and the plainest earrings she could lay her hands on. For once, the others kept their suggestions to themselves. Martha Lee didn't look all bad, just not like herself. Still, I wished my mama could see her like that. It would have made her smile. Right after she was done, Martha Lee scooted out, not staying around like the others. I could tell by her stiff expression that she was heading straight home to give her face a good scrubbing.

It was after six by the time the last customer cleared out. I finished putting in a load of towels. We must have gone through two hundred, and the machines had been going nonstop. When I came out of the back room, the *Glamour Day* ladies were packing up their things. I saw Raylene slip them some bills and then she said something I couldn't hear, but it was none of my beeswax and besides I was so tired, I didn't care if she was telling them to rob a bank. Now that the excitement of the day had worn off, I was feeling the disappointment. It lodged in my chest and sat in my mouth, clogging my throat with a bitter taste.

"Tallie," Raylene called, and I thought, if she wants me to do one more thing, I'll collapse on the floor and it won't be an act. Then she was taking up one of the plastic capes we used for shampooing and settling it around my shoulders. The Glamour ladies had these dumb smiles on their faces.

"Come on, Tallie," Raylene said. "It's your turn now."

I couldn't believe my ears. I thought she must be teasing, but then I could tell by her eyes that she meant it. I had to look away 'cause I knew if I didn't, the dark thing perched in its usual tight place inside my chest would break free. I loved Raylene so much then, I almost told her I'd work the rest of the summer for free. And I was thinking of Mama and her belief in miracles and wondering if she'd arranged this one for me. Then I slid onto the shampooing chair and prepared to be *transformed*.

★ Tallie's Book ★

Apply blusher with an upward stroke.

Life is full of miracles.

*r*aylene tuned the radio dial to 99.7, for once forgoing gospel. Reba was singing, which couldn't have been better, 'cause Mama just loved Reba and that made it almost like Mama was there, too. The Glamour ladies announced that while Raylene was doing my shampoo and set, they'd take themselves over to the Briar Bush for some barbecue and beer.

It felt good to have Raylene's fingers working my scalp. It reminded me of the way it felt when Mama used to brush my hair, or when she'd scratch my back with her fingernails, writing out letters and making me guess the words. I used to love the lazy feeling of lying on the bed while her nails played on my back. Not having her to touch me was one of the things I missed.

Raylene used her best shampoo, the one that smelled of mint. She rinsed twice, cool water, not warm, because cool closed the follicles in the hair shaft and made your hair shine. Next she blow-dried my hair and curled it with the iron so it held a nice wave. She brushed one side back and held it there with a plastic clip. The other side was turned forward. Raylene held the hand mirror so I could get a look at the back. The latest styles weren't Raylene's strong suit, but I had to admit it looked good. Front, back, and sides. It looked shiny and thick, and I could tell Raylene was pleased with herself. She said what I could really use was some highlighting, and I nearly passed out cold when she said if I stayed late someday she'd foil me for free.

When the Glamour ladies came back, they were toting a six-pack they'd picked up at Winn-Dixie. Sylvia, the makeup lady, flipped the tops for the three of them. They'd brought Coke for me and it was like we were having our own private party. I stayed in Raylene's comb-out chair while Sylvia brought her purple case over. She told me I had real nice bones. She said I didn't need all the layers of paint the way the other women did, 'cause I was young and had a natural radiance. That's exactly what she said. *A natural radiance.* I wrapped those words up and stuck them in my mind so I could pull them out later and hold them in my mouth. She used a light foundation—to even out my color, she said—and then a little blusher. When she leaned close, her beer breath didn't even bother me. She brushed some shadow on my lids, a brownish shade, 'cause she said I was an "autumn," whatever that was, and that the earth tones favored me. She chose the palest pink pearl color for beneath my brows. She said I didn't need liner, that my eyes were perfect just the way they were, only some mascara because my lashes were light and needed defining. I held so still while she was doing it, I hardly took a breath. She applied two coats and when she was done you wouldn't believe how long they looked. They reminded me of the picture of Bette Davis in Mama's Hollywood scrapbook, one where Bette was young and blond and, looking at that photo, a person would never even guess it was Bette Davis, that's how fine she looked.

They all had an opinion about what I should wear. Sylvia said definitely the cowgirl look and chose the Western hat and a fringed leather jacket. The photo lady, who was named Patty and was one of those bossy women who thought they were an expert on everything, wanted me to wear a satin halter in black. Black looks good on blondes, she said, and the halter would show off my nice, wide shoulders. Swimmer's shoulders, she called them. Then Raylene told her how I was the star of the Eden swim team, making it sound like that was the same as being head cheerleader *and* chief twirler on the Sparkettes.

And Raylene, well, Raylene wanted me to wear it all: sequins, velvet and satin, leather and silk. The choker of pearls and the dangling earrings. Armfuls of jewelry and gloves that went so far past my elbows, I couldn't picture anyone wearing them in real life. But no hats, Raylene said, 'cause they'd spoil my do, just a rhinestone clip instead of the plastic, though finally she agreed I could wear the cowboy hat if we saved it for last. No one was acting tired anymore. Especially me. I was a doll they were all playing dress-up with, and I didn't want it to ever stop. And if I could have had one dream come true—just one—it wouldn't be about Spy being my boyfriend, or about going to Hollywood, or my daddy staying away from CC's and acting like a regular daddy who felt some affection for his daughter. My one wish, the one I would have given up just about anything for, was that Mama could be there. I wished she could see the miracle of me.

When we finished, Sylvia and Patty each gave me a hug and

told me I looked beautiful. "Smashing," Sylvia said, and I tucked that away with her comment about natural radiance. Patty even let me keep the rhinestone hair clip. We tossed the empty cans in the trash, and Raylene said everything else could wait until morning. She offered to drive me home, but I said, no, I needed the exercise. Truth tell, it wasn't just my mama I wanted to see me, I wanted everyone in Eden to have a look. Mama was entirely right about the amazing power of makeup to effect a transformation. Even if underneath I was still just a girl who looked like her daddy, I didn't feel the same. I could understand why Miss Tilly sat so still in the tiara and blue velvet, like she was made of air, like one quick move and the magic would blow away.

I pedaled real slow, disappointed there weren't more cars on the road and hoping the Queen of the Universe would drive by in her graduation-present-a-year-early Jeep. A horn sounded behind me and as it drew even, I looked over, smiling like I was riding the homecoming float, but it was only Joe Morell in the Mill Ridge Auto Body wrecker. At the Cash Store, I pulled my bike up to the air pump and pretended to check a tire, prolonging the day so I didn't have to go home where for sure there would be no one to notice. Now if Mama were there, that would be something. I could just picture how it would be. There'd be a big celebration and she'd make a fuss and get out her little Kodak camera and take about three hundred pictures. Then she'd get dressed up and when Daddy came home she'd tell him he had to take his girls out to dinner. We'd go to Lynchburg for Chinese, and Daddy'd sit there all proud and saying how he was the luckiest man in the world, having a date with two women who looked like movie stars, and he'd let me have a sip of his beer when no one was looking. About every five minutes, I'd go to the ladies' room so people could get a good look at me. When we got back home, Mama'd crank up old tunes—Little Richard, Jerry Lee—and they'd start to dance. Me, too. The three of us, boogying till we were sweaty and out of breath. Finally Mama'd fall on the couch, legs splayed, fanning herself and telling us she was *pooped*. I could see it all so clearly, for a minute I could almost believe it might happen.

A horn startled me, and the image of Daddy, Mama, and me vanished. I turned and saw the red T-top Camaro, and it seemed like the magic that started back at the Kurl just kept on growing, like this was my birthday and surprises I couldn't even imagine were just around every corner.

"Tallie?" Spy said, like he wasn't sure it was me.

"Hi," I said, bolder than usual. Transformations give you what Mama'd call spunk. I stood tall, so he could see my swimmer's shoulders. Then I remembered that he'd seen a hell of a lot more of me than my shoulders. I wanted to tell him about everything that had happened that day. I was bursting to tell someone about how pretty everyone had looked when they were getting their pictures done, even Sue Beth Wilkins and Miss Tilly. And how Raylene sent out for pizza, and how the two Glamour ladies, Sylvia and Patty, turned out to be so nice. And how Raylene fixed it so I could have *Glamour Day* after all, even if I didn't have the money, and about how I felt when it was my turn, and about the feathery touch of Sylvia's brush on my cheeks, like a fairy's wand or something, and what she'd said about me possessing natural radiance. Then I remembered what Mama told me. She said the secret of all gorgeous women was that they never let anyone see the work behind the magic.

She said, believe it or not, without their makeup, most actresses looked plain ordinary. Always remember that, she said. *Never let anyone see the work behind the magic.* Later I wrote it down in my rule book.

There was another reason not to tell Spy about *Glamour Day.* I didn't want him teasing me. Everyone knew Spy hated women who paraded around acting glamorous. Women like his mama. At school, he referred to his mama as the Dreck Girl. Mrs. Reynolds's major claim to fame was that a long time ago she'd been a Breck Girl, and believe me she didn't let anyone in Eden forget it. Back when she was about five, she'd modeled for an ad together with her mama 'cause they both had blond, beautiful hair and that was what the shampoo people looked for. Sarah told me that Mrs. Reynolds had about a zillion pictures of herself all around their house including a big one— life-size—done in oil of when she was in the ad. It hung in their living room. Another time, Sarah told me her mama'd had a face-lift. I called her a liar, 'cause I knew only old people did that and her mama wasn't more than thirty-five, but Sarah swore it was true. She said her mama told everyone she was taking a vacation, then she went to Richmond for the operation, and no one knew but the family. And now me. Sarah made me promise not to tell. According to Sarah, when her mama came home her face was all purple and puffy and she couldn't go out of the house for two weeks. She had stitches that ran behind each ear like giant question marks. I pictured zippers. I asked why she did something like that and Sarah said her mama needed to be firmed up and that she was afraid of growing old. Sarah said her daddy liked her looking young. The scars from the stitches were why Mrs. Reynolds wouldn't be caught dead at the Klip-N-Kurl. She knew Raylene would see them. Once a week she drove to a salon in Richmond to get her hair done, and she'd make Sarah go there, too.

Spy was kind of squinting at me now, like he was trying to figure out what was different. "What're you doing?" he said, and his voice was too loud and not like his at all.

"Nothing. Just hanging."

"Well, how about hanging with me?" he said, like it was an everyday normal event, although it was as unexpected as a sneeze.

"Okay," I said. And it *was* okay. So what if I wasn't wearing a new store skirt like I'd planned for my first ride with him, I smelled good from Raylene's mint-scented shampoo and looked better. That was enough. Before he could change his mind or I lost my nerve, I stashed the Raleigh behind the trash cans out back of the store.

I waited a minute for Spy to reach over and open the door, like Mama said well-mannered people did, but he didn't, so I opened it myself. As I was sliding in, he revved the gas in this impatient way and for an instant I got a little flicker in my belly that said maybe this wasn't such a good idea, but I shut it right off 'cause this wasn't just a good idea, it was a great one. What could be bad about going for a ride in a T-top with the best-looking boy in the entire county? The only thing that would make it better would be if the Queen of the Universe came by and saw me sitting there, but the only one who saw us was batty old Mr. Beidler from the county museum, and he was half blind.

"Where to?" Spy said.

"Anywhere," I said. It felt like my birthday for sure.

★ Tallie's Book ★

Blondes look good in black.

Never let anyone see the work behind the magic.

Dreams can come true.

*l*et's just drive," Spy said.

"Okay," I said, though I was hoping we'd go to the A&W or someplace where the popular kids would see us. Just driving meant we'd probably head over to Elders Pond, or maybe north past the Pedlar River, or out to the Natural Bridge, which was this granite bridge that grew that way by itself and was a big tourist attraction. It had George Washington's initials carved in it, and at night it was lit up with colored lights. Instead of any of these places, Spy took the road heading west over the Blue Ridge. I had to keep sneaking looks over to make sure he was real. I was riding with Spy Reynolds. Spy, the most popular boy at Eden High, who was going off to be a lawyer, and whose daddy was rich and his mama good-looking, just like in the song. He drove using just one arm, draping it over the wheel so it looked like he was steering with his wrist. The next time I went for a lesson with Martha Lee, I decided I'd drive that way, too.

The radio was so loud, you couldn't hear us if we did talk, which we didn't. Spy fiddled with the dial, twisting it past the

oldies station in Monroe, past gospel and bluegrass, finally settling on rock, which was my least favorite, one more thing that
made me a freak according to the popular kids. The DJ was
playing an entire Aerosmith album, the *Permanent Vacation* one,
and we listened to "Angel," and even if I didn't usually like
Aerosmith and the volume was up too loud, I felt like they
were singing this song just for me. I *was* an angel. *With natural
radiance.* Once he had the tunes set to his liking, Spy reached
under the seat, not even looking at the road or slowing down,
and pulled out a bottle. He used both hands to twist off the cap,
and I got another little flicker in my belly. I bit my lip to keep
from telling him to pay attention to his driving.

"Want some?" he said.

The label said *Vodka,* which was what the popular kids drank
'cause they said no one could detect it on your breath. The only
thing I'd ever had was beer, but I didn't want to look like a baby,
so I took it when he passed it. There wasn't any way to wipe the
rim without him seeing, but I figured maybe the alcohol would
take care of germs.

Vodka looked like water but it tasted like lightning, burning
my throat and leaving a streak all the way to my belly. I had to
swallow twice to keep from coughing or puking. Spy took the
bottle back, putting his mouth exactly where mine had been.
When he was done, he wiped his mouth on his sleeve, which
was something my daddy might do. His shirt was all wrinkled.
I started noticing other things, like his hair was mussed and he
was wearing a pair of chinos with a rip in the knee, looking
nothing like his usual "Best-Dressed" self, which he was in the
Eden yearbook.

Aerosmith was singing "Rag Doll." Spy passed me the bottle

again. This time I was prepared and it wasn't so bad. It helped ease the nervous place inside, so I took another drink before I handed it back. We were up by the parkway now, and Spy pulled into an overlook and switched off the engine. It was getting dark, so there wasn't much of a view, but I could picture it clear in my mind. The dips and swells of the valley, the way the mountains rose toward the sky, holding every variation of green in creation, even green dipping into blue, which was how they got their name. Mama loved the Blue Ridge. Sometimes we'd hop in the old Dodge and drive up there for a picnic. She'd sit for a while, staring out like she was seeing it for the first time, then she'd tell me to imagine crossing these mountains without out aid of a car, doing it on horseback or by foot, doing it before there were even roads. She said imagine what courage it took, heading off into unknown territory, where no one had gone before and there were no trails to lead you. While Mama was talking about the wonder of it, I couldn't help but think about how a person could get lost. I'd wonder if it was possible for a person to get lost if she didn't even know where she was heading in the first place, though now I understand a person can hold a road map in her hand with the path lit in front of her and still manage to lose her way.

Spy hadn't said more than two words since I'd gotten in the car. The radio was still blaring, even though the engine was off, and I was worrying what if the battery got low or died and we couldn't get home. He was sipping from the bottle and I thought, damn, if I wanted to spend the evening with someone drinking, I could have tracked my daddy down. The idea made me so mad, I reached over and switched off the radio. The silence was big. It was like the whole world stopped, frozen, maybe even ended, and then, gradually, I heard little sounds. At first it sounded jumbled, but when I concentrated I could hear each one distinct. The distant sound of a truck engine climbing somewhere on the highway behind us. Then birds and tree frogs and insects and, off in the brush below the guardrail, a rustling, maybe a squirrel. Mama would have recognized each bird by its call. She never missed. I could only get the easy ones. Chickadees and crows, like that.

Even with the vodka easing me, Spy's silence was making me nervous. I wondered if he'd try to kiss me. I wanted him to. I'd been wanting him to for years. But I thought we should talk, too. I didn't want him to think he could just drag me off somewhere and begin the kissing part without even pretending to first conduct a conversation. In the girls' room at school, I'd heard about how guys only wanted one thing and when they got it they told all the other guys the girl was a slut. From what I could gather, there was a fixed order to things. First the guy had to talk to you in school, stand by your locker with you between classes so everyone would know he liked you. Then you went on a real date. A movie, or a meal at the A&W or Micky D's, or maybe even a Wild Cat game over in Lynchburg. Rula Wade said Ronnie Duval took her bowling on their first date, which she hated because you had to wear those ugly shoes and half the time your ball landed in the alley and everybody laughed. After two dates, you could let the boy French you and get to second base. When you were wearing his ring around your neck, he could get to third base. The girls swore they were still all virgins, but Rula said the only true virgins in the school were me, the born agains, and her, her only because her stepmama watched her like a hawk. I was wondering if Spy thought

I was cheap. I ran my hand over my styled hair, fingered the rhinestone clip so I'd remember I'd been transformed, that I was pretty.

Spy finally looked at me. His eyes were rimmed with pink, like Sylvia the makeup lady was let loose with her liner. Or like he'd been crying. He kept staring at me, but not at me exactly, like I was suddenly invisible. It was the inward stare of someone gazing at a place no one else could see. It didn't feel like my birthday anymore.

I tried to remember all the subjects I'd practiced talking to him about and rolled them around in my head—when exactly was he going off to college and did he truly want to be a lawyer or was it his daddy's idea and was he going to be going to Virginia Beach with the other kids—but when all the thoughts quieted down, the one they stopped on was Sarah and all the things I'd never told him, like how sorry I was I didn't go to her funeral, especially since he'd come to my mama's. That was most important, and so I settled on that. "I'm sorry about Sarah."

He didn't answer, just leaned forward and rested his head on the steering wheel, like he was tired.

"And I regret not going to her funeral," I said. "I really appreciate that you came to my mama's."

"It's okay," he said. His voice was as ragged as torn silk.

"I miss her on the swim team," I said. "She was the best one." I wasn't sure Sarah really was better than me, but I said it anyway, like it was a gift I could give him.

He didn't look at me or answer, and I thought I'd better stop talking because I didn't want to end up saying something dumb like she was in a better place or she was happier in heaven, stupid stuff like people said to me after Mama passed. Finally I just reached over and took his hand. He sat up and his face was stiff and shut, but I knew it wasn't because he didn't care about Sarah or didn't miss her. I knew because his face looked exactly like the hard place inside me felt, like he had to hold it fixed or he might die. And it wasn't boldness or wickedness that made me do what I did next. And I didn't think it was love, because, though I never got to learn this from Mama, I didn't think real love could come on you sudden-like. And it wasn't sex, although I'd had the wanting feeling for Spy for as long as I could remember. It was more like when I used to have a nightmare and Mama'd come in and sit on my bed and smooth back my hair until things quieted down and I could go back to sleep again. It was what I wanted someone to do to me when the dark, hard place hurt so, it made it so I couldn't breathe. And that was why I bent over and kissed him. When I finished, he looked straight at me and the hard, clenched look slipped for just a second, then it was back.

When he pulled me to him, I went without resistance, natural and automatic, with no more will or desire to resist than those iron filings rushing to a magnet. Up close, I could see the tiny whisker specks on his skin, so tiny they hadn't even grown out. It wasn't true you couldn't smell vodka on a person's breath, but I was smelling other things, too. I was getting to know the scent of his hair, sweet and strong and salty like a mixture of Prell, aftershave, and sweat, and another smell, too, that came from inside him and was his alone, and I inhaled deep so my brain and lungs could memorize it.

He kissed me, soft, like our mouths were melting together. The place where the vodka had turned my belly warm was heating up again, and it wasn't only the liquor that was making my head spin. I didn't think it could be true, what the girls said in school about having to go to the movies before a guy could kiss you. That kiss was the sweetest thing, just filled with his feeling for me. I didn't believe it was possible to fake something like that. His hand slid to my shoulder and he rubbed his thumb in little circles over my collarbone and in the hollow right above it, then it moved lower, near my breast. I didn't want him to stop, but he did. He drew away and leaned back against the door, then he looked at me and his eyes didn't have the faraway look. He took his finger and ran it down my nose, like something my daddy used to do, and I thought maybe that was it, that was the end of the kissing, but it turned out it was just the beginning. He pulled me to him so we were both lying back against the door and I could feel his chest and hip where I was pressed against him. I could hear my own heart beating and I thought he must have heard it, too. We started kissing again, harder. He opened his mouth and I must have opened mine without even planning on it, 'cause our teeth clicked. Then his tongue was pushing between my lips and into my mouth and we were Frenching.

Back in eighth grade, Rula Wade told me boys liked to kiss like that but it sounded like pure barf to her and she'd bite off a boy's goddamn tongue if he tried. I agreed because I kept thinking about all the germs you'd get, plus I didn't even like a dentist looking in my mouth. But this was different. You couldn't imagine.

Spy ran his tongue over my teeth and up over my gums, way up to where they attached to my cheeks, then around my tongue, under my tongue, like he was trying to know every part of me, till there wasn't one secret part he hadn't touched.

I opened my eyes a slit. His were closed, and he had the tight, shut look on his face. He moaned, like something hurt, and cupped his hand against the back of my head. I closed my eyes. His shirt was moist beneath my hand and I could feel the beating of his heart, fast and strong. I couldn't think straight. My body started moving of its own accord, like it was trying to get closer. He took his tongue out and started running it over my lips, round and round, in no hurry, like he could do it forever, and I felt that *attraction* pulling on me, turning me weak. When he slid his tongue back inside my mouth, I welcomed it. I wasn't thinking about germs or anything except how I liked the feel of him filling me and I wanted more. The hollow place in my belly began to ache, deep, like my moon ache, but different, too, a wanting ache. Between my legs was damp. It was lovely. Spy was lovely. For an instant, the dark, hard place in my chest softened, like it was wanting to open, too.

A bird called then, shrill and scolding, and close to the car. It brought me to my senses. It was like Goody was in the car, calling me cheap-cheap-cheap, a piece of trash like my daddy, and other things worse. I tried to ignore her, to return to that lovely place of aching, of opening, but the vodka was swirling in my belly and this time it was working its way up, not down. I pushed Spy away, hard, and grabbed for the doorknob, fighting the sourness rising in my throat. I got out just in time, not even making it behind the car, but puking right in full view, like a dog who'd eaten bad fish. My face heated thinking of Spy seeing me hunched over and puking like that, hearing the ugly sound of it. If I'd had a choice I would have walked home rather than get back in the car. My mouth tasted sour and I knew I smelled that way, too, from where I'd puked a little on one of my shoes. I cleaned myself up the best I could and got back in the Camaro. "Spy?" I hated my little girl voice.

He was still slumped back against the door, just like I'd left him, with his head tilted back and his eyes shut.

"Spy?"

He sat up and looked toward me, but that inward look was back.

"Do you have any gum? Mints, or something?"

He reached across and opened the glove compartment and started pawing around. A comb fell out, and a car manual and some Kleenex. Then a gun.

"Jesus," I said. "What the hell is that?"

"What's it look like?" His words were pushed together, all icy, and I hate-hate-hated the sound of it. He picked up the gun.

"Jeez," I said. "It's not loaded, is it?" That warning flicker started up again. Even my daddy knew guns and booze were not a combination you'd want to be fooling with.

Spy laughed, like I'd said something really funny. He opened the door and got out, then he pointed that gun—a revolver, I guess it was—down toward the valley and fired. Just like that. The noise hurt my ears so bad I thought I might go deaf. It wasn't at all like you see in the movies, with people running around, shooting and talking, and I had to wonder why they never showed people covering up their ears when the shooting starts, because, believe you me, that was what you wanted to do. Then he started waving the gun around and firing fast, one after the other, *bang-bang-bang*, and I was afraid he was going to kill a bird or maybe even me.

"Spaulding Reynolds," I screamed. "You stop that. You hear."

He turned and stood there, staring at me like he didn't even know my name, like he didn't know where he was. The kissing and the sweet, aching feeling were like they'd never been. We got back in the car and he tossed the gun on the floor by my feet. Then he switched on the ignition and threw it in reverse. He backed out so fast, gravel shot up all around, and the tires squealed when we hit pavement. I sat tight, praying we wouldn't be killed. It was hard enough to drive on the Blue Ridge stone sober. He didn't say a word, just drove me home, forgetting to let me out at the Cash Store so I could pick up my bike.

"Bye," I said. "I'll see ya." I waited for him to say something, even just *so long*, but he didn't. Not one word. He just stared straight ahead waiting for me to move, like he couldn't wait for me and my puke-spotted shoe to get out. When he took off, he left another stretch of rubber. I figured in spite of the kissing, he hated me, hated the way I turned into such a baby, puking all over the place. I figured within twenty-four hours every one of the popular kids would know about it.

I could hardly stand to look in the mirror. There were dark smudges of mascara beneath my eyes, and my lipstick was smeared on my chin. It was like *Glamour Day* had never been. Somewhere along the way, I'd lost the rhinestone hair clip, which would have made me cry if I'd been the crying kind. I washed my face and brushed my teeth, scrubbing every place Spy's tongue had touched. The tree outside the front room was scratching at the window, a sound I usually found comforting, but now the *screetch-screetching* of it sounded like someone trying to get in, like there were eyes staring in. I wanted to turn the TV on so I wouldn't hear it, but if the set was on, I wouldn't be able to hear if someone really did try to get in. Stop being a baby, I said, but I couldn't help it. I turned the lights off so it would look like no one was home. I would have locked the door, but I'd done that one time after Mama passed, and when Daddy came home late from CC's, he broke the door, just kicked it in. He didn't listen when I told him I'd been scared. He told me never again to lock a man out of his own house. Finally I stumbled through the dark to my room and pushed stuff around in the closet until my hand located Mama's red sweater. It had to be ninety degrees, but I put it on and sat on the bed, listening for the sound of someone on the porch, someone at the door, someone coming in. I kept picturing Spy with the gun.

I tried to hold on to the good parts of the day. How I had looked in the sequin top with the crystal earrings and in the cowboy getup; how it felt to be pretty; sitting in the front of Spy's car; that first, soft kiss. Just remembering the good parts made the jumping settle down in my chest, but it made me sad, too. If God was so good, why did He give you a thing so beautiful that it could make you ache with the beauty of it and then take it away? Why didn't He make it so that once—just once— things that were perfect and true stayed that way without the bad stuff mixing in? Good things like my mama's laugh, or her brushing my hair, or how it was to watch her dance with my daddy. Things like *having* a mama. Or feeling beautiful and deserving of attention. Or being kissed in a way that made your whole body ache with the wanting for more.

Why couldn't the good ever stay?

★ Tallie's Book ★

A girl is not a slut if she Frenches on the first date.

thirteen

On the radio, the weatherman was yammering on about the weather and about how we were in the midst of an official heat spell. Like we needed him to tell us that. Just breathing, a person got sweaty. Lawns were turning yellow, and Old Straw had collapsed under the tree in our yard and didn't even wag his tail when you called his name. The heat was all anyone talked about. At the Kurl, Raylene kept the AC cranked on high and even so, the ladies fanned themselves with magazines. Mamas brought their sons in for buzz cuts.

Everything was back to normal there. *Glamour Day* had rolled through our lives like a spring storm, leaving us with only the memory. Raylene took the poster down from out front, and she didn't mention anything about foiling my hair again. It was like when the clock struck midnight in that movie *Cinderella* and her ball gown turned to rags and the coach became a pumpkin and the horses were mice. That was how it felt. At least Cinderella had a glass slipper. I had nothing, not even the rhinestone hair clip, not even a picture, since Raylene said it would be another two weeks before the company came back with the photos.

Spy had disappeared, too. I didn't see him at the Cash Store or at the creek or even at the lake when I went one afternoon to check. I called his house once, but no one picked up. I thought maybe his family was on vacation. I dialed his daddy's office, too, but lost my nerve and hung up before anyone could answer. I wondered if he thought about me at all and if he remembered the kissing. For sure, I hadn't forgotten. The memory occupied my mind night and day and turned my legs to water. Sometimes, thinking about Spy shooting the gun and driving off without saying good-bye, I thought I didn't care if I ever saw him again, but mostly I wanted to have him kissing me again.

I had my Hollywood plan to hold on to and that helped get me through. I kept telling myself how Mama'd always said if a person could dream something, she can do it. The possibilities seemed stronger after my *Glamour Day* transformation. My original idea was to head for L.A. in the spring, right after graduation, but I began to consider the possibility of leaving sooner. You didn't have to graduate high school to be an actor—half the people in Mama's Hollywood scrapbook hadn't, including Clark Gable—and there was less and less to keep me in Eden. Finally I called the Lynchburg airport and inquired about the cost of a flight to L.A. I wrote down all the information, including how long the trip took and where the stopovers were. I decided I'd ask Uncle Grayson for the money. He'd never let Mama down, and I was hoping he'd extend the same courtesy to me. At night, I studied Mama's scrapbook. I looked at the pictures of the old-time actors like Lana Turner and Rita Hayworth, Veronica Lake and Grace Kelly. And the new ones like Farrah Fawcett, though there weren't as many of those. Mama just loved the old ones. I pretended she was there with me, encouraging me and giving me advice. No one knew how I missed Mama. Sometimes it was like the flu the way the missing made my whole body ache, a giant hole that never went away and no one could understand. Girls at school would say things like how dumb their mamas were, or how they hated them. Once, I heard Ginny Wheeler going on about how mad she was that her mama wouldn't let her buy this dress she had her heart set on and how she wished her mama'd die. I wanted to shake her and tell her what it was like to have your mama gone. For real. Forever.

Even when Mama got real bad, I couldn't truly believe she was *really* going to die. Mamas didn't die. I imagined one morning I'd get up and go in the kitchen and she'd be making corn bread. Mama, you're up, I'd say, and she'd nod and say, well, thank God that's past, like she'd only had a summer cold. So I kept waiting for a miracle to happen. I'd move the flowers people sent close so she could see them without turning her head and I'd hold a Popsicle for her to suck on because her mouth was always dry. And I'd keep waiting for her to be cured.

In the middle of November, Mama had Daddy cut down a fir tree, though it was way too early and the needles would drop off before Christmas. She watched while I decorated it, pointing out the spots that needed tinsel. She wanted the lights turned on round the clock. One morning I went in and she was talking to the tree, like it was a person who'd dropped by to visit. Martha Lee explained it was the morphine that made her act that way. Mostly she didn't talk at all, like silence was required, but Martha Lee seemed to know what she was thinking. Once, when I was about ten, Mama and I'd had a conversation about the silent languages and we'd made a list of all the animals that

didn't make a sound, and bugs, too, like butterflies, and deer
and snakes. Mama said she thought they communicated by
mental telepathy. I wondered if dying people could do that, too.

In movies, they made people pretty when they were dying.
They never showed the truth of it. The truth wasn't pretty. It
was messy. Hard to watch. One night the doctor told Daddy
there wasn't much time left. How much? Daddy asked. Weeks?
Dr. Cullen said he didn't think so. Not weeks, he said. Not even
days. Fact was, he said, we were down to counting hours. Dr.
Cullen had known Mama since she was born and you'd think
by then he'd know she wasn't going till she was ready, no matter what he said. I stopped going to school, but no one cared,
not even when I missed a week.

Mama lived for two more weeks. One day when I'd gone to
the kitchen to make some tea, I heard Mama make Martha Lee
promise something, but I didn't catch what. "Promise me," she
said. "The exact day. It will make me close to her." I thought
she was talking about me.

Mama passed on November 29, the exact same day Natalie
drowned. Martha Lee had been there all night and had made
me leave the room for a while in the morning. When I came
back, Mama was barely breathing, and you only knew that because of the sound it made. You could stare at her chest and not
even see it move. And then she died. One minute Mama was
alive, and the next she was gone, no more than a piece of clay,
her hand turning colder by the second, drawing the heat from
mine. Martha Lee cleaned her up, wiping away the snot that
dripped out of her nose and straightening the sheets, and then
she made the phone calls while Daddy sat at the kitchen table
and cried. She called Goody and Uncle Grayson and Daddy's

sister, Ida. Finally she called Dr. Cullen and he came over and examined Mama and then told Daddy that it was official, she'd passed. Like we couldn't see that for ourselves.

Then they took Mama away and the house got real empty, even with us still there. We just sat around and said thank you to the folks who brought food and waited for Goody to arrive. She was flying up that very night.

The next morning, when we weren't even used to the idea that Mama was truly gone, Mr. Wesler came by. He had this little notebook and he kept asking all kinds of things: what hymns did we want played at the service; when could Daddy come and pick out the coffin; where was Mama to be buried; would we write out something about Mama for the paper; had Mama left any personal instructions. He wanted us to answer all these things when we weren't able to think straight to save our souls. He wanted to know if we wanted him to arrange to send a limousine for the family. Daddy said no, not if it cost extra. When Goody heard that, she hit the roof. She called Daddy a cheap son of a bitch and told Mr. Wesler to order the limousine, she'd pay for it herself. Fact is, from the moment she'd arrived, Goody took over everything. First thing she got me aside and told me she didn't want me to spoil everything by crying and carrying on like a baby and that I was to behave myself. Then she made the arrangements for the flowers and the viewing hours and what was going in the notice for the *Eden Times*. I asked her if I couldn't put something of mine in the coffin with Mama, like the teddy bear they'd put in with Sarah, but she said no, it was a tacky thing do to, and so that was that.

First there was the viewing, which is exactly what it sounds like. Mama was laid out in a casket with a cream satin lining and a two-part lid. The top part was open and the bottom closed, so you couldn't see her from the waist down, which made me glad because if her feet hadn't returned to their normal size, I didn't want everyone to know. Two things Mama was vain about: her feet and her hair. Her hair they'd fixed real pretty. Raylene did it. She did all the funerals. You'd think it would be creepy, but she didn't mind. I'd heard her talk about it whenever Mr. Wesler had a job for her. "Only got to do the front half of the head, but I get paid full price," she said. They put flowers in Mama's hair. Roses, not the gardenia Daddy wanted. Mr. Wesler said a gardenia would turn brown before the first visiting hours even ended. Everyone said Mama looked beautiful, like she was sleeping. A fat lie. There's no mistaking a dead person. They don't look one goddamn bit like they're sleeping.

She wore a pale green dress with pearl buttons down the front, and a sweater with a lace collar attached, the one she kept in a plastic bag in her bureau and never, ever wore, exactly like the one Natalie Wood wore in *Splendor in the Grass*. Once, she told me it *was* the sweater Natalie Wood wore. At the time I thought it was a fib, the only lie she ever told me. At that time, I had no idea of the secrets a person could hold.

At the funeral, Martha Lee sat next to me. She let me hold her hand and ignored all the black and evil looks Goody sent her way. Daddy sat on my other side, shrunken and wiping his eyes. His sister, Ida, was there, cracking her knuckles till I could have screamed, and passing Kleenex to Daddy since Goody hadn't told him he couldn't cry. Goody was next in the row. She sat there straight as a yardstick, muttering things about Martha Lee having the nerve to sit in the front pew with the family like she was kin. She was too far away to continue her lectures warning me not to start crying or make a scene, but every now and then she'd turn her attention my way and one look was enough to get the message. As if I needed it. I knew I wasn't going to cry. All my tears were locked in that tight place in my chest and I didn't think they would be coming out for the rest of my natural life. Uncle Grayson didn't come from Atlanta. Daddy'd phoned him earlier and when he heard about Mama, he started to cry and couldn't talk. He sent every gardenia in the local flower shop and probably the rest of Virginia, too. Then he sent a bunch of roses and daisies. According to what he'd written on the card, daisies meant beauty and roses meant love and he said that was Mama all over. Just filled with love and beauty. The arrangements he sent were nearly as big as the casket. "Show-offy," I heard Ashley Wheeler's mom whisper at the viewing, like she was one to talk. Later, Uncle Grayson wrote a letter to me and Daddy telling us how much he loved Mama and that he hoped we'd understand, but he just couldn't bear to come to the funeral.

No one talked while we were waiting for the service to begin, but there were the whispering, shuffling sounds people made in a church. I turned around once to look, but Goody reached over and pinched my knee and told me to sit still, for heavens' sake. Then the organ started up "Rock of Ages," which Mama would have hated, but Goody loved. Even the whispering stopped. Then they played "Abide with Me," and there was the sound of wheels rolling along the wood floor as they brought Mama in. If it wasn't for Martha Lee giving me her hand to hang on to, I don't think I could have stayed. I could understand why Uncle Grayson hadn't come.

After, the ladies at the church set up a table in the social hall and everyone perked up, like suddenly this was a party. The men went outside to drink from the bottles they kept in their cars. The ladies kept telling me to eat. As if I could swallow one bite. As if I'd ever want to eat again. They'd come up and say things like, "At least she didn't suffer long," like it was a good thing Mama was gone. Or they'd say, "You're a big girl, now. You'll have to be the woman of the house and look after your daddy," like I was twenty, instead of twelve and needing care myself. "She's happier there," Cora Giles said. And I wondered what kind of dumb thing was that to say? "No, she isn't," I said. "She liked it here with me and Daddy." Then Goody was there telling me not to be getting a fresh mouth.

The newspaper man took what Goody wrote and changed it around. Here's what was in the paper about Mama:

Dinah Mae (Adams) Brock, wife of Luddington Brock and one of Eden's brightest stars, died at 38. Daughter of the late Dr. Taylor Adams, she was a graduate of Eden High and the Cushman Secretarial School in Lynchburg. Renowned for her striking resemblance to the actress Natalie Wood, she performed in a number of amateur productions. The performance of her lifetime, a struggle with cancer, ended November 29, when she died quietly at home. In addition to her husband, she is survived by her mother, Jessie Adams, of Sarasota, Florida, a daughter, Natasha Brock, of Eden, and a brother, Grayson Adams, of Atlanta, Georgia. Services will be held 11 A.M. Friday, December 1, at the Methodist Church, with burial immediately following. Those wishing to make memorials please consider the Monacan Indians of Tobacco Row.

They printed Mama's high school photo, too.

Goody and Daddy had a big fight about the donations to the Monacan Indians. "It was what Deanie wanted," Daddy said, and something about his voice made Goody shut up. I cut the newspaper article out and put it in the cigar box with Mama's postcards, even thought I thought it was stupid. Especially that part about the performance of a lifetime. I mean, jeez. Every printed line of it was just a tiny reduction of a person who could have been a stranger. It held none of the truth of Mama. I thought they should have let me write it. At least then people would know what she was really like. Shortly after that I began making my own list about Mama, so I'd never forget. Another thing about the notice was I think they should have mentioned Martha Lee. Mama always said she was her sister, even if they weren't blood kin.

After the funeral Goody started in on Daddy about how I should go back to Florida with her, so I wouldn't turn cheap and get myself in trouble. I could only imagine what she'd think if she ever heard about what I'd done with Spy. She'd probably fly straight up to Virginia and haul me personally back to her stupid gated community.

Well, I had no plan to be heading off to Florida. Or staying for the rest of my life in Virginia. I was going out to Hollywood. I was going to follow Mama's dream.

★ Tallie's Book ★

Daisies stand for beauty, roses for love.

If you can dream something, you can do it.

Even if your heart is broken, you can make yourself not cry.

f o u r t e e n

*t*he Tyree sisters weren't in their usual spot on their porch when I went by, and there was no sign of Easter Davis at her place either, no laundry hanging on the line, like the heat had driven even that inside. The dirt road off High Tower was nothing but pure dust. The Raleigh kicked it up, coating me and leaving a little cloud as I passed. It was a good thing I didn't have asthma. All that dust would have about killed Rula Wade.

I was on my way to Martha Lee's for another driving lesson, though I was torn about in half between wanting her to be there, so I could have another lesson, and wanting her to be off, so I could help myself to one of those pictures of Mama I'd found in her dresser drawer. Those pictures had been occupying my mind ever since I'd seen them. Daddy and I only had two photographs of Mama, an old grainy one taken before I was even born, and the yearbook one they put in the newspaper with the obituary. Goody had all the others. So they'll be safe, she'd said when she'd packed them up after Mama's funeral. When I die they'll be yours, she'd said. Like she didn't even consider that maybe I'd want one before then or wouldn't know how to take care of it if she did give me one. She took everything of Mama's that had value. She wasn't having Daddy sell Mama's stuff for beer money, she said. She'd put a stop to that plan before it got started, she said. When I asked her who'd want to buy Mama's pictures, she told me not to be fresh-mouthed. When I saw she meant to take everything, I hid the silver syrup pitcher and Mama's red sweater and scrapbook or she'd have taken them, too. That's why I'd been thinking about the photos in Martha Lee's bottom drawer. For sure, she'd have given me one if I asked, but if I did, she'd know I'd been snooping around.

Martha Lee was home when I got there, hauling a hose around the garden. "We could sure use some rain," she said. It'd been weeks since we'd had even a shower. All traces of her Glamour transformation were gone, and she'd reverted to her usual self. Her hair was shoved up under an old Orioles cap, and she was wearing a pair of denim shorts, displaying legs that revealed every doughnut she'd ever eaten. I hadn't seen her since *Glamour Day*, so I told her how, after she'd left, Raylene had fixed it so I could get the makeover, too. I would have told her about Daddy taking the money from the silver pitcher, but that might have led to questions about how I'd managed to get twenty dollars in the first place, so I let it go. Instead, I told her in detail about all the clothes I'd worn for the photos, and how Patty, the photographer, had given me the rhinestone hair clip. If I were talking to my mama, that would have been the time I'd have told her about losing the clip and about Spy. Because I'd told Mama everything, I would have told her what had happened, even about the vodka and kissing, and I would have gotten some advice about what to do next, but Martha Lee wasn't Mama and she wouldn't be any help with matters of love or sex. As far as I knew, Martha Lee had zero experience in the man department. Instead, I told her the company was due back that week with the photos.

"This week?" she said.

"Thursday," I said. Then I told her she was the last person on earth I expected to see at the Kurl for the *Glamour Day*. She said it was my fault and that all the carrying on I'd done about it had made her want to see for herself, which sounded like a flat-out lie. I knew it had to be something more than that that got her to the Kurl, that got her to let Raylene fix her hair and call her honey, and some stranger pile on makeup, but I could see whatever the real reason, she wasn't about to tell me. Mama always said people were full of surprises, but I didn't think she meant someone like Martha Lee. As a rule, I thought most people were predictable. Especially adults.

I helped with the hose. She'd rigged up her own personal irrigation system using empty liter Coke bottles and gallon-sized bleach bottles that she'd half buried neck side down beside the tomatoes. She'd sawed off the bottoms and filled each one with water. "Water the roots," she said. "That's what you want to do." She explained how watering the leaves could cause mildew and leaf rot and was wasteful, too, because so much water evaporated.

After we finished up, we took turns splashing our legs and faces with the hose, then we got ourselves a couple of Cokes, hopped in the pickup, and drove out to the place where she let me practice my driving. It was my third lesson and I was shifting smooth as lemon pie, no bucking. I could go up a rise riding the clutch just right, so I didn't stall, not even on the steep ones. Martha Lee said I was getting to be an old pro. We practiced going in reverse and doing three-point turns, something I'd need to do on the driving exam.

On the way home, she pulled into Shucks Discount and when she said she was taking me shopping, I about fainted. She said it was time I got some clothes that fit. First thing we picked out some bathing suits for me to try on. I selected a turquoise one, another in black, and a hot pink one. All three had built-in bras and high-cut legs, not a bit like the ugly ones we used for swim team. When I came out of the dressing room in the black suit, Martha Lee whistled right out loud. "Jesus, Cookie," she said. "You'll be swatting the boys off like flies from molasses." I was afraid that meant she wouldn't let me keep the suit, but she didn't say a word when I put it in the cart. Next I picked out a blue skirt with tiny white flowers on it, the kind I'd imagined myself wearing when I rode in Sky's Camaro, and two cotton T-shirts with narrow straps. One blue and one white. Martha Lee also threw in some sandals. On the way to the checkout, she picked out a tube of lipstick in frosted pink, but I told her that color didn't look good on me. You could have laid me flat with a chicken feather when she told me the lipstick was for her. I thought she was teasing, but her face said no. Mama was right, I thought. People are full of surprises.

We swung by her house to get my bike, then she dropped me off at home. I told her I could ride the Raleigh, but she said it was too hot for anyone to be pedaling around. I wanted to hug her or something to thank her for the lesson and the clothes, but Martha Lee wasn't the hugging kind, so instead I asked her if she wanted to come in. "Thanks, Cookie," she said, "but I've got to be going." She hadn't set foot in our house since Mama died.

*   *   *

Sundays and Mondays, when the Kurl was closed, I usually did
housework, but it was too hot to think of dusting or doing
laundry. I put on my new suit and checked myself out in the
mirror. Martha Lee was right about the way it made me look.
The high cut made my legs seem longer, and the built-in bra
made my tits look bigger. Goody'd have a stroke if she saw me.
Even the Queen of the Universe would be impressed, though
she'd probably think of something mean-spirited to say. I
thought about riding out to Elders Pond where everyone hung,
but then I decided on the creek. What I was really thinking was
that maybe Spy'd be there. A girl could hope. In the black one-
piece, I definitely didn't look like a baby, so maybe he'd remember the kissing part and forget about me puking, just like I was
trying to forget about the gun part with him.

The creek was deserted. I swam for a while, not laps or anything that required real effort. Just cooling down. When I'd had
enough, I spread out the old blanket near the willow and
stretched out, still hoping Spy would show. After a while I noticed the birds weren't singing. It was too hot for even that.
Lying there, in the total silence, I could almost believe I was the
only one existing on the planet. Rula would have hated it. She
wouldn't have lasted five minutes. She always was asking me
how I could stand spending so much time alone. I didn't mind.
Being alone gave a person time to get their thinking straight.
Rula couldn't go a minute without talking or cranking up the
radio. She got a Walkman last Christmas and about kept the
battery company in business the way she played it night and
day. I guess you could say Rula was my best friend, but I knew
we wouldn't be friends for life, like Mama and Martha Lee. I
guess we'd become friends because we were the only ones

whose mamas had died and that set us apart, even if she had a step-mama.

The thing about Eden was that anything that made you different meant you had zero chance of being in the popular group. Even before Mama died, I wasn't exactly winning medals in the popularity department. It wasn't 'cause we didn't have money. Half the families in Eden were poor. When I asked Mama, she said what set me apart was that I had imagination. In Mama's book, imagination was right up there. She said it was their capacity for dreaming that led most people to Hollywood, not any excess of good looks or talent. According to Mama, imagination and luck were the unbeatable combination. She said imagination had power, like electricity. Both were invisible, she said, but they had energy and could make things happen. She said when you think about it, all the mighty forces in the world were imperceptible to the eye. Like love. And hate.

Mama believed it was a lack in the imagination department that led most people to keep their expectations for life too low. As a rule, folks didn't allow themselves the pleasure of a dream, she said. They *settle.* "Your daddy's problem is he doesn't have aspirations," she told me once. "He was born without the imagination gene, the gene to dream." It was the only time I ever heard her say anything bad about my daddy. Then she said that was all right because she had enough dreams for both of them.

"Hey, Tallie."

I jumped about ten feet. "Jeez, Wiley, you about scared me to death."

"Didn't mean to. You sleeping?"

"No," I said, cross at being startled.

"What were you doing?"

"I was thinking, if it's any of your beeswax."

"Penny for your thoughts," he said.

I hated when people said that. *Penny for your thoughts.* A person's thoughts were worth a hell of lot more than one copper cent. "Nothing special," I said. "Where's Will?" I hardly ever saw them together anymore. I wondered if they'd had a fight.

"Working." He sat down on the blanket and started poking at the ground with a stick. "Hot, isn't it?"

"Well, duh," I said.

He flushed red. "Well, isn't it?"

"Yeh," I said.

"Nice suit," he said, still working that stick into the ground.

"It's nothing special," I said.

"Looks new."

"It isn't." I didn't know why I lied.

"You look good in it," he said.

"Thanks."

"You always look good." He about buried the stick, he was digging so furiously.

"Martha Lee's teaching me to drive," I said. Anything to get off the subject. I used to feel comfortable around Wiley, like he was a brother or something, but lately things had changed.

"You always look good," he said. "With or without a suit."

"Wiley, what the hell are you talking about?" He was freaking me out.

"You know."

"No, I don't know."

"A couple of weeks ago," he said. He poked at the ground some more, avoiding my eyes. "I saw you."

"You saw me? What does that mean?"

"You know."

"Wiley Bettis, I don't have a clue what you're talking about."

He swallowed hard. "Here. At the creek. When you were skinny-dipping."

"Jesus, Wiley, you were spying on me?"

"I didn't mean nothing. I came for a swim and you were here and I didn't want to spook you. I didn't mean anything by it."

Wiley saw me naked. Jeez, it was like letting your kin see you. My face heated at the thought of the way I'd posed, proud and showing off, thinking it was Spy watching me.

"I didn't mean nothing by it," he said again. He looked like he was going to cry.

Just at the moment, a ladybug landed on my knee. Like fireflies, ladybugs were really beetles. I thought about how Mama'd said beetles signify change. It seemed like change flew into your life whether you wanted it or not. It didn't matter one whit if you were prepared. Change just happened. Nothing you could do to stop it. Wiley was changing from the friend I'd known my whole life into some nervous creature who spied on me and couldn't look me in the eye. Martha Lee was buying lipstick and changing in some other way I couldn't figure. Daddy'd changed from a man who was proud of his daughter and took her to his job to a person who didn't even know she was alive. I was changing, too. I thought of how I'd lied and stolen and strutted naked. I remembered the bold way I'd acted with Spy, kissing and such. And then I thought how one of the things that had made me bold was that I'd believed he'd seen me the day I'd been skinny-dipping. But it had been Wiley all along. Then I reflected on how it could change your whole life if you acted on something you thought was true and it turned out to be false.

★ Tallie's Book ★

Imagination has power.

Water the roots of tomatoes, not the leaves.

People are full of surprises.

Add mulch to clay soil. Mulch is the secret.

There's nothing you can do to stop change.

*b*reaking a one hundred-year-old record," the radio weatherman said. He was all worked up, exactly like Mr. Baldock when he got on the P.A. system to announce that the football team won a game or that the junior class test scores were higher than last year's. Mr. Baldock spit when he talked, and you could hear his germs splatting all over the mike. When it was your turn to read the absentee list, he watched you like a hawk, like you were going to steal the goddamn P.A. system or something, so you couldn't wipe the mike. It made you want to puke.

"Crops are being lost," the announcer was saying, "which means a bad year for the farmers." Well, duh. Like we couldn't figure it out. He said nearly a thousand chickens had perished over at the poultry farm in Duncan. He didn't mention what they did with all the dead chickens. I'd heard they ground them up for dog food, which I thought must be against some law. Next the man said two people had died of heat prostration. It was amazing to think a thing as natural as heat could kill a person. It wasn't like it was a disease or anything. You'd

have to be as old as Easter Davis or the Tyree sisters to die of
something like heat. It was slowing me down, for sure. It'd
made me oversleep and I was going to be late for work. At least
the Kurl was air-conditioned. All we had at home were these
lame fans in the windows that only stirred the air but didn't
cool it one degree.

Daddy'd made coffee, and the pot was still on the stove. I
swear he'd drink hot coffee if the thermometer read two hundred, but all I wanted was iced tea. I poured a large glass and
stirred in some sugar, watching it swirl around the ice. Just the
thought of food made me queasy. Outside, heat was rising off
the road in waves thick enough to walk on.

It was Tuesday, Seniors' Day at the Kurl, and I prepared myself for the usual bowel complaints. Gas, indigestion, constipa-
tion. Last week Hattie Jones said it was getting so she had to
order Metamucil in the industrial size. She said things like that
flat-out without a trace of embarrassment, like we were sincerely interested in the state of her intestines, like getting laxa-
tives by the barrel was something to brag on.

"Sorry," I told Raylene. "Overslept." She was busy talking
and hardly looked at me.

"Some families attract tragedy," Raylene said. "They just
draw it to them."

"Like the Millers," Lenora Mallows said. She was soaping up
Easter Davis. "Remember the Millers."

The Miller family moved to Louisiana years ago, but whenever someone was having a string of misfortunes, people always
brought up the Millers. Misfortune dogged that family to such
a degree that they were famous for it. Even children knew their
history. First off, their baby died of pneumonia, and one year later

they lost their house in a fire. They didn't save one stick of furniture. Nothing. Chief Newman said they were lucky to get out alive. After that, the linen factory over in Redden closed down, so Mr. Miller was laid off and they'd had to live on charity. Like Raylene said, they seemed to attract bad luck. Even their good luck had a way of turning bad. Like when the oldest boy, a running back for Eden, got news of a full scholarship to Georgia. The next day, he was hitching home on 29—which everyone knew was dangerous, cars whizzing through like there was no tomorrow—and he got hit by a truck. His football scholarship was crushed as flat as his hip. "Some people just draw it to them," Raylene said again. "Seems like they got a lightning rod for misery."

Raylene's theory seemed dangerous, like just believing in something could make it true. Mama always said you had to be careful of your thoughts. She said they had power. They were on that list of invisible stuff like love and prayer and imagination. Imagination, she said, was just another kind of thinking. She said the first place anything existed was in our minds.

It made me exhausted to even think of having to police my mind all the time, watching what I thought, thinking of how an idea could just shoot out like a piece of lightning to take up residence in the world. If thoughts had power, why hadn't they cured Mama? Did some thoughts hold more power than others? What made that so?

"Who found him?" Cora Giles was saying.

"His wife," Hattie said.

"How dreadful," Cora said. "Imagine. Discovering him like that."

"Who?" I asked.

"It wasn't more than four years back the daughter died," Hattie said. "Swimming accident, wasn't it?"

"Well, that's what the family said," Cora said. "If I remember, there was talk."

"That's right," Easter Davis said. "There always was something funny about it. Her drowning and all. Wasn't she supposed to be a crackerjack swimmer?"

Cora turned to me. "She was in your class, wasn't she?"

I was still playing catch-up. "Who?"

"The Reynolds girl," Cora said. "Can't think of her name to save my soul."

"Sarah?"

"That's right," Raylene said.

My mind finally caught on. They were talking about Spy's family.

"Lawd, that poor woman," Cora said. "Imagine. First her daughter, and now her husband."

"Mrs. Reynolds?" I said.

"That's right."

"What happened?"

"Her husband's dead."

"Mr. Reynolds is dead?" I remembered when I'd called the house and how angry Mr. Reynolds had sounded, how he'd threatened to call the police. Maybe it was a heart attack. All that anger couldn't be healthy. Or an accident. Then I remembered what the radio had said about people dying of heat prostration. "Was it the heat?"

"What, honey?"

"Mr. Reynolds. Did he die of the heat?"

"Lawd, no, child," Hattie said.

"He was murdered," Cora said.

"Sheriff Craw must be in his glory," Lenora said. "I imagine those TV people will be arriving with their cameras. First murder in the county in I can't count how many years."

"Mr. Reynolds was murdered?" I said.

"Last one was back in the fifties," Easter Davis said.

"I remember that," Lenora said. "Lillie Grigsby."

"The husband did it," Easter said. "John, his name was. Accountant for some company over in Lynchburg. Little squirrel of a man. You wouldn't think he had it in him."

"It's surprising what people are capable of," Cora said.

I was picturing Mr. Reynolds at the school picnic all dressed up in a three-piece suit, wearing a hat similar to the one he'd worn in the picture on the front of the *Eden Times* when he was cutting the ribbon at the new chamber of commerce dedication. I was remembering how Sarah had said her mama'd had a face-lift, with stitches behind her ears, 'cause her daddy wanted her looking young.

"The fifties?" Hattie said. "You sure it was that long ago?"

"Summer of fifty-six," Easter Davis said. "I remember Swannie was busy campaigning for Eisenhower, doing the phoning for the county, and Sissy couldn't get through on the phone. Six months along and she walked all the way over to tell us."

"Wasn't there one after that?" Hattie said.

"You're thinking of that hippie they found in the woods up by the Pedlar," Lenora said. "They never did determine that was murder."

"Mr. Reynolds was murdered?" I repeated.

"Right in his own office," Cora said. "Sheriff's looking into it. Thinks it musta been some drug-crazed kid, looking for money. Or maybe a client."

"Must have been someone he knew," Hattie said. "He wouldn't let a stranger in his office."

"No," said Easter. "Especially not one with a gun."

"A gun?" I said. "Mr. Reynolds was shot?"

"Right through the head, I hear," Lenora said. "Close range, rest his soul."

"That poor woman," Raylene said. "All the money in the world can't heal the wounds she's having." Even though Mrs. Reynolds had never once set foot in the Kurl and drove all the way to Richmond to get her hair done, I could tell Raylene was genuinely sorry. But that was Raylene for you. Heart as big as Texas.

"Wonder if they'll have the funeral here?" Hattie said. "Aren't his folks from Roanoke?"

"That's her kin. His hail from Lynchburg."

"I suspect the funeral will be here," Lenora said. "They'll bury him next to the daughter."

"Isn't there another child?" Easter said. "Lawd, it's getting so I can't keep up."

"I don't think so," said Hattie.

Spy, I thought. Then I remembered the thing I'd been working hard to forget.

"There's the boy," Cora said. "You know the one. Drives around in his car like he owns the road. Going up to Charlottesville in the fall. Studying to be a lawyer like his daddy."

"Tallie?" Raylene said. "You okay, honey?"

"Yep," I said.

"You look peaked."

"I'm okay." I was picturing Spy taking out the gun, and I was hearing it go off, hurting my ears. I concentrated on stopping the thought in its tracks, stopping it before it flowed like electricity all the way to Sheriff Craw.

Hattie let out a long, satisfying burp. "Bacon," she said. "Bacon and doughnuts for breakfast. In this heat. I should know better. Raylene, you got any Tums around here? I got so much gas in me, I could blow the place up."

I got busy straightening out the magazine table, relieved the conversation had reverted to the usual Tuesday topics. I didn't really believe Spy had anything to do with his daddy's death any more than I'd had anything to do with my mama's. When I looked up, Lenora was looking at me funny, like she could read my mind as easily as she divined soap bubbles. Like she knew all about Spy and his gun.

★ Tallie's Book ★

Thoughts hold power.

It's surprising what people are capable of.

*C*ora was right about the TV people. By Tuesday noon, they covered the town like fleas on Old Straw. It got so crowded in Wayland's Diner that Mr. Wayland had to take on extra help. The reporters acted like the place was their own private club and the booths were their personal desks. Mainly they were from Lynchburg, but some came all the way from Richmond. I thought about how people passed every day, and wondered what made some people more deserving than others of special attention. Raylene said it was because Mr. Reynolds was rich. If it'd been one of us, she said, the only reporter interested would be Miss Gibbons from the *Eden Times*. There were vans all along Main Street, dish antennas on their roofs big enough to contact Mars, and camera crews had set up on the sidewalk outside Mr. Reynolds's law office. "The scene of the brutal murder," I heard one reporter saying into her mike, her voice all edgy and excited. I swear some people would dance on the grave of the newly dead. I could never figure what caused people to be so taken with the misfortunes of others. A couple of

reporters tried to set up over on Carlton's Way, outside the
Reynoldses' house, but someone complained, so Sheriff Craw
blocked the road off with sawhorses and said only residents
could drive through. He put extra men on duty to enforce this
rule. After work, I rode by on my Raleigh, trying to catch sight
of Spy, but the front curtains were drawn tight and his red
Camaro was nowhere in sight. When I got home, I phoned, but
I got an answering machine telling me to leave a message, so I
hung up.

On the six o'clock news a reporter "live on the scene" (like
they'd use a dead one?) said the murdered man had been a
prominent lawyer in the community. There was a picture of
Mr. Reynolds and one of Mrs. Reynolds, too. They called her
a former model and mentioned she'd been a Breck Girl. They
said stuff about how this was "the second time the family had
been visited by tragedy," and told how Sarah had drowned.
And they showed her picture, too. Then the reporter said the
local sheriff had no leads and the people in Eden were locking
their doors at the thought of a killer in their midst. Which was
a big fat lie. You wouldn't believe they could just make up stuff
like that and get away with it. Raylene said they did it all the
time. She said the only ones who told the truth were Dan
Rather and the weatherman, and you couldn't always count
on them.

It was crazy like that for twenty-four hours; then on Wednesday afternoon a huge scandal broke in the mayor's office in
Lynchburg, something about a secretary and misspent funds,
and the lot of them cleared out like they'd never been. "Sex, pol-
itics and money," Raylene said. "That beats a murder anytime."
Then on Thursday morning, the *Glamour Day* people returned

to the Klip-N-Kurl with everyone's pictures, and for a while, believe it or not, we all forgot about Mr. Reynolds's murder.

We were expecting the two blondes, Sylvia and Patty, but this time the company sent men, as if ladies weren't to be trusted with this part of the transaction. There were two of them and they wore suits with narrow legs and narrower lapels and sported slicked-back hair, the kind of men who called you honey and made you hold tight to your purse.

I'd observed that most men felt out of place in the Kurl, but these two waltzed in with giant-sized cups of take-out coffee and fake leather briefcases, acting like they owned the lease. Without even asking Raylene, they shoved the magazine table over by the sinks, where we'd have to walk around it all day, and set up a card table.

Miss Tilly was first on the schedule. They made a big fuss over her, calling her the "lovely Miss Pettijohn" and pulling out a chair for her to sit in. After they had her settled in, one of the men reached for his briefcase and took out a large white envelope with *Glamour Day* in pink letters in one corner. Raylene and I left off what we were doing and went over to watch. The pictures were wrapped in two sheets of tissue, which one of the men unfolded slowly, making a big deal of it. Then he spread them out on the table: one 9 x 12, three 8 x 10s, five 5 x 7s and twelve wallets, in a combination of the five poses.

"Will you look at that," Raylene said.

"Oh, my," Miss Tilly said, her voice hushed like you'd use in church.

"You'd have to go far to find a prettier picture," the first man said. He picked up the one of her in the tiara and set it in front of her.

Miss Tilly reached out to finger her image. She looked like she might cry.

At this point, the second man took over. "Here's what we're going to do. We're going to let you keep the nine by twelve at absolutely no cost," he said. He smiled like he was giving her a special treat, like the 9 x 12 wasn't already included for the original twenty dollars.

Miss Tilly's eyes were stuck on those pictures. I didn't even know if she was listening to him.

"The complete package, all twenty-one photos, is yours to keep, too," said the first man.

That got her attention. Miss Tilly looked up at him, her mouth shaped in a perfect O.

"That's right," he said. "All twenty-one photos." He moved them around the table, drawing Miss Tilly's eyes back to the pictures. She reached out to pick one up.

"The whole package," he said, "for only ninety-nine dollars."

Miss Tilly's hand fluttered to her lap.

"That works out to less than five dollars apiece," the second man chimed in.

I looked over at Raylene. I wondered if she knew about this part of the deal.

"Oh," Miss Tilly said, her voice gone all flat.

"Now, we can offer an installment plan if that's convenient," the first man said. "We can break it down into payments for you."

"How much would that be?" Miss Tilly asked in that flat tone.

"Let's see," said the second man, as if he were only at that moment doing the figuring. "We can give it do you for—let's see—for twenty dollars a month spread out over a period of five months."

"Interest free," said the first.

"Twenty dollars?" Miss Tilly said.

"That's right," said the second. "And absolutely no additional interest for the entire five months."

"None," said the first.

Willa Jenkins was next on line, and she crowded in to look at Miss Tilly's photos. "Jesus, be praised," she said, "but, girl, don't you look *fine*."

And she did. The way Raylene had fixed her hair you couldn't see her scalp shining through, and Patty, the camerawoman, must have played some photographer's trick with the lighting, which Mama'd told me was a technique photographers used. Lighting, Mama said, was everything; it could be your friend or enemy, add ten years or take them away. They must have done something like that, because most of Miss Tilly's wrinkles were ironed out. She looked like she could be the queen of some important country. England, maybe. Or France. It didn't take five minutes for Miss Tilly to decide on the installment plan, her hand barely trembling at all as she signed on the line. I imagined her drinking watery tea for the rest of her natural life.

Willa settled in the chair next, and when they unfolded the tissue and brought out her shots, she tossed back her head and laughed right out loud. "Praise, Jesus," she said. Her two friends elbowed their way in and repeated the praise to Jesus. I had to admit she looked amazing. Sparkling in a red satin top. All cleavage. Like Aretha, only fatter. "Praise, Jesus," she said again.

Just like Miss Tilly, she couldn't seem to stop staring at her pictures. As she was putting her signature to the installment payment contract, I was wondering how she'd break the news to Baylor, who was still looking for work. But maybe, seeing his Willa look like a star, maybe he'd think it was worth five months of grits and boiled greens. When it was their turn, her girlfriends took the whole package, too. They left, sashaying out like they'd won the lottery.

With customers coming in all morning and us leaving off shampoos and sets to go take a look, we ran behind on the schedule, but no one complained. It was the same story whenever anyone saw the photos. They were intoxicated, plain drunk on these visions of themselves, and every single one of them ended up buying the whole lot. I couldn't imagine what they were going to do with all these photos. How many pictures of yourself in rhinestones and elbow-length gloves could you hang on the walls of a four-room house? How many wallet-sized ones could you hand out? How much could you sacrifice to get them?

I understand a lot more about the power of dreams, now, but until that day I didn't know that you could make a living by selling them. I didn't understand that people would spend a lot of money, money they didn't have and had no way of getting, spending it to buy something that wasn't real in any sense except in their heads. I hadn't yet discovered that people yearned to taste *possibilities,* to see what it would be like if only they had the chance to live another life, to look like a star.

At lunch the men sent me over to the diner to pick up sandwiches. Extra bacon on the BLTs, and double sugars with the coffee, they told me, like I was their personal slave. I was supposed to be sweeping up from two cuts and folding a load of towels and I expected Raylene to tell them to go get their own sandwiches, that I worked for her, but she didn't say anything.

Just after three, Martha Lee came in. She was wearing her stained nurse's uniform, and her hair looked like it hadn't seen a comb in a week. I caught one of the men winking at the other, but I didn't think she noticed. She wasn't looking at much. She didn't even want to see all the shots, though I was dying. "Just give me the nine by twelve and throw the rest away," she told them straight out. The one who'd winked lost his smile. I could see they weren't used to dealing with someone like Martha Lee. The second man put on this real phony voice and said surely a handsome woman like herself would want to see them all. No, she said, she just wanted the one, like she'd told them. This made the first man get pushy. I could have told him to save his breath, that he was taking the wrong tack, but I was on Martha Lee's side. Somehow her not taking all the pictures, or even wanting a look at them, was making up for Miss Tilly and Willa Jenkins and all the other women who'd been signing up for the installment plans all day. Martha Lee asked him was he deaf, what part of this wasn't he hearing, she wanted the one 9 x 12, that was the deal, and if they wanted a suggestion what to do with the others, she'd be happy to give it to them. The first man's face got all flushed. He muttered something too ugly to repeat and pulled the 9 x 12 out of the white envelope. Then he made a big show of ripping up all the others. Without another word, he thrust the photo at Martha Lee, like it was suddenly contaminated. She grabbed it and beat it out of the Kurl, not caring one bit that the men were mad.

After she left, things settled down and the men got back

their smiles. Sue Beth came in and Bitty Weatherspoon and Aubrey Boles, and every one of them took the whole package. Ashley Wheeler was the only one who paid cash. Finally, *finally*, it was my turn.

First thing, I didn't even recognize myself. In the cowgirl outfit, I was pure Wynonna Judd. You wouldn't even know it was me. I swear I looked twenty. "Oh, Tallie," Raylene said, and gave me a little hug. I was filled with so many feelings, I couldn't speak. I was stunned to see this vision of myself, this *transformation,* and I was deeply regretting Mama wasn't there to see, too. She'd be so happy. Then I remembered what Preacher Tillett had told me about how now Mama was watching over me and could see everything, how she was my guardian angel. I was thinking that if it was true and Mama really could witness everything, she must have been mostly disappointed lately what with me drinking beer and Frenching with Spy and stealing from her very best friend on the planet. But, I was hoping that maybe somehow she'd understand all that. For sure if she was looking down at that photo, I know she'd be happy. "See, sugar," I could hear her say, "listen to your mama. Didn't I tell you you were beautiful?"

One of the men was explaining about the installment plan, like I hadn't heard it so many times, I could have recited it to him. All day long I'd been thinking about it and I'd been knowing no installment plan was possible for me. I didn't even bother asking for a miracle. Ninety-nine goddamn dollars was as far away as the moon, and if they agreed to let me spread it out over two hundred months it wouldn't help one bit. But looking at these glossy pictures of me, facts didn't matter. I didn't want the one 9 x 12. I wanted them all, and I swear I'd have promised just about anything to get them. I wanted to paper the walls of our house so that no matter where I looked my eyes would rest on this creature staring back at me, this glorious creature who was saying, yes, you're beautiful, yes, you can be a star. I wanted to divide up the wallet-sized sheet and send one to Goody in Florida and another to Uncle Grayson in Atlanta and one to Elizabeth Talmadge, just to show her who was the true Queen of the Universe. I wanted to tack one of the bigger ones up on the school bulletin board where they posted clippings about the football team. I wanted to put one up at the Eden Post Office next to the poster of the newest commemorative issue. I wanted to blow them up and plaster them on the billboards on the way into town. On the way out of town. I wanted to own them. I wanted to *eat* them.

Most of all, I wanted to paste them on the bathroom mirror so that when I brushed my teeth and washed my face, a different me would look back, a face that could belong to a movie star or a country singer, a woman who could wear flowers in her hair, a woman a boy like Spy Reynolds could love. I wanted to see this vision instead of the face I was used to, a face that had a lot more of my daddy in it than my mama.

When I could trust my voice, I told them thank you very much, but I'd just be taking the one.

The second man started in on how maybe I should call my mama and have her come and take a look 'cause for sure if she saw them she'd want to have them all. That's when Raylene came over and told them my mama'd passed four years back.

I could have killed her for telling these two men with their greasy, slicked-back hair something so private that was none of their goddamn beeswax. They got that fake, sad look people put on when they heard about Mama. Then one of them wrapped the 9 x 12 in tissue and gave it to me, calling me honey and acting like he was doing me the world's greatest favor. I took it with me to the back room and got busy refilling bottles of shampoo and conditioner. I folded towels and then started on the ladies' room, scouring the toilet and refilling the paper towel box and taking the Ajax to the stubborn rust spot in the sink. I planned on keeping busy back there until the men packed up and got out. Then I heard Raylene calling me and when I came out she was standing there with the men and one was holding a *Glamour Day* envelope.

"Here you go, little lady," he said. "You just take these with our compliments."

They were waiting for me to thank them and act like they were deserving of some big prize for being so generous, which I had no intention of doing. I was going to tell them no, thanks. I planned on telling them that just 'cause I didn't have a mama didn't mean I had to take charity. I was going to copy Martha Lee and tell them I had a suggestion for what they could do with the goddamn photos. I took a second to get the words straight and when they came out what I actually said was, "Thanks." Then I grabbed the envelope right out of his hand before he could change his mind.

Wanting is a powerful thing. You'd be surprised at what it could make a person do.

★ Tallie's Book ★

Wanting is a powerful thing.

seventeen

*a*fter I left the Kurl, I rode directly over to Martha Lee's. I figured I'd show her the shots of me and she'd make a big fuss, like Raylene had, but when I got there, Martha Lee wasn't home, a huge disappointment. I'd been looking forward to showing the pictures to *someone*. I sat on the steps and opened the *Glamour Day* envelope, carefully unwrapping the photos from the tissue. The one good part of being alone was that I could take my time looking without anyone saying I'd gotten too big for my britches. Each one was perfect: the one of me in the blue sequined tube, long gloves, and blue dangling earrings, my mouth curved just a little, like I knew a secret; the Wynonna cowgirl one, all sass and attitude; the one of me dressed in the square pearl earrings and the low-cut velvet, where I was displaying some cleavage and grinning like a bad girl. But the best by far was the shot of me in the black satin halter. No jewelry, just the rhinestone hair clip. Patty was right about my shoulders, and I was glad she'd insisted on that top. I wasn't gazing directly at the camera, but off a little, like I was half dreaming and half looking at something no one else could see. But what made it the best was the way the light reflected in my eyes, like they held little suns. Mama would say it was a picture that *glowed*. That was the one I'd be using in L.A. Sure as sunrise, that was the photo that would make me a star.

After a while, I wrapped the photos back in the tissue and slipped them into the envelope. I wondered if Martha Lee was ever coming back. I fished the key out from its usual spot and let myself in. I helped myself to a beer and did a little straightening up. The envelope of money was still on the kitchen shelf. Curiosity killed cats, according to Goody, but I couldn't help counting it, just to see how much was there. Well, believe it or not, there was more than a thousand dollars. I mean, hadn't Martha Lee ever heard of banks? I knew Martha Lee's daddy was rich, but I hadn't pictured Martha Lee as actually having money. Believe it, if I had that kind of cash lying around, I'd sure be driving something better than a rusty old pickup and living like white trash in a place no better than a trailer. So would most people, I guess. But Martha Lee was different from most, and that wasn't fresh news. I replaced the envelope exactly where I'd found it and went back outside. To keep myself occupied, I checked the garden. The grass all around was yellow as straw, but in spite of the heat and continued lack of rain, nothing in the garden had wilted. The irrigation bottles were nearly empty, so I unrolled the hose and got to work filling them. I helped myself to the bush beans, snapping the ends off, eating them right off the vine. The cherry tomatoes were ready for picking, too, so I had some of those, popping them in my mouth like candy till I had my fill.

*   *   *

By six-thirty, when Martha Lee still hadn't arrived, I went back inside. I headed straight for Martha Lee's room and opened the bottom drawer. The pictures of Mama were still there. Only weeks had passed since I'd seen them, but this time looking at them was different, like I was looking at someone I used to know a long time ago, someone who'd moved away. You wouldn't think it was possible, but in spite of thinking of her every day and hearing her voice speaking clear in my head, in spite of my lists and my rule book, I was losing Mama. Without a picture to hold, I feared she'd disappear entirely.

Half listening for the sound of Martha Lee's truck, I went through them all, slowly this time. There was no way photos could capture the truth of Mama, they could only suggest the liveliness of her. I looked at the ones where she was with Daddy and Grayson and Martha Lee, and the ones of her in school, always in the front row near the framed board with the class and year spelled out in block letters. The ones where she was older could have been photos taken out of her Hollywood scrapbook. That's how pretty she was.

There was sound outside then, and I froze, straining to catch the rattle of the pickup, but everything fell quiet. Still, it made me nervous and I began to put everything back. I'd nearly shut the drawer when I saw another envelope, shoved toward the rear. I knew, even before I looked, that it was about Mama. There were two photos inside. The one on top was of Mama in the front seat of a fire-red convertible, sitting close to a blond boy I'd never seen in my life. Mama was smiling out at the camera and looking like she was queen of the homecoming parade. There was a dog in the backseat, which surprised me. Mama was afraid of dogs, even Old Straw, who was completely harmless and so old he didn't even chase squirrels. Because of the dog, I thought maybe it wasn't Mama at all, maybe it was a picture from her scrapbook, one of the real Natalie Wood, but when I turned it over, there was Mama's round handwriting, as familiar as my own. *Gordie and Me,* it said in blue ink. *April, 1965.* I did the math quick and determined Mama'd been fifteen. Almost the same age as me. I stared at Mama and the man named Gordie. Now that I had a name for him, he seemed real. He was real good-looking, a look-alike for this movie star named Tab Hunter who was another actor in Mama's scrapbook. He and Mama looked just right together, though it made me feel disloyal to my daddy to be thinking that. I'd never heard Mama or Goody or Martha Lee ever mention anyone named Gordie. For sure he didn't live in Eden. It was weird to think of Mama having another life, a life before she married my daddy. Before me. I wondered where she'd met this Gordie guy and if it was when she was in school in Lynchburg and doing some theater there, but the date on the back didn't match up. I wondered what had happened to him and why she'd never mentioned him. Had she ever kissed him, like I'd kissed Spy? I wondered if she'd had that first shock at the hardness of him and if she'd felt that melting, aching feeling of wanting deep inside. I wished the picture could come alive like a TV show, so I could hear what they were saying, so I could hear what music was playing on the radio. For sure, there'd be music playing in that car. You couldn't think of Mama without putting her together with music. For the first time I really understood that Mama had a whole history before

I was born, and there were whole parts of my mama that I didn't know at all.

The second photo was of Mama, too. She was standing in front of a tree, and as impossible as it was to believe, she was with a girl who could have been her twin, like somehow the photographer'd made one of those trick double images. Except not really double, 'cause each person was dressed in different clothes. And one wore a bracelet on her left wrist. I looked on the back. *Natalie and me. September '65,* it said in blue ink. I'd have sworn on the Bible, Mama had never met the real Natalie. Never. If she had, for sure, I'd have known. Mama couldn't have kept something like that quiet if you'd paid her a million dollars and promised her the sun. If this picture was real, it would have been hanging on our living room wall instead of being stuck in a drawer in Martha Lee's bureau. I stared at it a long time, trying to understand, but nothing about it made sense.

The last thing in the envelope was a postcard. It was a picture of the big Hollywood sign, just like the one Mama'd sent me, except it was addressed to Martha Lee. *I found her,* she'd written on the back. That's all. *I found her.* Found who? For a minute I thought she must have meant Natalie. Who else? Of course that was impossible. That summer Mama left Daddy and me and headed off to Hollywood, Natalie'd already been dead for seven years. My head was dizzy from trying to make sense of it. I almost missed one other thing in the envelope. A slip of paper holding a name and an address and phone number. I stared at the name. Sasha. Sasha Upton; 344 Mississippi St., Los Angeles. I put everything back in the envelope and when I left Martha Lee's I took it along with me.

The last thing I expected was to uncover a mystery about Mama, but one had been placed right before my eyes. I wondered if Uncle Grayson knew about what Mama'd been doing the year she was fifteen, and if she'd really met Natalie Wood. And if she had, why she wouldn't have told me. The mystery was so big, it took my mind right off all the things that were happening in Eden. That's how I pretty much forgot about Spy until Saturday, the day of Mr. Reynolds's funeral.

The funeral was this really big deal, so I was glad I'd worn my new skirt and the blue cotton top, even if I had been saving it for a more festive occasion. The church was full up, and Mr. Wesler was running around telling people to move over and make room so other people could sit down. When he'd packed us in so tight you couldn't breathe, when I swear you couldn't slip a blade of sour grass between us, he ordered some men to set up folding chairs in the back. They formed a little assembly line, passing the chairs from one to another, snapping them open with efficient clicks. Even so, people had to stand. I figured every store in Eden must have closed up, like it was a national holiday instead of a funeral. It was three hundred degrees in the shade, and the overhead fans were going top speed. Between the heat and the overpowering smell of lilies and roses, you had to concentrate not to faint. Everybody was fanning away with this program that had been printed up, like it was a regular Sunday service except the program was all about Mr. Reynolds, even had his picture inside.

Just as the church bell was sounding one o'clock, there was a stir at the door and this group of strangers came in. They headed for the front pews that had been tied off with black ribbons, so I knew they were Reynolds kin from Lynchburg. An old lady led the way, making her way down the aisle with the aid of one of those ugly aluminum walker things, taking so long, it made you just itch to pick her up and carry her. Someone should have arranged for a wheelchair or something. It took her about three hours to get to the front. The rest of them shuffled along behind her like her own personal little parade. One of the men looked so much like Mr. Reynolds, he could have been a twin, right down to the black suit and hat. After they got themselves seated, there was a pause and people made those little impatient waiting noises with their feet, then Mrs. Reynolds came in. She had never been a big woman—Sarah took after her in that way—but now she looked plain tiny, all shrunk up like cotton washed in hot water by mistake. Spy was holding her arm. He was dressed in a suit, and you could see the white skin on his neck where he'd had a recent haircut. As they made their way to the front, Mrs. Reynolds stopped to touch people's hands and thank them for coming, but Spy looked straight ahead, his eyes blank, like overnight he'd lost his sight.

When the family was finally seated, six men rolled in this huge casket, big enough to be a bank vault and looking like solid brass. It made my chest hurt to look at it and I was glad my daddy hadn't come. I knew he'd be thinking about Mama, too. Then, from outside somewhere, came this wailing sound that raised the hair straight up on your arm and made your heart about break, like an invisible hand had reached right through your skin and grabbed hold and squeezed. Everyone turned as the rear doors swung open and a man came in playing a real bagpipe. It gave out the most sorrowful sound I'd ever heard, worse than a woman crying. The hand was clenching hard around my heart, so I found the dark place inside and held on to that and held on to that until things settled down. Behind me I heard Aubrey Boles's mama say, "Just like them to be different." Then the piper walked to the front, taking his time, head held proud, shoulders straight, little plaid skirt swaying with each step. When he was done, he stood for a moment until the last echo faded away, then he left through the side door, the one usually reserved for the preacher. Things were quiet for a minute, then up in the choir loft, Mrs. Duval started up, singing "Amazing Grace" in her screechy voice, erasing the ache the bagpipe man made, and the funeral got under way.

It lasted about a hundred hours. You wouldn't believe a service could last that long, even for an important man like Mr. Reynolds. The preacher talked first, saying how this was not a sad occasion, but a celebration of a life and like that. Then Mrs. Duval sang again. Then the preacher read some passages from the Bible, the one about the mansion with many rooms. I think it's a law or something that you have to read that at funerals. Then we all had to stand and sing from the hymnal. "Nearer, My God, to Thee." *All five verses.* One would have been more than enough, as far as I was concerned. But that was only the beginning. Mr. Reynolds's brother got up and stood at the pulpit and read some more from the Bible, and another man got up and said he knew Mr. Reynolds from working with him at the chamber and a finer man never was born and ours was not to reason why or question the will of God but to remember the good things about Mr. Reynolds and carry on his work. It sounded like he wanted people to send money to the chamber in memory of Mr. Reynolds. Then we had to sing another hymn, "Abide with Me," which only had three verses, thank the Lord. Everyone was sweating, and my new skirt was getting all wrinkled from all the sitting and standing and sitting again. After a while I stopped listening to what was going on up front. I found if I moved a little to the left, crowding so close to Mrs. Purvis I was practically sitting on her lap, I could catch sight of the back of Spy. He didn't move at all. Not once. Then I looked at the picture of Mr. Reynolds they'd printed in the program. Gone to clay. Just like Mama. And Sarah. And Granddaddy Adams. And the people on the train in that tunnel collapse in Lynchburg. And all the people in the Eden Cemetery. And in the black cemetery out by Elijah Baptist. And movie stars, like Natalie Wood. And all the people who had ever died anywhere in the world, since time began. And dogs, too. And birds. And butterflies. It didn't seem like there was enough ground to hold all the dead, even with the dead people in India being burned. It made me wonder why the earth didn't weep, just holding all those bones.

When it was over, the preacher announced that Mrs. Reynolds had invited everyone back to the family's home for libations. I couldn't imagine how they expected to fit everyone in, but later Raylene told me they'd set up a tent and that caterers brought in all the way from Lynchburg did the food. I went directly home. I stripped off my new clothes and put on one of my daddy's old shirts and sat on the glider, trying to figure out the puzzle of life. The summer she'd passed I heard Mama tell Martha Lee that life was short. "Even if you get the full measure of years, it's brief," she'd said. "Why don't we know that? Why do we waste time?" Sitting on the glider, I thought about Mr. Reynolds and how he must have thought he was going to live to see Spy graduate and become a lawyer and take over the business. And Mama—what had she believed she'd live to see? And the people buried beneath a tunnel in Lynchburg? What would they do different if they had the chance? "Regret," Mama'd said to Martha Lee, "regret is a pitiful thing, and I don't know which is worse, regret for what you've done or remorse for all the things you never got to do." "You can't live life backwards," Martha Lee'd told her. "Best we can do is go forward, doing what makes sense at the time."

I thought they were both right. Then and there, still holding the memory of Mr. Reynolds's funeral and Mama's words about regret being a pitiful thing, I decided to move forward. You might not believe this, but I marched straight to the phone and dialed the Lynchburg airport. When she asked, I told the lady my departure was Wednesday. That would give me enough time to get prepared. And I wanted to go to the Kurl one more time. I wanted to say good-bye, even if Raylene didn't know that's what I was doing. I believed a person should always say her good-byes when she had a chance. Just in case. The reservations lady said if I wasn't charging the ticket on a card, I'd have to pick it up within twenty-four hours, and I told her no problem. I knew where I'd get the money, and it didn't seem wrong. Not one bit. Life was so short, you had to grab what you wanted. You had to move forward. I started packing that night. I didn't have much to take. My stuff didn't begin to fill Mama's gray suitcase. I had just the clothes Martha Lee had bought me, my *Glamour Day* photos, my rule book, Mama's red sweater and her Hollywood scrapbook. I put in the postcards she'd sent me, too, and the envelope I'd taken from Martha Lee with the mystifying pictures of Mama and the paper with the address and phone number of Sasha, whoever she was. I'd tried to call the number Mama'd put down but had just gotten a recording telling me that number had been disconnected at the party's request. Then I'd called the information operator, but she'd said the only listing they had for a Sasha Upton on Mississippi Street was unlisted. I figured I'd just have to look her up when I got there.

The other thing I planned to do when I arrived in L.A. was to go see all the places Mama'd written about: the sidewalk with the handprints of the stars; the Hollywood sign the actress had jumped off; Paramount Studios. I figured I'd go to the studio since someone there might remember Mama and that would help me get started. Then, in the back of my rule book, I copied my Uncle Grayson's number. And Goody's number in Florida, too, in case I had a real emergency, though I'd have to be close to dead to call her. I was finishing up when I heard my daddy's truck pull in.

I shoved the suitcase back in the closet and listened while he came up the steps. No stumbling or falling. Still, I held my breath. You could have knocked me over with a sneeze when he stopped at my door. "Hey," he said.

"Hi." I wondered if somehow he could tell my plans, if my face revealed my thoughts.

"You okay?" he said.

"Yeah," I said.

"How was the funeral?"

"Crowded," I said. "And hot." It was weird, talking to him like this, and it made me about crazy with wondering what was wrong.

"I'll bet," he said. "No telling how long this dry spell will last." He came in my room and sat down on the foot of my bed. He'd had a few, I could smell the beer, but he wasn't drunk.

"They had to set up extra chairs," I said.

He leaned forward, elbows resting on his knees. "Guess he was an important man," he said. My daddy never spoke ill of anyone, even Goody; in that way he was like Mama, but the funny way he stressed *important* told me he hadn't liked Mr. Reynolds.

"There was a bagpipe," I told him.

He looked up, surprised. "A piper?"

"Uh-huh."

He shook his head. "Nothing like a pipe," he said. "They can crack a grown man's heart in half."

"I know," I said. "It kind of hurt to listen."

"I knew a man once who played. Friend of my daddy's. Your Granddaddy Brock."

"Really?" My daddy never talked about his mama and daddy, who'd died before I was born.

"You know, he played the fiddle."

"Who?" It was weird, having a real conversation like normal people, but nice, too. It reminded me of when he'd take me to the mill and explain about the different grains, real patient, even when I couldn't tell the difference. "Who played the fiddle?"

"Your granddaddy. He could make a cat dance just with the pleasure of hearing him play." He stood up. "It's getting late. Best you be getting some sleep."

I didn't want him to go.

At the door, he looked directly at me. "You're getting tall, girl," he said, and shook his head like he was trying to remember something.

I looked over toward the closet where I'd hid Mama's suitcase. Up to then I hadn't given a thought as to how it would be to leave my daddy. It seemed he'd pretty much forgotten I existed. It was peculiar him coming in that way, suddenly behaving like a father, acting like he liked me, now that I was preparing to leave. It made me sad, like the music of the pipes. But if I was going to be having regrets, I'd rather they be 'cause I'd gone rather than 'cause I'd stayed.

I was dreaming of my Granddaddy Brock, at least I guess it was him. He looked a little like my daddy, but he was old and he was playing a fiddle and there was a cat dancing a jig. It was dressed in a little suit, like this picture I had in a book when I was a little girl. Someone was calling my granddaddy and whistling for him and they kept it up and I was sorry because I didn't want him to stop the music. Then I woke up. There was a sound at the window, the old willow I thought, and turned over, wondering if I could settle back in the dream of my granddaddy, like sometimes you can if you don't wake too much, but the noise came again. It wasn't the willow, it was someone scratching at the screen and whispering my name.

I held still, barely breathing.

"Tallie? It's me. Spy."

"Spy?" It was a night for big surprises. First my daddy, coming home and talking to me regular-like, then Spy showing up at my window. "What're you doing here?" I whispered back.

"Can you come out?"

"Now?" I was wearing nothing but my daddy's old shirt.

"Yeah."

"In a sec," I said.

"I'll wait," he said. "On the porch."

I brushed my hair and put on the clothes I'd worn to the funeral. It seemed like a million years ago I'd sat in the church and heard the bagpipes and squeezed next to Mrs. Purvis so I could get a better look at Spy.

When I went outside, he was sitting on the glider. I looked around but the Camaro wasn't in the drive or anywhere as far as I could see. "How'd you get here?"

"Walked."

"You walked? From your house?"

"Yeah," he said, like it was normal to walk five miles in the middle of the night and scratch at someone's screen until you woke someone you hadn't seen in days and who you'd acted like you never wanted to see again as long as you lived.

"I was there today," I told him. "At the funeral, I mean."

"A Dreck Girl production," he said, his voice tight and mean.

I didn't know what to say to that, so I shut up. I was filled with a million questions, but I didn't ask one. I figured if he came all this way, he must have something on his mind and I'd let him tell me in his own fashion.

We sat on the glider and stared out into the night. Whatever brought him to my window, he wasn't in any hurry to get around to it. I was real conscious of him sitting so close, and it was a mixed-up feeling, sort of comfortable, like we were friends, but nervous, too, with that electric feeling he always caused in my stomach. I wondered if he could hear my heart beating. Fireflies flickered over the grass. I told him what my mama'd said, about them being a kind of beetle and how beetles signified change. Sitting next to him in the dark, I was seized by a feeling I couldn't name and I told him a secret I hadn't told

anyone. Not Rula or Martha Lee or Goody. I told him about
burying the Queen of Cures that Allie Rucker had given me.
But that wasn't the real secret. The real secret was something
close to a miracle, 'cause there was no other explanation for
how it had occurred. The real secret was that the spring after
Mama died, in the *exact* spot I'd buried that mess of seeds and
bark Allie called a Cure, in that *exact* spot, a butterfly bush appeared. I'm not making that up. Honestly. In the exact same
spot. I thought Spy might laugh or think I was making it up,
but he didn't.

"You miss your mama?" he asked.

"Every day," I said. "I guess you'll be missing your daddy,
too."

He didn't answer, just stared out at the dark. I wished there
was a moon, something to give a little light on his face, something so I could get a hint of what he was thinking.

Then he turned and put his hands on my shoulders and
pulled me to him. The electric feeling shot straight through
me, so strong that, if I'd been a lamp, I would have lit up like
neon. Then he kissed me and there was hunger near desperation in that kiss and it roused something answering in me,
something I hadn't even known was there, but that had been
building all day, starting with the bagpipe music and the
knowledge that everyone died, even me someday. He kissed me
long and deep and it was nowhere near enough. The feelings
ran so fierce, I thought it must mean we were made for each
other.

Of course, now I know that being around death always
makes you hunger for life, makes you reach for it however and
wherever you can find it, but that night I thought it was magic

reserved for us. He pushed me back on the glider and I welcomed the weight of him, welcomed the astonishing hardness of him, knowing what it was and that it came from wanting me. When he slipped his hand beneath me, I shifted my hips to make it easy. My body rose to meet his in a rhythm that flowed as natural as the water in a stream.

He pulled back and looked down at me. "Is your daddy home?" he whispered.

"Sleeping."

"Can we go in?" he said. "Your bed?"

I didn't hesitate one instant. I figured before it was my time to pass, I'd be answering for plenty of regrets and I'd have my share of sorrows, but that night I didn't think there was one thing about being with Spy that I could live long enough to regret. Not if I lived to be twice as old as Easter Davis.

★ Tallie's Book ★

Always say good-bye when you have the chance.

Regret is a pitiful thing.

Being around death makes you hunger for life.

Magical things rise up out of unlikely beginnings.

A boy who looks like a pirate can have a choir singer's soul.

eighteen

*i*n the morning, Spy was gone and for one moment, before I fully woke, I truly believed that everything had been a dream, that his coming to me had no more happened than my Granddaddy Brock'd played a fiddle and a cat dressed in green velvet had danced a jig.

But dreams didn't leave your body aching and sore, or the smell of a man on your skin. For sure dreams didn't leave blood on your sheets. Proof I was no longer a virgin, which was supposed to be some big deal or something. Truth was, I was happy to be done with it. I mean, virgin sounded stupid. Like a disease you needed to get over. Spy had been my cure.

My daddy was in the kitchen, whistling and making coffee. I was absolutely not ready to face him and I decided to stay right where I was until he left for the mill. I believed that all that had occurred in the night must show clear on my face, show as openly as a birthmark, like one of those port-wine stains Willie Purvis had, so dark, it made you avert your gaze.

While I was waiting for Daddy to leave, I replayed the night from the beginning, running it through my mind like a Technicolor movie, starting from the instant when I woke to Spy calling at my window. I saw myself get out of bed, unpack my new skirt and shirt from Mama's gray suitcase, then slip out to the porch. I saw Spy and me sitting on the glider, listening to the cicadas, watching the signals of fireflies. I remember telling him the secret of the butterfly bush. And I recalled that first hungry kiss, which just remembering made my belly heat up. I remembered how right it felt. All of it. I thought of how I'd led Spy inside, to my room, my bed.

In the clear light of morning, it seemed impossible—crazy—that we'd have used my bed, that we'd head there without the least concern or fear that my daddy'd wake and find us. There was only the urgent need. Nothing else. My daddy could have been sitting in the front room with a shotgun laid 'cross his lap and it wouldn't have prevented me from bringing Spy to my bed. I was pure amazed to find myself capable of such desire. That's what I remembered most, the deep, insistent desire and the fiery need to meet it. Spy'd undressed me. (My skirt and shirt were still pooled on the floor, exactly where he'd dropped them.) I remembered the sharp, quick sound of his breath—nearly a sob—when his fingers touched my skin, my breasts and belly, and then his whispered *Jesus.* I'd started to undress him, too, but I was too slow. He was faster with the buttons and belt and zipper. I'd longed for a moon, even a crescent, so there'd be light. In the shadows, our fingers had become our eyes. I recalled the electric jolt when skin touched skin, our bodies sweat-soaked from desire as much as heavy summer heat. I remembered the salty taste of kisses, and the way our bodies moved, without thought, in natural rhythm, like they'd been made for just that. Exactly that. And maybe they had. More than walking or working or playing or praying, maybe *that* was what we'd been born for. I'd made cat noises, little moans I didn't even know I was making till Spy'd whispered in my ear *Shhhh, Shhhh, Shhhhh,* but I was beyond caution. Then his hand over my lips, gently muting my cries. Urgency drove us, drove me, so that nothing could stop me, not even the shock of that first cutting pain when he, grown harder than you'd imagine possible, entered me, and our bodies carried us forward, soaked and slippery with sweat.

I remembered Spy holding me and then I must have fallen off to sleep. I woke to someone's touch and I'd believed it was my mama. Oh, the pure joy of it. Of knowing she was there, holding me, rocking me, stroking me, telling me how sweet I was. I was so happy to have her back, so joyful her passing had only been a wicked dream. Then I woke fully and saw it was Spy, not Mama, and I felt a confusion of sorrow and joy. We kissed again, slower and more deliberate at first, with me still filled with the waking grief of knowing Mama was truly gone. I'd felt an answering heartache in Spy, as surely as if he'd spoken it aloud, and I believed he was thinking of his daddy. And of Sarah. It was like we were taking all the sorrow we'd ever borne and were pouring it into each other, trying to make something else of it. Something good. There was more I half recalled, not trusting memory. Had I licked tears from Spy's cheeks? Had he really wept? Or was it sweat? Or had I dreamed that, too, like Granddaddy and the cat?

Guitar music floated in from the kitchen. Daddy'd turned on the radio, and I was wondering if he was ever going to get going for the mill. I was desperate to pee. I was hungry, too, like

I hadn't seen food in days. Then I smelled the nutty, burnt smell of butter frying in the skillet and knew he was making pancakes. That's how I remembered it was Sunday and he wouldn't be heading off to the mill. I got up and stripped the stained sheet off the bed. I'd have to soak it in vinegar water later. I left the pillow slip on my pillow. It still smelled of Spy, his aftershave and sweat. Then I saw the rhinestone hair clip sitting on my dresser top. I picked it up and held it, the edges of the little stones digging in my palm. It was proof Spy'd really been there, as if I needed more beyond the stained sheet and my sore body. I took out Mama's suitcase and put the clip inside, so I'd have it with me. It was all I had of Spy to take, all I had to remind me of our night, and I was glad for it. In the bathroom, it stung when I peed, a fleeting reminder.

"Another hot one," Daddy said in the kitchen. He smiled at me, and I caught my breath, but he didn't notice anything after all. He told me the weatherman was predicting it'd go over a hundred. If the farmers lost the crops, it would hurt the mill. He said other things, too, but I wasn't paying attention. Ronnie Milsap was on the radio. Later, I remembered that 'cause he was singing "Daydreams About Night Things," and it seemed the perfect song for that morning. I wondered if somewhere Spy was listening to it, too. I hoped so. It was funny, the way I was calm thinking about him, not like the girls at school, who'd gather in the girls' room and go on and on about some boy they'd gone parking with the night before. They'd carry on like it was some disaster, holding conferences about whether they would dare phone the boy if he didn't call. Elizabeth Talmadge would be combing her hair and giving out advice, she who never in her life had to wait for any boy to call her. Ronnie

Milsap stopped singing and a man came on with a bulletin, but I was still lost in a reverie of Spy. Daddy went over and turned up the volume and that was when I finally listened. "An arrest had been made in the murder of an Eden man," the man said. "The son of prominent businessman George Reynolds has confessed to the fatal shooting."

He promised more news to come, but I didn't—couldn't— listen fully. I felt like a yard dog sideswiped by a truck, lying in a ditch too stunned to move or to rise and see if walking was a possibility. I must have made a sound, said something, 'cause Daddy said, "You know the boy?" Of course he knew I did. Everyone knew everyone in Eden. I nodded. The part of me that could think—the little part that seemed to be standing apart—wondered what my daddy'd say if he knew Spy had been in his house, in my bed. The other part wasn't thinking, it was just saying over and over that it was all a mistake. Boys like Spy didn't kill their daddies. They just didn't.

The pancakes stuck in my throat like sawdust, and after a while I gave up even trying to eat. In my bedroom, I buried my head in my pillow, inhaling Spy. He couldn't have done it, I told myself. Couldn't have done it. I cleaned up the sheet and pinned it on the line. I washed my skirt and top and hung those out, too.

Finally I headed out. "I'll be back," I yelled, slipping away before he could ask where I was going. I rode the Raleigh straight downtown. It was a zoo there. I swear it was worse than right after Mr. Reynolds died. Reporters and cameramen were swarming the streets, taking over the diner and standing outside the courthouse, even though it was Sunday and the place was shut up tight. I headed for Wayland's and ordered a cherry

Coke. The reporters were talking a mile a minute and I listened hard, trying to sort fact from pure rumor and there was plenty of that, no surprise. Rumors were spreading through the place like spilt milk on linoleum. You wouldn't believe some of the things they were saying. One reporter said Spy was a student at Washington and Lee, reporting it like gospel, and then another said, no, he was enrolled at Liberty University, a Bible student. It almost made me laugh. The only thing they all agreed on was that Spy'd confessed. They'd gotten that directly from Sheriff Craw. The sheriff said Spy'd even turned over the gun, case closed. The lady who was sure Spy went to Washington and Lee said she'd heard Spy was protecting his mama.

"The son's covering for the wife," she said. She had a nasty, nasal voice.

"No way," said the man who'd made Spy a Bible student. He had greasy hair and a bad case of dandruff. "The boy did it. Open and closed."

"I don't think so," said the nasty lady. "I say it was the wife. She killed the husband and got the boy to take the rap."

"Didn't happen," the man said.

"Motive," the lady said flatly. "That's why I think it's the wife. What would the son's motive be?"

"Who knows," the man said. "Probably drugs."

They acted like they were talking about people in a movie or something, and I hated them, even if hating was a sin.

"My money's still on the wife," the lady said.

"How much?" said the man.

"Ten bucks."

"You're on." They actually bet on it, shaking hands and everything.

You're wrong, I wanted to shout. You're stupid and you're wrong and you have dandruff all over your shoulders. I didn't care what the hell they said. Not one damn thing about it made sense. I recalled Spy's hands on me, stroking my back, caressing every part of me. I tried to imagine those same hands pointing a gun at his daddy's head, pulling the trigger. It seemed impossible. Even knowing he had a gun, even remembering the night up on the Blue Ridge when he'd fired it, I couldn't believe Spy'd really shot his daddy.

On the way out of the diner, I pretended to stumble and bumped the table where the stupid reporters sat, spilling their coffee.

"Fuck," the lady said right out loud, brushing furiously at her skirt with a handful of napkins.

"Sorry," I said in a perfect imitation of Elizabeth Talmadge, a tone that said I wasn't sorry in the least. I didn't just want to get away from Wayland's, I wanted to run from Eden, too. I needed to escape and I didn't think I could wait until Wednesday. You might think with all that was going on—Spy and me making love, his confessing to his father's murder—all that would make me want to stick around, but in some way I couldn't explain, it made me want to go more than ever. My chest felt tight, like I wasn't getting enough air. It was like everything was closing down, like I could suddenly see my whole life playing out in front of me. If I didn't escape, I'd go to the cosmetology school in Lynchburg and then work for Raylene and we wouldn't talk about it but there'd be an understanding that someday I'd take the shop over from her, like she had from Lenora. Jeez, I'd probably end up marrying someone like Wiley Bettis.

I thought about Mama heading to L.A. and Goody going all the way to Florida after my granddaddy died. In science class, Mr. Brown told us that genes determined the color hair you got and the color of your eyes and height and things like that. Everything, he said, was determined by genes. So I had to wonder if our family carried an Escape Gene and if so, was it a dominant gene, one that twisted our hearts into always wanting something more. Just as another family might have girls with curly hair, I wondered if the women in my family were born wanting to escape. Goody wanted to get away to Florida, and before that, she drove my granddaddy to becoming a doctor so she could avoid the life of a store clerk's wife. Mama wanted to go to Hollywood and be a star so she could live the life she was truly fated to live. And I wanted to become famous, too, and flee a future that went no farther than cosmetology school in Lynchburg.

Maybe it wasn't exactly an Escape Gene we had. Maybe we had the chromosome for Wanting so that we were always desiring something more, confusing our lives by longing for something other than what life handed out. As Mama would say, we were capable of imagination, and imagination—the power to dream—could make you discontent. Mama said once we're denied something, we want it even more, like the denying was what held the power. For years I'd been wanting Spy Reynolds, but now that we'd made love—and I didn't regret one moment of it—the terrible desire had eased.

Still, I wanted to talk with him. I owed him that before I left. With my daddy off from the mill, I knew I couldn't use the phone at home, so I headed over to the Cash Store. In the pay booth, I dropped in my dime and waited, expecting to get the machine with the "leave your number and name" message, but on the second ring, Mrs. Reynolds picked up. I wasn't prepared, and she had to say hello twice before I managed to ask for Spy. "Who is calling?" she demanded. She said that in a precise way, three clipped and separate words, unlike her normal tone. I remembered how shrunken she'd seemed at the funeral, leaning on Spy, and what Rula'd said about her at Sarah's funeral, grasping at hands and not letting go, talking of how her beautiful angel'd gone to heaven. Now her voice sounded as hard and shiny as a sheet of steel. *Who is calling?* I remembered what the reporter said about her being the one to kill Mr. Reynolds. For the first time I believed it could be true. Someone with a voice that'd cut through stone would be capable of anything. "It's Tallie," I said. "Tallie Brock." I was hoping she'd remember me from when I used to swim with Sarah. "I'm sorry," she said, her voice brittle as baled hay. "Spaulding isn't taking any calls." She hung up before I could say more. For the moment, it calmed me, knowing he was at home, that at least he wasn't sitting in the county jail.

Daddy was asleep when I got home. He was sprawled on the sofa in the front room, TV blaring out some ballgame. There were empty beer cans on the floor. The dirty dishes were still on the kitchen table. Wednesday, I thought, I'm out of here on Wednesday.

I put the dishes in the sink and was squirting detergent on them when the phone rang. I picked it right up, hands still wet, sure it was Spy.

"Tallie?" Rula said.

"Hi," I said. Rula hadn't called since school ended in June, and I couldn't imagine why she was calling now. "What's up?"

"Have you heard? About Spy?"

"Yeah," I said. "It was on the radio." I didn't want to talk about it.

"Isn't it awful?" she said.

"Yeah."

"God, it's so creepy. It makes me sick to think about it."

"Me, too."

"My Daddy says it didn't surprise him a bit. He never liked him."

"Your daddy didn't like Spy?"

"Jeez, Tallie. Where're your brains? Mr. Reynolds. He didn't like Mr. Reynolds."

"Oh."

"But I can't stop thinking about poor Sarah. It's soooo creepy."

"Rula," I said. "What the hell are you talking about?"

"You don't know?"

"No."

"I thought you said you knew."

"Well, I don't."

"You don't know about Sarah and her daddy?"

"Shit, Rula," I practically screamed. "I don't have a clue what you're talking about. Stop driving me crazy and just tell me."

According to Rula's daddy, who worked nights mopping floors at the courthouse and county jail, Sheriff Craw'd been talking about Spy and how he'd shot his daddy.

"They *think* he shot his daddy," I said.

"Oh," Rula said, "he did it, no lie. He did it 'cause Sarah killed herself, just like some of the girls at school were always whispering. She drowned herself because her daddy'd been coming to her bed," Rula said.

Rula had that wrong. She had to. "But she was only eleven," I said.

"Exactly," Rula said. "Don't you want to puke just thinking about it?"

I couldn't even answer. My mind shut down. What I wanted to do was go back to when before Rula called, back to when I hadn't heard anything, back to before the picture of Sarah and Mr. Reynolds took hold in my mind. Rula kept on talking. Spy had known about it, she said, and he hated his daddy for what he'd done to Sarah.

I just couldn't talk about it anymore.

"You still there?" Rula asked.

"I'm here."

" 'Cause there's more. Spy told the sheriff that their mama'd known, too."

"Mrs. Reynolds knew about it?"

"According to Spy. But then Mrs. Reynolds told the sheriff it was all a bunch of lies. Every bit of it. She said she didn't know why Spy had killed his daddy or why he was making up all those terrible lies. She said he was clearly disturbed but he was her son and she'd see he got the best counsel money could buy. And that was all my daddy heard," Rula said, finally out of breath.

The black place in my chest hurt so, I thought I might be having a heart attack. "Gotta go," I told Rula. She'd be mad I hung up like that, but I couldn't help it.

I had to sit quiet-like for a while, until the stone sitting in my chest eased a bit. The ballgame was blaring in the living room and beneath the sound, I heard the soft snoring of my daddy. I thought back to when I used to wish Mr. Reynolds was my daddy, and I came as close to crying as I had since my mama got sick. My daddy was weak, no question, but he was a good man. He wasn't rich and he didn't wear fancy suits, but he'd loved my mama as much as it was possible to love someone and that was his strength and his weakness. Mr. Reynolds had a weakness, one I could hardly bear thinking on, but his wasn't born of any strength. His was pure evil, and just then sitting there thinking of my little friend Sarah, I was glad Spy'd shot his daddy. I wished he'd shot his mama, too.

★ Tallie's Book ★

Vinegar water washes out bloodstains.

Don't believe everything you hear.

There are two kinds of weakness: one born of evil and one born of good.

*a*s soon as Daddy left for the mill on Monday, I set out for Martha Lee's. I figured it would take me about an hour to bike over to Lynchburg and of course I had to stop by Martha Lee's on the way. The only hitch in the plan—the huge hitch— would be if Martha Lee was home, preventing me from taking the money. The whole idea that I was turning into a major league thief made me such a wreck, I practically got in an accident turning onto the main road. As I passed the Tyree place, the sisters were on the porch. They lifted their hands to wave as I went by and I wondered if later they'd tell anyone they remembered seeing me ride by. I figured Martha Lee'd call Sheriff Craw when she discovered the missing cash and he'd go snooping around. I was hoping he'd think some tramp broke in. Or that it was someone needing money for drugs, like the reporters thought when Mr. Reynolds got shot. The idea of an official investigation got me so riled, I almost got in another accident turning onto High Tower Road. By the time I got to Martha Lee's and saw the pickup was gone, I honestly didn't know whether I was relieved or not.

I found the key and let myself in. She'd fried up some bacon for breakfast, and the greasy smell hung thick in the air, making me queasy. One thing about Martha Lee, she loved pork. All kinds. Bacon. Ham steak. Pork barbecued or roasted, even sliced cold, which I personally couldn't stand 'cause of the way the fat coated your mouth. One time when she and Mama were playing gin rummy she said, "I'm so hungry I could crawl up a pig's ass and eat a pork sandwich," which made Goody slap down her magazine and stamp out of the room. Martha Lee was always saying things like that in front of Goody just to get her goat. The time she said she was sweating like a whore in church, Goody near turned purple.

The gray envelope from the bank was on the kitchen shelf, right where I'd last seen it. Taking it was harder than I'd imagined. It was one thing to steal fifteen dollars and another to take a thousand. I briefly reconsidered, thinking maybe I'd call Uncle Grayson. Hadn't Mama said I could always count on him? I just wasn't sure I could count on him for that much money without him insisting on an explanation. Plus, even if he gave to it me, I'd have to wait at least a week for the money to arrive from Atlanta. My choices seemed clear. I could take the money from Martha Lee and pick up my ticket for L.A. or I could leave it where it was and head back home, probably staying in Eden for the rest of my natural life. Finally I convinced myself it was just a loan I was taking and I had full intentions of paying it back.

That wad of money heated up my pocket all the way to Lynchburg. Still, none of it seemed real until the lady at the counter handed me the ticket. That was when it hit that I was actually going to L.A. The lady explained that the flight had two connections—one in D.C. and one in Denver—and was scheduled to depart at nine-forty, Wednesday morning. Then she told me I should plan on arriving an hour before my flight and that I'd need some identification—driver's license or birth certificate or something—to show at the gate before they'd let me on the plane.

"No problem," I said, as natural as you please, like I flew to L.A. every day of the week.

On my way back to Eden I stopped at the dollar store and bought myself a pocketbook. I still had six hundred and forty-three dollars of Martha Lee's money and I didn't want to risk losing it. I figured I'd be needing every penny when I arrived in Hollywood.

The rest of the day hung heavy, and I was riding by the Eden library when I was struck by an idea straight out of the blue. I parked the Raleigh, marched straight in, and asked old Mrs. Boles if they had the yearbooks from Eden High.

"Yearbooks?" she said, squinting at me through glasses thick as half-inch plywood. She was so old, I swear she must have been librarian back when Easter Davis was a child. "That'd be the Resources Room," she said. "You'll find it over there, directly beyond the nonfiction department." Then she pointed me off to this little section that was divided by one of those movable partitions, and it turned out that the "Resources Room" was really comprised of three long shelves. There were a bunch of telephone directories, one dictionary and a world atlas, a set of encyclopedias that was missing the second and seventh volumes, and *The Reader's Guide to Periodical Literature*. Way off to the far end I caught sight of a bunch of yearbooks that I recognized by the blue and gold writing on the spine. To my immense disappointment, there were only the ones from the past five years. I headed back to the front desk.

"Did you find them, honey?" Mrs. Boles said.

"I found a few," I told her. "What I was really looking for was the old ones."

"Old ones?"

"That's right," I said.

"Oh, honey," she said. "I don't know what to tell you. We only have them from the last five years."

Well, I could see *that*. "Where would I find the old ones?"

"Well, we don't keep them here," she said. "I'm afraid I can't help you. You might want to try over at county historic museum."

"The historic museum?" I said.

"That's right." She squinted up at the big clock behind the desk. "You hurry over there right now and you might get there before Mr. Beidler closes up for the day."

When I arrived, Mr. Beidler was sitting at a card table. Before he'd answer a single question, he made me put a dollar in the donations jug and sign the official visitors book. According to the book, I was the first visitor he'd had in more than a week. I was writing out Tallie Brock when it hit me that that would probably be the last time I'd be signing my old name. Once I hit Hollywood I'd be Taylor Skye. The idea made me smile.

"Yearbooks?" Mr. Beidler said when I repeated my request. "What year would you be looking for, little lady?"

"Nineteen sixty-five," I said.

"Well, I think I can help you with that." It took him about two hours to make it up the stairs and to the section where they stored the yearbooks. Then it took him about another two hours to locate the correct year. Finally he slid it out and set it on the table. "Now, when you're done with it, you leave it right here," he said, tapping the table. "Right here. I'll put it back."

"All right," I said.

"Be sure about that," he said. "We don't want things going back on the wrong shelf."

Honestly, sometimes old people just killed me. When I'd promised to follow his exact directions, practically swearing an oath not to return the book to the shelf, he went back down the stairs, which only took him about an hour going down. Finally I opened the book. I was operating on instinct, and Mama always said if you trusted your instincts, they wouldn't let you down.

I flipped open to the A's and found Mama's picture straight away, the same one the *Times* had printed with her obituary. Beneath the photo there was a list of everything Mama'd done, including her four years in the Drama Club and being Queen of the Prom and Homecoming, too. It hurt my throat just to look at it, that burning kind of hurt, like when you're coming down with a real bad cold. After a while, I flipped back to the first page and started through the whole book, taking my time and checking every picture. I found him in the W's. His full name was Gordon Allen Wheeler. The only Wheeler I knew was that stuck-up Ashley, and I wondered if she was related to him. For sure, I'd never heard of him, and sure as shooting I'd never seen him before, except for that photo with Mama. According to the yearbook, he'd been class treasurer, played baseball and football, and had been captain of the debating team. I liked that about him. Brains and brawn. A good match for Mama. I knew I could probably go to jail for what I was about to do, but that didn't stop me. I just ripped the page right out, folded it up, and stuck it in my new pocketbook. I left the book on the table and went down to find batty old Mr. Beidler. He was back at the card table.

"You all done up there?" he asked.

"Yes, sir," I said.

"Did you leave the book out on the table like I told you?"

I said I had—neglecting to mention that I'd ripped out a page—and then I asked him if he'd ever heard of a boy named Gordon Wheeler. Gordon Allen Wheeler.

Mr. Beidler repeated the name twice, staring up at the ceiling like he expected to find the answer written there. "Name sounds familiar," he said after a few minutes of checking the acoustic tiles.

"Class of sixty-five," I said.

He shuffled over to this filing cabinet, pawing through until he located the right folder. "Yup," he said after he'd looked over a couple of pages. "Here he is right here. Gordon Allen Wheeler."

My fingers pure itched to grab the folder right out of his hands. With a name to go on, I was figuring it would be easy to track him down, even if he had left Eden. And that was when Mr. Beidler told me where to find him, for all the good it would do me. The Baptist Cemetery, he said. Then he told me that Gordon Wheeler had been killed over in Vietnam. Six months after he graduated from Eden. Thinking about it, remembering the picture of Mama sitting with him in the fire-red car, I had to wonder what would have happened if Gordon Wheeler hadn't died. Would my mama have ended up with my daddy? It was weird to think how close I'd come to not even being born.

Tuesday I went to work, same as usual. As soon as I walked through the door, I got busy with the regular chores—folding towels and such—and tried to avoid Raylene. I was sure she'd be able to read my plans plain on my face. I needn't have worried. No one was paying the least bit of attention to me. Spy's murder confession was the main topic of conversation, and the women were mostly talking about Mrs. Reynolds. Clear as springwater she wasn't winning any popularity contests.

"Never did like her," Hattie Jones said, going through a roll of Tums like they were peanuts. "Always 'yes ma'am-ing' me to death and acting like butter wouldn't melt in her mouth."

"Always did act better than anyone else," Easter Davis said. "That woman believed her farts smelled sweet."

"Do you think she knew what was going on between him and the girl?" Raylene said.

I knew she was talking about what Spy had said about his daddy and Sarah.

"I just can't imagine how a woman could know what was going on right in her own house, right in front of her nose, and pretend she didn't," Hattie said.

"I'd a thrown his ass right out the front door," Easter Davis said. "I don't care how much money he had."

It made me sad to think about what Spy had said about why he'd killed his daddy. I pictured Sarah smiling at everyone as she stood in front of the school auditorium in her pretty dress with the wide lavender sash, the same one they'd buried her in. I remembered her at the spelling bee, acting so confident, like she had nothing more important on her mind than where to place the vowels, sailing right through every word Miss Banks gave her: Odyssey. Eucalyptus. Resplendence. Decoupage, a word I couldn't spell if I had the dictionary to help me. I remembered the times we sat together on the bus rides to swim meets. All those times she might have said something and didn't. Then I wondered if I'd been her, if my daddy had been doing what hers had, if I would have told anyone either. I pictured Mr. Reynolds dressing up in his suit and shaking hands with the teachers at the school picnic, and cutting the ribbon to the new chamber building, not giving the least sign that at night he was going to his own daughter's bed. Deception ran deep in that family. Then I thought about Spy setting to go off to UVA and becoming a lawyer, and kissing me like he meant it, all the time planning on killing his daddy. My mama told me once that a person could never tell what was going on in another person's house or in his mind. Experience was proving this true as a plumb line.

Just about then, I caught sight of myself in the mirror, and I looked the same as usual. If Raylene or Lenora looked over at that moment, they'd see me sweeping up and preparing to water the ivy, and nothing about me would indicate in the least that I'd stolen more than a thousand dollars from my mama's best friend and that right at that moment hidden in my closet was a packed suitcase and a new black bag holding a ticket to L.A.

It was spooky to think about. It made me wonder if everyone had a secret self. A secret story. But if it was possible to hide what you'd done and what you were thinking, how was it possible to ever trust anyone? Thinking about all this made me get real quiet, and Raylene asked if I was feeling all right.

"Just thinking," I said.

She said I was looking a little peaked.

"Really," I said. "I'm okay."

"You thinking about that boy?" she asked. "You knew him, didn't you?"

"Do you think he'll go to prison?" I asked.

"No need to worry about that," Raylene said. "Rich folks don't go to jail."

I took comfort in her words, but she would prove to be

wrong. Sometimes rich people did land themselves in jail, and all the high-priced lawyers in the world couldn't prevent it.

Easter Davis was under the dryer, and Lenora was putting the last of the wave solution on Hattie. Raylene went and poured herself a cup of coffee, then checked the schedule. I thought she'd forgotten about me, but the next thing she told me to go and sit at one of the sinks. She said she had a half hour before the next set. She said that wasn't enough time for her to do a foil, but she could give me a shampoo.

"You sure?" I said. I loved having a shampoo. Some people can't stand being touched, but not me. I lay back and let her get to work. She'd done the first rinse and was just working up the suds again when the phone rang. Lenora got to it first.

"It's for you," she yelled to Raylene. "It's Jackson."

Jackson was Raylene's husband. Her *first* husband, she always told people, when she talked about him. Like she was auditioning for another one, though everyone in Eden knew Raylene would never leave Jackson. Easter Davis always laughed when she heard Raylene say that, and she'd tell her she'd better get busy if she wanted to beat her record. Easter liked to say she'd had five husbands, three of them her own. Raylene said that was just talk.

When Raylene went to answer the phone, Lenora took her place at the sink. "I'll finish up with Tallie," she said, and smiled like she'd been waiting all year for the opportunity to get her hands on me.

The last thing on earth I wanted was to have Lenora anywhere near me, but short of jumping off the chair and running out with a head full of soap, there was no way to avoid it. No telling what she'd see. I had a lot to hide. The money I stole

from Martha Lee. My plans for L.A. The night I'd taken Spy into
my bed. Take your pick. I was praying I'd get off without her
seeing anything. She started scrubbing away, working up a
head of suds. Her fingers were stronger than you'd expect,
given her arthritis and all. I said a little prayer that she wouldn't
see anything, and crossed my fingers under the shampoo cape.
Not that it did one bit of good.

"Well, I'll be goddammed," Lenora said. "Will you look at
that?" Heat rose up from my chest, flooding my cheeks.

"Clear as can be," she said. Everyone in the whole place
looked over. Whatever the hell she was seeing, I didn't want to
know and I most certainly didn't want every busybody in town
to hear.

"Is it a boyfriend?" Easter Davis said, practically cackling.
"Has Tallie got herself a boyfriend?"

Lenora was chuckling to herself. Honestly, I wanted to
throttle her.

Hattie got up and came over to the sink, dripping wave solution the whole way.

"See," Lenora said. She pointed into the sink with a crooked
finger.

Hattie squinted into the sink. "What?"

"Right there. See?"

"Don't see nothing but a bunch of soap," Hattie said.

"There," Lenora said again. "And there. And there. Couldn't
be any clearer if you took a picture."

Raylene was off the phone and she came over, too. "What
is it?"

"A baby," Lenora said.

"A baby?" I nearly shouted.

"Not just one," Lenora said. "Lots of them. Oh, yes, I see lots of babies ahead for you."

Hattie was oohing, like isn't that the cutest thing, and Raylene was saying, yes she thought that she could see them, too, and that got old Easter Davis out from under the dryer to come take a look.

"Yes, sir," Lenora said. "Looks like there's babies in your future."

I sat there frozen, thinking it couldn't be true and trying to remember what I'd heard the girls say in the locker room about whether or not you could get pregnant the first time. All the while I heard Goody's voice saying I was stupid, stupid, stupid, no better than white trash.

★ Tallie's Book ★

If you trust your instincts, they'll never let you down.

You can never tell what's going on in another person's mind.

People hide their secret selves.

t w e n t y

*W*hile Raylene was blow-drying my hair, I tried to calm down. I kept telling myself there was no sense freaking over g.d. soap bubbles and that it was not possible that Lenora could actually be seeing a person's destiny in a sink full of suds. Soap was only soap, I told myself. Besides, my future was already decided, and I had the packed bag and ticket to prove it. Still, it wasn't as easy as you might think to forget the absolute certainty in Lenora's voice. Babies, she'd said. Lots of babies.

For about the eighty millionth time, I was missing my mama and wishing she was there. She'd know what to do. She'd know for sure if it was possible for a person to get pregnant even if she'd only done it once. Course if my mama were still living, I'd never have gone to bed with Spy in the first place. If Mama were alive we would be heading out west together, preparing to be movie stars, and I wouldn't be left alone trying to figure everything out by myself.

Say it *was* possible to get pregnant that easy. How long before a person'd be getting some sign? Wouldn't a person feel *something* if there was a baby growing in her belly? I'd seen kits you could buy at the drugstore, but I hadn't the least idea how far along you had to be for them to work. More than a few days, for sure. Besides, before I'd even walked out the door, Mrs. Albert at the drugstore would be on the phone spreading the word all over Eden and the next thing Miss Gibbons would probably have it written up in the *Times*.

Raylene was combing my hair under her round brush, setting the curl with the dryer, and our eyes locked in the mirror. She smiled, real sweet, probably thinking my future with babies was waiting a ways down the road. For a minute, I thought about seeking her advice—later, in private—that's how desperate I was, but I wasn't sure I could count on her to keep quiet about something that important. She'd probably feel obligated to tell my daddy. Fact was, I didn't think there was anyone I could trust. Not even Rula. I knew Rula. Even if she promised on a blood oath, she wouldn't be able to keep my secret. Like the time she'd told everyone that Rita Jean Purvis had gone all the way with Dusty Newman, even though she'd sworn on her dead mama's grave not to. All I'd need was to be having Elizabeth Talmadge and the rest of the Sparkettes hearing about Spy and me.

Calling Spy was out of the question, even if he wasn't under house arrest or something for killing his daddy. It didn't seem to me a girl could be with a boy twice—neither time on a real date—and then call him up and tell him she might be carrying his child. I knew Martha Lee would have information about this kind of thing, being a nurse and all, but I couldn't ask her. Not after I'd stolen her money. For a fact, I didn't think I'd ever be able to look her in the face for the rest of my natural life. I'd got myself in a pickle and it didn't look like there was any way out. Just then I wished I could be more like Scarlett O'Hara and put the entire mess off to another day, but if I knew one thing for sure it was that trouble didn't evaporate like smoke just because you decided not to let it occupy your mind.

Raylene held up the hand mirror so I could look at the back, but not even the soft way she styled my hair could cheer me up. If Lenora really had seen my future, my life was pretty much over. I'd probably be packed up and sent to live with Goody, who'd spend every waking moment reminding me of what trash I'd become. She'd say I only got what I deserved for sinning with Spy. If she knew about the money I'd stolen from Martha Lee, she'd probably say I was paying for that, too. Goody wouldn't give one hot damn that every dream I ever had would be over, ended before I even turned seventeen. The burden of not being able to tell one living soul weighed on me all afternoon, festering inside, but when we closed up at five I said good-bye to Raylene same as normal, just like I'd be seeing her in the morning, not giving her one clue that in the morning I'd be sitting on a plane heading for L.A.

When I got home, I poured myself some tea, then settled on the glider and tried to be practical. Mama always said losing your head only caused bad problems to get worse, and the thing you had to do was stay calm and reason things out. Just recalling her advice helped quiet my heart. I closed my eyes and tried to figure out when I'd had my last moon. I wasn't always regular and generally didn't pay much attention. Then I must have fallen asleep, 'cause that's when my mama came to me.

Right after she passed, I used to pray that Mama'd give me some sign that she was still with me, like Preacher Tillett at

Elijah Baptist said. I'd sit by the creek and listen, trying to hear her in the liquid song of birds. Or I'd wake in the night and watch the fireflies, studying their fitful light as if it held a code she'd sent. Oh, I looked and listened everywhere for Mama, but in four years I hadn't had as much as a whisper. Now here she was appearing plain as day. If I'd been capable of tears, I would have wept from the joy of it.

"Hi, baby," she said.

I'd heard that when people were dreaming, they couldn't smell or taste things or see beyond black and white, but it wasn't true. I could smell her perfume—My Sin—coming through clear as my daddy's coffee perking in the morning, or the wave solution at the Kurl. And she appeared in full and living color, dressed in the green dress we'd buried her in, with three pink roses Mr. Wesler put in her hair. For the first time since she passed, Mama was truly with me. "Hi, baby," she said again. Not aloud, because we didn't exactly converse. It was more like we had ESP or something, like the silent communication of butterflies, like there wasn't any need for speech. Right off, she knew about everything—even about me being with Spy and what Lenora had said about seeing babies all around me. I thought for sure that would make her real mad, but it didn't. You might not believe this, but she wasn't even disappointed I'd gone to bed with Spy. Or that I'd taken all that money from Martha Lee. All the time I'd spent worrying about her looking down watching me behaving like a bad girl and now it seemed like there was nothing on God's green earth I could have done to gain her displeasure or disappointment. She had the sweetest smile, like she had a secret, the good kind, and there wasn't one thing worth the effort of worrying about. She was so full of love and forgiveness, I could feel it around me, enfolding me like the softest fabric you could imagine, softer even than her red cashmere sweater. With all she seemed capable of, I expected she would have the power to tell me if I was truly carrying Spy's child, so I asked her that, but it turned out she couldn't tell about things like that. When I asked her what I should do, she told me straight out, surprising me with her advice. Then Old Straw must have barked or something, because I woke up.

Imagine every beautiful and precious thing you've ever known. Imagine the wet miracle of a newborn calf, or late spring in the Blue Ridge; imagine the rainbow lines of sunlight shining through a prism, or the evening sky streaked with rose in that precise moment before the sun disappears behind the mountain. Imagine the smell of a lilac bush, or a spice cake your mama's just taken from the oven. Imagine the touch of a loving man. Now imagine holding all this in the palm of your hand. Then imagine having it disappear, cut off, your hand gone with it. That was how it hurt to wake and have Mama gone. The hard dark place in my chest burned so I might as well have been swallowing knives as dreaming.

When I was capable of moving, I got up and did exactly what Mama'd directed me in the vision. I wasn't even afraid. It was like there was a tiny bit of her left behind. I left a note on the table for my daddy and headed straight out for Allie Rucker's. In the dream, Mama'd told me Allie would know if I was carrying and—if that's what I wanted—she'd help me get rid of it. Well, that was definitely what I wanted. There was no way I could be having a baby. Mama'd understood that. She'd known a baby meant no movies. No Hollywood. No dreams coming true. I'd be just another Eden girl who got knocked up. End of story.

This time I didn't even hesitate when I got to Allie's. With Mama giving me courage, I marched straight through the overgrown yard, up the steps, and rapped on the door, startling a jay with the sound. I waited a minute, then knocked again. It hadn't occurred to me that Allie wouldn't be home. Maybe she wasn't even alive. Maybe she was lying inside, dead as roadkill, and I'd be the one to find her decaying body. I was fretting on what I was going to do if she wasn't around to help me and wondering how I'd explain to people how I happened to find Allie's body if she was dead, when she appeared from the stand of trees that led to deep woods, where it was rumored she kept her copper still. I hadn't seen her since before Mama'd passed, but she hadn't changed one bit in four years. She wasn't in the least surprised to see me, just crossed to the house without a word. A couple of dusty hens pecked at her feet, which were about the ugliest feet I'd ever seen. They were worn and misshapen with bunions so big, they looked like extra toes.

"I'm Tallie Brock," I said.

"I know who you be." She narrowed her eyes and spat, the brown stream of tobacco juice barely missing the hens and her own ugly toes.

I was trying to figure out how to tell her why I was there, but as if she had the same ESP as Mama, as if girls showed up on her porch regular with troubles like mine, she got right to it, asking straight out when I'd had my last moon. That's what she called it. My moon. Same as Mama always did.

Next thing she was heading into the cabin and motioning me to follow. It held the same sour, mildew smell I remembered from before. Inside, a live crow—I swear—was sitting on a windowsill. It ruffled its wing feathers and turned a black eye on me. One thing always made me nervous was a bird loose in a house, but I consoled myself with the thought that at least it wasn't a bat. I couldn't have stood that. Except for the crow, not one thing had changed since the last time I was there. Without further conversation, Allie went to the cupboard and pulled out some jars, taking a pinch of this and some of that.

"This here's what you be needing," she said, chuckling like she'd thought of something funny. "Same as I gave your mama."

I remembered the vile smell of the herbs she'd made for mama. I didn't think I was capable of swallowing something that awful without puking it up. "The Queen of Cures," I said. "That's what you gave my mama when she was sick." I was wondering if she knew I'd buried the Cure out in our backyard or that a butterfly bush had grown up in that spot.

She laughed, a big laugh, not a weak old lady one. "T'other time," she said. "The one I made your mama t'other time."

"Mama came here?" I said.

"Girl, half the womenfolk in Eden been coming through my door. You and your mama be no different."

"When?"

"Long time. She be about your age. Same as you. Messing with some fool man who be carrying his brain 'tween his legs."

Mama? Mama came to Allie looking for help, same as me? I couldn't believe it. But then lately it seemed I was learning about whole new parts of my mama's personal history, things that could fill another book and that might just be the beginning of uncovering all the mystery in my mama's past. I recalled the picture I'd found of Mama in the red convertible with the boy named Gordie, a boy who was strong and smart, according to his yearbook, but apparently not smart enough to keep Mama from getting pregnant. The date Mama'd written on the back of the pictures was 1965. I did some quick figuring. Mama'd been fifteen. For sure, Goody'd have about killed her if she was pregnant. No wonder Mama'd turned to Allie for help. Still, it made me sad to think of Mama getting rid of a baby, a baby who'd have been a brother or a sister for me. I used to dream about having a sister. I never told Mama, but I always wanted more family. With Uncle Grayson the way he was, I didn't even have a cousin.

Allie handed me the bag and told me how to mix it up, same as before. She warned me not to wait too long before I drank it and said not to worry if it made me sick. She said there'd be some cramping, but no worse than with my moon.

Well, surprise, surprise, surprise. When I got home, who was sitting on the glider but Spy. You might think with him being a murderer, I'd be a little nervous or something, but as peculiar as it sounds, I hopped off the Raleigh and went right up to where he was sitting. He studied me like he didn't know what to say, and I surprised us both by walking straight over and giving him a hug, like it was the only natural thing to do.

"Oh, God, Tallie," he said, breathing the words into my hair.

I didn't say a word, just stood there drinking in the scent of him, a smell I already knew by heart. We held on a little while longer, then we both sat down.

"I don't have a lot of time," he said.

"I was afraid you might be in jail," I said. I said it flat-out, and it was like we could say anything to each other, like there was no time for anything but truth.

"They released me in the Dreck Girl's care," he said.

I took his hand and ran my finger over his palm, tracing the web of lines they say hold the directions and true facts of a person's life. I didn't know what I was looking for, but nothing I saw in Spy's hand indicated he was a boy equal to killing his daddy.

He curled his fingers over mine. "I need to talk to you," he said. "To explain."

I pictured Mama then, how she'd come to me in the vision and the way she'd understood every bad thing I'd ever done, understood with no need for explanation, and how she'd loved me in spite of my sins. "No need," I said.

"I have to, Tallie," he said. He lifted a hand to my chin and made me look directly at him. "I don't give a goddamn what anyone else thinks, but I want you to know."

Then Spy told me everything. He told me how he'd gone to his daddy's office, only meaning to scare him with the gun. "I wanted him to confess," he said. "I wanted him to admit what he'd done to Sarah. To own up to at least one person that he was responsible for her dying. I swear I didn't mean to hurt him." But Spy said his daddy hadn't confessed. He'd called Spy a stupid son of a bitch and said he'd show him what happened to people who threatened him. Then Mr. Reynolds had punched Spy in the face and tried to take the gun. That's when it went off. He said he'd thought a lot since Sarah died about making his daddy confess, but the thing that caused him to finally confront him was that he saw his daddy hugging his youngest cousin. He said he had let Sarah down, but at least he could protect one girl.

"I swear," Spy said again. "I never meant to kill him."

"I believe you," I said. "It wasn't your fault."

"I should have been able to stop it," he said.

I told Spy there were some things that, once set in motion, can't be stopped or derailed no matter what our will or intention. I think we could have sat there talking for the rest of the evening and all through till morning, but he had to go home. Before he left he told me he was sorry about a lot of things but not about the night we'd spent together and he hoped I wasn't sorry either.

Then Spy Reynolds said the sweetest thing a girl could ever hope to hear. He told me he thought that I was beautiful, beautiful in a real, true way, the kind of beauty that was a lot more than surface. He said he knew I'd still be beautiful even when I was an old lady, as old as Easter Davis. He said he'd thought that was so for a long, long time, even years back when I was just a kid on the swim team with Sarah. Then Spy said I was the kind of girl a person could trust to hold his secrets and hold his heart and not betray either one, and that that was a rare and precious thing. He said he was sorry the way things had turned out, him shooting his daddy and all, sorry it had happened before we'd had a chance. I memorized every single word he said.

I supposed that was the time to tell him about the baby. I almost did. It seemed like there should be no secrets between us. Then I figured he already had enough worrying his mind and there was no sense adding to the list a baby that neither of us was ever going to see. That was one sorrow I'd be bearing by myself.

He kissed me and asked me if he could call me and I said yes, no more able to tell him I was leaving in the morning than I'd been able to tell Raylene. I had this feeling that the more people I let know I was leaving, the harder it would be to go. It hurt to tell this lie, hurt to imagine what he'd think when he learned I'd gone, but I locked the hurt up with all the others and waved good-bye, whispering God bless. And I meant it, too, me who didn't even believe in God, saying it like just for a minute I'd been transformed into Reverend Tillett or one of the ladies at Elijah Baptist.

You might think as soon as Spy left I'd get right to mixing up Allie's cure, drinking it down and being done with it, but I didn't. I stuck the bag in Mama's suitcase, along with the rest of what I'd need. I figured I'd wait until I arrived in L.A. Another day or two wouldn't matter. Besides, if I got sick, like Allie said, it was best I was alone without anyone around to ask questions.

Just before I fell asleep, I pressed my hands against my face and inhaled the smell of Spy.

★ Tallie's Book ★

Losing your head causes bad problems to get worse.

It is a mighty and terrible possibility that a person can do great harm without the least intention.

twenty-one

*i*t started to rain in the night and by morning it was coming
down like it'd been saving up all summer for just this occasion. The radio was tuned to the weather station, and the man
was going on about flash floods and washed-out roads. I lay
there waiting for my daddy to head off to the mill and trying to
figure out how I'd get to Lynchburg. Riding the Raleigh was
clear out of the question. I stared up at the ceiling and looked
at the little stars Mama'd stuck there so long ago, wondering if
I'd ever see them again. I'd been planning this for years, but the
idea of leaving Eden made me the tiniest bit sad. I wondered if
Mama'd experienced the same confusion of feelings that summer she left us.

At the last minute, I heard my daddy revving up his truck. I
jumped out of bed and tore to the kitchen door, but was too
late to catch more than the sight of the rusted-out tailgate as it
disappeared around the curve. I waved anyway. I fried up a
couple of eggs, checking the sky about every two minutes, but
like the weatherman said, the storm showed no sign of letting

up. After breakfast I made up my bed and washed the dishes, then I retrieved Mama's suitcase from the closet and checked the contents one last time. Then, without planning on it, I took out the bag Allie Rucker had given me. I pulled on one of my daddy's rain slickers and took that bag and went out to the yard by the miracle butterfly bush. I dumped the stuff out—stuff that would get rid of any baby I might be carrying. Even now I can't say why I did that. It wasn't 'cause I thought I'd be sinning if I took it. Or because I suddenly was attached to the idea of having Spy's baby. A baby would complicate my life and mess up my plans and I surely didn't want one. Preacher Tillett would say I dumped it out because I was trusting that whatever God sent me I would take, no matter how it turned my future on its back. He'd say I was operating on faith, and maybe I was, although I didn't think Mama was wrong when she'd gotten rid of the baby she was carrying. Before I returned to the house, I took a good look at the seeds and bark and stuff and wondered what, if anything, would be growing out of it.

I was soaked through by the time I finished up and was still fretting about how to get to Lynchburg. I considered hiring Mr. Tinsley, but that meant spending some of the money I was saving for L.A. Finally I thought of Wiley. I gave him a call and asked for a ride to Lynchburg and he said yes, no questions asked. Five minutes later he pulled into the yard and I was on my way. Anyone else would have to be knowing exactly what I was up to, but Wiley just plunked the suitcase on the seat between us and shifted gears. Tired of keeping it to myself, I nearly blurted out my plans, but then I told him I was going off to Florida to visit Goody, same story I'd left in the note for my daddy. My plan was to have Wiley drop me outside the airport, but he insisted on coming in. I practically had to be rude to get rid of him. He surprised me by grabbing a kiss at the last minute, and I astonished myself by kissing him back. He was my oldest friend and even if he had been acting weird all summer, I was going to miss him. Leaving a place was more complicated than I'd realized.

I sailed through the gate, prepared with my birth certificate and acting like I'd done this a few hundred times. The rain continued and I was wondering if they'd call off the flight, but pretty soon they told us to get on board and then we took off. I didn't have a window seat and had to lean way over in order to see Lynchburg disappear. Except for the part where the plane took off and you rose up to greet the sky, boring right through the clouds, I thought flying was mostly overrated. I was crammed in the middle seat between a lady with the worst head of hair you could imagine and a man with a bad cold. I about broke my neck twisting away so as not to get his germs. About halfway to our first connection in D.C., he complained about his ears hurting and I thought it served him right for flying with a cold, spraying bacteria everywhere.

At Washington, we had to wait for a while before we got on another plane, and I spent the time getting a Coke and using the ladies' room, checking my panties to see if my moon had come yet. When there was no sign of it, I felt I must have been crazy to dump out Allie's baby cure. The thing about operating out of faith was that faith didn't always stay steady. When we got back on the plane, I was glad to see I had a window seat. After about two hours, they gave us each this little tray of food, all divided up with salad and chicken with some kind of sauce that even Goody would say had too much salt. There was some foil-wrapped cheese, a little cellophane packet of crackers, and another containing three cookies. The woman sitting next to me offered me hers, but I declined, mindful of the extra weight a camera added to a person's frame. Then, believe it or not, I fell asleep. I woke up hours later, drool running down my chin.

From then on, for the rest of the trip, I was torn between imagining my future in Hollywood and thinking of everything I was leaving behind. I figured by then my daddy must have discovered the note I'd left telling him I'd gone to visit Goody. I wondered if he'd believe it or would think I'd run away, and if he'd be relieved to be rid of me or if he'd miss me a little. And I wondered when Martha Lee and Raylene would hear about it and what they'd think. I figured Martha Lee must have discovered the missing money and known I'd taken it. I'd probably have to spend the rest of my life begging her forgiveness. Then I thought about Spy and that warm, wanting feeling spread through my belly. Maybe it was a train-wreck romance, but it sure was powerful. I remembered what he said about not meaning to shoot his daddy and wondered what would happen to him. I wanted to believe what Raylene'd said about rich people not going to jail, but I didn't think they let a person completely off the hook if he'd shot his daddy, even if it was an accident.

The oddest thing was, believe it or not, I wasn't one bit nervous and that was because Mama was with me. I could almost hear her voice, getting me prepared, telling me everything about Hollywood, stuff she'd told me a million times, like how the movie stars live in big mansions, and people stand on street corners selling actual maps so you can drive by and look at them, and about how Lana Turner had been discovered sitting at a drugstore soda fountain, and how Rita Hayworth had married a real prince, and Grace Kelly, too, which just went to show you that Hollywood was a place where dreams could come true beyond a person's liveliest imaginings.

There were two things I planned on doing as soon as I got there, even before I got a job. One was for Mama and one was for me. First thing, for Mama I was going to find Natalie's grave. When I found it, I was going to leave some flowers there, gardenias if I could find them, no matter what the cost. I knew that's what Mama would have done if she'd been able to go there like she'd wanted. Before she ran out of time. Then, for myself, I was going to track down the Sasha woman. I was determined to discover who she was and exactly why my mama'd had her name written on a paper.

For just a moment, when I got off the plane and was waiting to retrieve Mama's gray suitcase, I came near to panicking. People were shoving and pushing and speaking in about three hundred languages and it was so crowded, you couldn't imagine. It was enough to turn a person dizzy. Off to one side there were about two dozen men holding up signs with people's names written on them, and if I could have wished for one thing at that moment, it would have been that there was someone there holding up a sign saying *Tallie Brock,* or at least someone telling me where I could find a bus that would take me straight to Hollywood. I located the baggage claim and waited for Mama's gray suitcase to show up. I was just beginning to think maybe it had gotten lost somewhere along the way when it came riding by on the conveyor belt. I was reaching for it when this man wearing a white suit and baseball cap grabbed it up. I thought he was trying to steal it, but it turned out he was only trying to help. I thanked him, polite as can be, and he inquired whether I had someone meeting me or if I needed a ride. "My car is right outside and I'd be happy to give you a lift," the smiling man said. I was thinking that people in L.A. were just as nice as people in Eden and was just about to accept his offer when this bossy girl butted in and told him to get lost. Before I had a chance to tell her to mind her own beeswax, the man disappeared, melted right into the crowd like he'd never been there at all.

The bossy girl told me the man was as nice as he looked and was always trying to pick up girls who'd just arrived. She said I had *virgin* written all over me. I told her I didn't care what she *thought* she saw written on me but one thing for sure was that I wasn't any virgin. If I'd said something like that to Elizabeth Talmadge or anyone back at Eden they'd have fainted for sure, but not this girl. She laughed and said, "Not that kind." She said I was an L.A. virgin. "Don't tell me," she said. "You're here to be an actress." I said I was, and next thing we were talking like old friends. She said everybody called her Jazz, but her name was Jasmine Jade, which I thought was perfect since it matched her eyes, which were an astonishing shade of green. (Later I learned she had colored contact lenses, and that her real name was Cynthia.) She said she was a professional dancer, and was presently employed at Jumbo's Clown Room, but only temporarily. I told her my name was Taylor Skye. She asked if I had a place to stay, and the next thing I knew we were sitting in this VW Bug painted hot pink and heading for Hollywood. She was staying in a youth hostel. For the time being, she said. Until she got her big break. It was cheap and located right in the middle of the action, she said, and that suited me fine. I didn't tell her that if she was looking for a big break she should think about wearing something besides combat boots and a baggy house-dress that looked like it belonged to Etta Bird.

She drove the little Bug like a maniac, zipping in and out of traffic. Talking a blue streak the whole time. She said she'd been at the airport—LAX, she called it—to pick up a friend flying in from Denver, but the girl never showed up and she must have been there to meet me. I agreed. I knew Mama was directing things, and all I had to do was relax and go along. We passed a giant, round building that looked like a pile of long-playing records stacked one on top of the other. Jazz said it was the Capitol Records Building. For sure Elizabeth Talmadge had never seen anything like that. Then she pointed out the Grif-fith Observatory and asked if I recognized it. She was surprised I knew it was where they'd filmed the final fight scene in *Rebel Without a Cause*. I didn't tell her I knew everything about Natalie Wood, since that was private between Mama and me, and even if I wanted to I couldn't have gotten a word in sideways. Next she pointed out the famous Hollywood sign, the one the girl jumped off. She said the letters were fifty feet tall. It looked ex-actly like it did on Mama's postcard. Then I saw a boy sitting under an umbrella right by the curb holding an orange sign that said *Maps to 300 Movie Stars' Homes*. There were palm trees, and the sky was brown in the distance—smog, according to Jazz—and I might as well have landed on Mars. The hills were brown, too, and Jazz said they were always brown in the sum-mer because they don't get enough water. It made me wish I could show her the Blue Ridge, all green, like mountains should be.

The hostel was located right on Hollywood Boulevard. It was quiet when we got there—everyone was working or asleep, but Jazz said I would meet them later. She said there was a party that night up in the hills. She said "industry" people would be there, and why didn't I come along. Well, I almost fainted right on the spot. I hadn't been in Hollywood one day and I was already going to a party. She said parties were important. "All you have to do is meet the right person and your career is set," she said.

First thing, she said, was that I had to get myself some clothes. She said I needed to fit in. People look at you and you're either Us or Them, and the way I was dressed, I might as well be carrying a neon sign saying *Them.* This from a girl with no more fashion sense than Rula Wade. I thought if I was going to be taking advice from anyone about style, it wouldn't be from someone wearing combat boots and a dress with ugly squiggles all over it.

She said I should take myself over to Aardvark's Used Clothes, but if I was too tired to get there she'd lend me something for that night. The next thing I knew she had me dressed in leopard-print tights and an oversized top and was ratting up my hair. I didn't know if I looked like Us, but for sure I didn't look like me.

She said she was going to take a nap and we'd leave for the party around eight. Wesley'd pick us up, she said. He played lead guitar in a band called Electric Lash and knew the people having the party. Then she warned me not to go walking around by myself. She said it wasn't always safe, especially after dark. She said things had been crazy since the Rodney King verdict and I nodded, like I knew who Rodney King was.

They gave me a room with four other girls, not one of them overly neat, and I settled in. I thought about calling my daddy, just to let him know I was all right and not to worry, but then I figured it was night back in Eden and he was probably sitting at CC's. Then I went down to the shower room that everyone shared and checked again to see if my moon had arrived.

★ Tallie's Book ★

Faith doesn't run steady like a river. It takes working at.

Leaving isn't as easy as you might imagine.

twenty-two

*W*ell, the party was a gigantic disappointment. When Jazz said it was an "industry party," I was expecting we'd be meeting some stars, even if they weren't the big ones, but it turned out to be mostly people who worked on movie crews or played in some kind of band. There were a couple of set carpenters, a makeup man, a girl who worked for Craft Food Services, which is this catering business that goes to movie sets, and the dog walker for some star no one had ever heard of. The most important person there was a personal assistant to the personal assistant to the head prop man on *Good Morning, Vietnam,* and she acted slow-witted, though Jazz said it was because she was on drugs, and I said for sure she wasn't going to be advancing anyone's career including her own if she continued like that. Everyone there was drinking and smoking dope and wearing dark glasses, even at night. One boy in leather pants that Rula Wade would have killed for talked to me for about five seconds. Once he found out I had just arrived from Virginia, he lost interest. I spent most of my time sitting on a stone fence by the swimming pool hoping I didn't still look like I was carrying a sign proclaiming *Virgin*.

I got up early the next morning, but the other girls in my room didn't look like they'd be waking anytime before Christmas. I didn't plan on wasting time waiting for Jazz to surface, so I got dressed and headed out. As I said, the hostel was located right on Hollywood Boulevard, directly across from the Chinese Theatre, where they held movie premieres and where the stars put their handprints in wet cement. Just looking over at the red and gold splendor of it made me smile. I wished Raylene could have seen it. I turned right and proceeded along the famous Walk of Fame. I went slow and read each person's name spelled out in brass letters. There was a little brass picture in the middle of each star, too, indicating what the person was famous for. An old-fashioned movie camera for movie stars, a record for recording artists, a microphone for the radio people. Like that. One thing Mama hadn't prepared me for was the length of the sidewalk, which went on for blocks and blocks. On both sides of the street. All the famous people you'd expect to see were there—John Wayne, Marilyn Monroe—but there were lots of people I'd never heard of and I was sure Mama hadn't either. Like Warren Hull and someone named Julius LaRosa. Most disappointing were the stars for the cartoon characters and animals. Woody Woodpecker. Lassie. Not even real people.

After a while, the sidewalk turned down another street named Vine, and I went down that, too. There was a man sitting on the sidewalk applying polish from a bottle to the brass parts of the stars and buffing away with a rag. I watched him for a while, and he told me his job was keeping the brass all shiny. He said when he finished the entire sidewalk, he went back to the beginning and started all over again. It took me almost an hour to cover the entire Walk of Fame. The blister developing from my new sandals slowed me down. I passed by tons of stores. It was possible to buy any tacky thing in the world you wanted on that street. There were T-shirt stores and guitar stores and shops with about eight hundred racks of postcards. I passed one place called "Exotic Shoes," and that's exactly what was in the window. Boots that reached near to your waist, and heels so high they could have been stilts—so that just walking in them a person would risk breaking her neck. There was a wig store that had about a hundred wigs in the window in every style and color imaginable. Pink and white and green and purple, along with the usual shades. Raylene would have flipped if she'd seen them. I wished she could have been there, then I thought that it seemed that ever since I arrived in L.A. I'd spent half my time thinking about people in Eden, the very town I'd been hell-bent on escaping.

I stopped at a newsstand to buy a paper called *Variety* 'cause Jazz said that'd be the place to look for job ads. While I was reading the paper, I got myself a cup of coffee and thought about Mama doing the exact same thing when she landed in L.A. I found an opening for a receptionist at Warner Brothers Studios, and another for a job in the mailroom at Paramount, so I borrowed a pen from the waitress and circled these as well as a few others that looked possible until something more promising came along. Jazz said if I had any sense of rhythm in me I could probably be a dancer at Jumbo's Clown Room, but when she'd driven me by there, I saw all these flashing signs that said *Nude Dancers,* so that was out.

After I finished my coffee I stopped by a drugstore to pick up some Band-Aids for my blister, which was practically bleeding, then I headed back toward the Chinese Theatre. Just as I got there a bus pulled up and all these tourists climbed out and right off started getting down on their knees and putting their own hands in the prints left by the stars, like they thought maybe some of the fame would wipe off on them. Every single one of them was taking pictures. I remembered what Jazz had said about acting like "you were one of us and not one of them," and was glad I hadn't brought Mama's old Kodak.

The place with Roy Rogers's name had an imprint of his horse's shoe, too, and an outline of a revolver. Naturally this turned my mind to Spy. That made my chest ache, not the burning kind of hurt that came when I thought of Mama, more a wanting ache, and I got to wondering if he was missing me at all and if his high-powered lawyers were being successful in keeping him out of jail. I sure hoped so. To get my mind off Spy, I walked around a bit more and found Shirley Temple's handprint. She'd been barefoot when she placed her foot in the cement, and her feet were tiny as a doll's. A star named Margaret O'Brien had been barefoot, too, and Judy Garland's foot was about the size of a midget's. At last I found the place where Natalie had signed. Then two women came over and asked me if I'd mind taking a snapshot of them standing by the theater.

"Imagine," one said. "We're standing exactly where all these famous actors have stood. Exactly in the same spot."

I thought about all the people traveling to this very place, who came from all over the country, all over the world, all coming to be in the movies or get close to those who were stars, like it was a kind of magic, the same kind of magic that made everyone in Eden sign up for *Glamour Day* at the Kurl. I thought about Mama and me and Jazz, and thousands of others, all of us wanting to be famous, no matter what it took or who you had to leave behind, even if they were people who truly loved you. Mama never told me that dreams had their own price and you had to be willing to pay the cost, but they did. Then, standing right there, for the first time I could remember, I found myself getting mad at Mama. It wasn't right for a mama to be leaving her girl behind just so she could go off chasing some dream. It wasn't right to mow down anything that stood in your way, especially if it was the folks who loved you. If Mama had been there, I would have told her she'd had responsibilities and I would have told her how it felt to be left behind, and nothing she could have said would have charmed me out of my anger. I was working up a righteous head of steam, and no telling how long I'd have been fuming, when suddenly I remembered the things I'd done. Stealing Martha Lee's money without a second thought, running off without a good-bye to Raylene or Spy or my daddy. I wasn't any better than Mama and for sure was as pigheaded in pursuit of the mesmerizing dream of Hollywood. After that, my anger settled down, not because Mama'd charmed me, but because I'd reached an understanding about the power of a dream and how it could turn a person's head backwards. I wondered if it was possible to work toward a dream without hurting people along the way.

Then, standing right there in front of the famous Chinese Theatre, I had myself a *revelation*. Etta Bird used to say a revelation could about knock the air straight out of a person's body, and that's exactly how I felt. It took me a minute or two to get to breathing normal. The revelation didn't come in any big flash of light or from voices like Etta said could happen. It was

quiet and came from a deep and true place inside. It told me
that as sure as dogwood bloomed in the Blue Ridge in spring, I
didn't want to be a movie star. Not really. Standing there looking at the handprints of big stars and listening to the women
talking foolish, I knew I'd taken money from my mama's best
friend and traveled across the whole country, all the time in
pursuit of a dream that wasn't even mine. Becoming a star was
my mama's dream and somewhere along the road, I'd taken it
as my own.

Learning this made me feel empty. I'd been planning on this
for so long, it felt like I'd lost something big, and that I'd let
Mama down, too. But then I felt Mama next to me and I heard
her voice clear, just like I'd been doing for the past several days.
She told me it was all right. She said I wasn't disappointing her
in the least. She said a person's job in life was to find and follow
her own dream, and it was time for me to be discovering mine.
That made me feel strong enough to get up and head back to
the hostel. It looked like I would be using the rest of Martha
Lee's money getting back to Eden, and I sure had a mess waiting for me to clean up when I got there. I figured I could get a
ticket home in the next day or two and that would leave me
time to finish up my other business.

I decided the first thing I'd do would be to find Natalie's
grave. I asked a lady selling maps at the corner and she said she
thought Natalie was buried in the cemetery over by Paramount, although she wasn't sure. When I got back to the hostel, Jazz was awake and said she'd drive me.

Paramount Pictures was in a part of Hollywood comprised
mostly of car wash and body shop places, and the entire studio
was bigger than all of downtown Eden, and that is the gospel

truth. A fence enclosed it, and on one corner there was this giant globe attached to the roof. There were big arched gates with black metal scrollwork, and you had to have a pass to get inside. I told Jazz my Mama'd worked there, but I could tell she didn't believe me. She pointed out a restaurant called Lucy's El Adobe and said a lot of people from the studio ate there, so I told her about Mama having lunch with Kelly McGillis, but she didn't seem to believe that either.

We found the cemetery on the street backing up to Paramount. Jazz drove right in, and I have to say I thought it was the prettiest cemetery I'd ever seen. There were big stones containing actual pictures of the person who was buried there. We asked the lady in the gift shop where Natalie Wood's grave was. She said there were lots of movie stars there, like Jayne Mansfield and Peter Lorre and Rudolph Valentino, nearly every important dead person in Hollywood, she said, but not Natalie Wood. She told us she thought Natalie was buried over at the Forest Lawn cemetery, which was across town, by the Warner Brothers Studios, the other place for famous people. Before we left, we took a little drive around the place. We saw Mel Blanc's grave, and his stone said, *That's All Folks,* 'cause he was famous for being the cartoon voice of Bugs Bunny. On some stones the engravings weren't even in English. Jazz said they were in the Cyrillic alphabet. Douglas Fairbanks's stone was off by itself at the foot of a long, narrow pool. Lots of people had carved their initials in a tree located nearby just to prove they'd been there, and that reminded me of the tourists putting their hands in the cement prints at the Chinese Theatre.

After we left that cemetery, Jazz said she was starving. We went to a Chinese place for lunch. Then she wanted to go clothes shopping, and it was late afternoon before we finally got over to Forest Lawn, which was more like a big park than a cemetery, with statues of people like George Washington. You might not believe this, but there was a wedding going on when we got there. With a tent and everything. Imagine. People actually got married there. Raylene wouldn't have believed it either. I could just hear her saying that only in Hollywood would people want to get married in a cemetery. The man at the gate made us stop and he gave us a list of printed regulations. There were rules for everything, like how long flowers were allowed to stay on the graves—five days—and no pets and no picnics on the grounds, which seemed peculiar to me. Why could you have a wedding and not a picnic? Jazz told him we were looking for Natalie Wood's grave, and he checked in a book he had and told us she wasn't there. Jazz asked if he knew where she was and he said he thought she was over at the cemetery by Paramount.

Then we had to get back because Jazz had to get ready for work. She said we'd look again the next morning. By the time we got back to the hostel, it was too late to do anything about finding the woman named Sasha. I showed Jazz Mama's paper with the address, and she said Mississippi Street was over in the flats. She said if I wanted to go in the morning, she'd drive me as long as I gave her some money for gas. Then she started getting herself all fixed up for work at Jumbo's Clown Room. I spent the rest of the evening making trips to the bathroom to see if my moon had come, which it hadn't. It looked like having Spy's baby was one more thing I'd have to be facing when I returned to Eden.

In the morning, as soon as Jazz woke up, we headed over to

the flats, which was this other section of L.A., and we found Mississippi Street without taking one wrong turn. There were rows of little houses, one right next to the other, not one of them much bigger than my daddy's. The number on Mama's paper was the only one on the entire street that was built of stone. And the front yard was filled with cactus plants, like the person living there couldn't decide if she wanted to be in California or Texas.

Jazz asked if she should wait, but I told her no. My stomach was jumping when I pressed the bell. You could hear music blasting inside. An old Billy Joel tune cranked up high. I rang again, holding the button in. Then the door opened and I swear I nearly passed out cold. Standing in front of me was a woman who looked so much like Mama, they could have been sisters. "Yes?" she said.

I'd practiced what I was going to say, but seeing Mama standing there just robbed me of my voice. Then, like in those cartoon strips, the lightbulb went on above my head and I understood who Sasha was. Mama'd told me that Natalie Wood had had two daughters, one with that awful Robert Wagner and one with another husband. It was clear as crystal I'd landed on the doorstep of one of them. There was no mistaking the resemblance. Same thick black hair and big eyes. She being Natalie's daughter explained the unlisted phone. Naturally she wouldn't want strangers calling her up all the time asking her about her famous mother. I couldn't believe it. Me, Tallie Brock, from Eden, Virginia, actually meeting the daughter of Natalie Wood. I wished I had the Kodak, even if it did make me look like a tourist.

"Can I help you?" she said.

"I'm Tallie," I blurted.

She frowned like she was trying to remember if she was supposed to know me.

"Tallie Brock." I stuck out my hand for her to shake, but she ignored it. She probably was thinking I was one of those nervy people who buy the maps to movie stars' homes, then beg for their autographs. Moving quick, before she could shut the door, I dug out the scrap of paper. "This was in my mama's things," I said.

She stared at her name and address written in blue in Mama's fine writing. "Your mama had this?"

"Yes," I said. "Her name was Dinah Mae."

"I know," she said. "Dinah Mae Brock."

"You knew my mama?"

She sighed, then looked real irritated. "Did she send you here?"

"Mama send me? No, I came on my own." I was still digesting the news that Mama knew one of Natalie's daughters.

"How is she?" she said.

"Who?" I asked.

"Your mama. Who else?"

"She passed," I said. "Four years ago. She was real sick."

She sighed again, then held the door open. "You better come in."

Believe it or not, every single thing inside that house was white. Walls, furniture, even the rugs. I'd never seen anything like it. It was the whitest house I'd ever set foot in. A person'd go crazy trying to keep a place like that clean. It made me nervous to even walk on the floor. A person didn't need to ask to know there were no children living there. Pets, either. It hardly looked like anyone lived there. Sasha headed directly for the kitchen and though it wasn't yet noon, she opened the refrigerator and took out a bottle of wine. She poured some into two blue glasses—the first speck of color I'd yet seen—and handed one to me. I'd have preferred a beer, but I didn't want to be rude.

She nodded toward the paper still clutched in my fingers. "She leave anything besides that?" she said.

"No, ma'am," I said.

She squinted like someone who needed glasses. "Tallie?" she said. "That's your name, right?"

"Yes," I said. "It's short for Natasha."

She rolled her eyes. "Don't tell me. After Natalie Wood. Right?"

I nodded, embarrassed. Probably I was the millionth person named for her mama.

"You live in Virginia?" she asked. "Like Dinah Mae?"

"Yes, ma'am," I said. "Eden."

"Do you know who I am?" she said.

I nodded.

"Your mama told you?" she said.

"No," I said. "It's just that you look exactly alike." I figured she probably heard this all the time and wondered if she ever got tired of people telling her this. I wondered if she wanted to be an actress, too, like Natalie.

She finished her wine and poured another glass. She stared at me like she was waiting for me to say something else, but I couldn't figure out what she wanted. "She came here, you know," she said.

"Mama came here?"

She nodded. "Four years ago."

"Why?"

She gave this tight little noise that sounded like it was trying to be a laugh, and it made butterflies start up in my stomach.

"Good question," she said. "That's what I asked her. What good does it do to go stirring up ancient history?"

I couldn't figure what history she was talking about, then I remembered the picture of Mama standing with Natalie Wood. "You mean about my mama knowing your mama?" I asked. When she didn't answer, I plunged on. "I was wondering 'cause I found this photograph of my mama and she's standing right next to your mama."

She looked at me like she was trying to figure out what the hell I was talking about, then she asked me if I'd run that by her one more time. And when I did, she said, wait a minute, you think I'm Natalie Wood's daughter.

"You're not?" I said. The conversation was getting like a Tilt-A-Whirl ride at the carnival.

She told me I'd better sit down and have another glass of wine, which is exactly what I did. And that's when I learned my mama held more secrets than I could have imagined. It took a while for Sasha to tell me the entire story, and by the time she'd finished we'd drunk one bottle of wine and started on another.

It seemed that Mama hadn't been able to take Allie Rucker's baby cure any more than I had. She'd run away from Eden when she was fifteen. She'd come to Hollywood and found a job working in the studio canteen, and when people noticed that she looked exactly like Natalie Wood, she got a job working as a stand-in on the movie *Inside Daisy Clover,* which explained why Mama knew everything about that movie. When Natalie learned Mama was expecting, she helped her find a home for the baby. The only thing my mama asked was that the baby girl be named Natasha, after Natalie, same as me. There were lots more details, but that was Sasha's story in a nutshell.

I had plenty of questions, like why Mama'd returned to Eden and why she never told anyone about working as Natalie's stand-in, Natalie Wood her idol, but Sasha didn't have the answers. I figured the two people who could tell me were both gone. Then I was hit with another revelation. "So we're sisters?" I said.

She looked at me steady. "The same woman gave birth to us," she said, "but that doesn't make us sisters."

"It doesn't?"

"Listen, Tallie," she said. "You seem like a nice girl and I don't mean this in any cruel way, but I already have a family."

"You do?" I said.

"I have a mother and a father and two younger brothers. I always knew I had a different mother, just like my brothers do, but I never once went looking for the woman who gave me up. I don't hold a grudge, but it takes more than an accident of blood to make a family, you know what I mean?"

"I guess so," I said, but I didn't. Here I'd finally found a sister, but before I had five minutes to get used to the idea, she was saying we weren't kin after all. She must have seen how I felt, because she reached over and I think she was going to give me a hug when we were interrupted. Just when I thought I couldn't take one more surprise if I lived to be three hundred, the doorbell rang. Sasha went to answer it and when she came back, who was right behind her but my daddy and Martha Lee, come to take me home.

When I found my voice, I introduced everyone, making

explanations, but no one was listening. Daddy was staring at Sasha like he was seeing a ghost, which I guess he was, in a way, her looking like Mama and all. Martha Lee was waving away every word I said. She just wanted to give me a kiss and seemed so happy to see me that for a minute I guess she'd forgotten I was a thief. Sasha was looking like she was getting a headache and kept glancing down at my daddy's boots and the dirt he was tracking through her all-white house. She didn't offer anyone any wine. In less than five minutes she had the three of us out the front door. But before I left, she handed me a paper.

"What's this?" I said, staring at the number she'd written down.

"In case you want to call me sometime," she said.

"Okay," I said, confused about whether that meant maybe we could be sisters after all.

"You okay?" Martha Lee said as we headed for my daddy's truck. I didn't know if she meant okay because I couldn't manage to walk a straight line after all that wine, or okay after learning all my mama's secrets.

On the way back to the hostel, Martha Lee chatted on and on, talking so it made me even dizzier, talking more than I'd ever heard her. She told me how when she saw the envelope holding the pictures of Mama and Sasha's address was missing, she figured out where I'd headed, and how it was a good thing she'd remembered the address on that paper or who knew how long before they'd have found me. She told me how my daddy'd been near hysterical when he discovered I'd gone, and how he'd driven all the way across the country to get me, hardly stopping to sleep. I started to tell her I was sorry about taking the money, but she said hell, she didn't care two sticks about that. I told her I'd make it up to her somehow, and she just gave me a squeeze and told me it wasn't nothing but money and not to worry. That's when I noticed she was wearing lipstick, but I was too dizzy from wine and all the surprises to think about it, or add two and two together.

When I got to the hostel, Jazz didn't seem the least bit surprised that I was heading back to Virginia. She wished me good luck, and I told her I hoped all her dreams came true, too. "Almost forgot," she said, and pulled a square of paper out of her pocket. "I don't know if you still want this." She'd called around all morning and had found out where Natalie Wood was buried. A cemetery called Westwood Memorial Park, she said. I told her thanks, but said it didn't matter anymore. Then Martha Lee surprised me by insisting we go anyway. We'd be doing it for Deanie, she said, because she'd never had the chance. I wasn't sure I wanted to do anything for a mama who'd kept secrets from me, secrets like a sister, a mama I felt I hardly knew anymore, but Martha Lee wouldn't be denied on this and, surprise, surprise, surprise, my daddy agreed with her.

We followed the address Jazz had written down, taking Stoner Street and then going down Olympic, driving round and round, and up and down the street, checking the directions about twenty times. We couldn't find that cemetery no matter how hard we looked. My daddy said probably the address was wrong. Finally Martha Lee made him stop a postman and he gave us directions. We must have passed by that cemetery a dozen times already, but it was up an alley, so hidden that if you didn't know it was there, you'd never find it. It was nothing like that Forest Lawn place or the cemetery behind Paramount. It was a memorial garden and there were no big headstones, just little markers flush with the grass and some benches and walls with places for people's ashes. There were lots of flowers and it was sweet and peaceful, like it could have been some rich person's private garden.

Daddy said he and Martha Lee'd wait in the truck while I found the grave. The man in the office started to tell me where to find Marilyn Monroe because she was there, too, and most people came looking for her, but I said no, I was looking for Natalie Wood. He pointed out this spot beneath a tree that had three big bouquets of flowers and a bench. I crossed over the lawn, walking right by Donna Reed's grave, an actress who'd played a mama on TV. When I got close, I saw that the flowers weren't bouquets after all, but potted plants, like little trees or bushes. There was a rose, a gardenia, and an orchid. That's when I remembered I'd planned on bringing a flower to leave there, but it didn't seem to matter anymore. I sat for a while, grateful for the shade from the tree. Between the sun beating down and all the wine I'd drunk, I wasn't feeling any too good. The stone on the grave said: *Natalie Wood Wagner. Beloved Daughter, Sister, Wife, Mother and Friend.* Someone had left two pennies there. I sat for a while, staring at the words and reflecting on Natalie and Mama, and considered the amazing coincidence of their looking like twins, and how this fact had changed my mama's life and how it didn't take much but a coincidence like that to alter the direction of a person's life. I thought about some of the things I'd written in my rule book, like how regret was a waste of emotion, and how not one single person lives a perfect life and that dreams were as true as what makes lightning bugs, or silence, or the dust on butterflies' wings, and how a person should be careful of what she dreamed.

In a way, it felt like both Mama and Natalie could have been buried beneath that stone, because for sure both of them had been a "Beloved Daughter, Sister, Wife, Mother and Friend." Before I knew it, that hard little chicken bone inside my throat and all the stones that had been growing in my chest just melted away. I was so tired of keeping it all in, I started to cry, shedding every tear I'd been storing up for four years. I just couldn't stop. Then my daddy was there, holding me tight and saying, let it out, girl, just let it go, let it all go. We sat like that, him holding me and rocking me until I'd gotten rid of every tear.

When I was all cried out, I was expecting him to tell me we had to get going, that we had a long trip ahead, but he continued to sit there on that stone bench, just like we had all the time in the world.

After a while, my daddy cleared his throat like he had something important to say. I readied myself for his lecture, which I'd been half expecting since the moment I'd seen him, and I wondered what punishment I could be expecting.

"Your mama would be proud of you," he said.

"She would?" I said, wondering exactly how lying and stealing and running away from home could possibly be the kind of behavior that would make my mama proud.

Then almost to himself, my daddy said, "My Dinah Mae sure would be proud of her litle girl."

I stared right at him. It was the first time since Mama'd passed that my daddy'd said her name aloud. I'd thought for a long time that that meant he'd forgotten about her, but suddenly I knew that he'd never, ever forget Mama. Never. No matter what.

"I'm proud of you, too," he said, surprising me.

"You are?" When were we going to get to the part about how disappointed he was about the stealing and lying?

He leaned over and picked up a stone from Natalie's grave and rolled it between his fingers. "You've had to put up with a lot, girl," he said, which was the closest my daddy'd ever come in his life to apologizing.

It was like somehow, sitting in this cemetery—or maybe it was on that mad-dash, three-day trip across the country to find me—my daddy'd found himself again.

Something has changed, that was for sure.

Then Martha Lee was there, too, and that felt right and I thought about what Sasha said about blood not making family and although it'd made me mad when she'd said it, I began to understand what she meant.

Before we left I plucked one of the roses from the potted rosebush on Natalie's grave. I didn't think anyone would mind. I wanted to bring it home and put it on Mama's grave 'cause I remembered what my Uncle Grayson had said about roses representing love. Mama'd have liked that, 'cause she surely had loved Natalie.

Then we got in the truck and headed for Eden. We were crossing over into Arizona when I got my moon.

★ Tallie's Book ★

Sometimes forgiveness doesn't have to be
earned.

A person's job in life is to find and
follow her own dream.

epilogue

i still have the pictures of me from *Glamour Day*. I framed the
9 x 12, the one of me in the black satin halter. I can see it from
right here where I'm sitting. It continues to remind me of life's
capacity to astound.

That summer when the Glamour people came to the Kurl I
thought I had already exhausted my life's full measure for surprise. Back then I was only beginning to learn about life and all
it holds in store for us, more things than we are capable of
imagining, both the good and the bad.

First thing, Daddy married Martha Lee. At first I thought
that was my fault. They'd crossed the country to come and get
me, and I figured that cooped up in my daddy's truck they
must have gotten to talking and something must have clicked.
Then I remembered Martha Lee going to the *Glamour Day* to be
transformed, and the day she'd bought the tube of lipstick for
herself, and I figured she must have had her own plans all
along. After the initial shock, their marrying made sense to me.
Like the only way my daddy could bear to be with a woman was

if she didn't look in any way like Mama. And Raylene proved right. All he did need was to be "taken in hand." Martha Lee is a determined woman. She's proved good at this job.

I still have my rule book. Sometimes I get it out and reread all the things I learned from the folks in Eden.

From Mama I learned about the power of dreams and the importance of imagination.

From Raylene I learned the power of honesty and kindness.

From my daddy I learned that love doesn't have to be loud and showy to be real. And I learned the many ways it can make you weak and the ways it can make you strong.

From Martha Lee I learned about patience. And friendship. And the amazing capacity we hold for forgiveness.

From Lenora I learned that life is filled with mystery and miracles, like the ability to see the future in a sink full of soap. Long before the rest of us had a clue, she saw Martha Lee married to my daddy, saw it when she was washing Martha Lee's hair on *Glamour Day*. And she was right about the other thing, too. I didn't become a movie star. Or enroll in cosmetology school over in Lynchburg, though it took me a while to figure out what I wanted to do.

After high school I went to a special school in Lynchburg and became a midwife, and now I live a life surrounded by babies, just like she saw in the suds.

From Spy I learned about the possibility for redemption. And much, much more.

I married Spy. He went to jail after all. They said he was guilty of manslaughter, and he served eighteen months at the county jail. I went to visit him every week regular. When he was released, the first thing he did was come see me. Goody would say I was breaking family tradition and marrying up, since Spy is a Reynolds and comes from privilege, but I don't see it that way. I don't think marriage is about marrying up or down. I think it's about marrying true. We've both had our share of heartaches and have known tremendous sorrow. We've tried to make something good out of it. Spy became a counselor, so girls like Sarah would have a place to go.

We have a baby. Mama knew what she was talking about when she said the sky's the limit, and that's why I named our daughter Skye. She's delicate as Spring Azures and looks exactly like my mama.

I learned how we heal, and about all the twigs and seeds and fungi that contribute to our healing. I learned how out of those seeds can come something as surprising and miraculous as the butterfly bush that sprang up from the ground where I'd buried the Queen of Cures.

I learned there is a cure for everything, what ails us and what fails us.

I learned the cure for life is to live it, to take it in. To take it all in.

★ Tallie's Book ★

The Queen of Cures is Love.

acknowledgments

*i*t is a truism that no author writes a book alone. This novel was written in a cradle of support, and many have helped along the way.

My profound gratitude to the Virginia Center for the Creative Arts and to the Ragdale Foundation for providing me with time and space in which to work. The VCCA has granted me seven residences—each in the spring of the year—and it was during these months that I first fell in love with the Blue Ridge, Amherst County, and her people. This book would not exist without the Center's astounding generosity. The Ragdale Foundation has been extraordinarily supportive over the past ten years, and it was during a lengthy residency there at my "home" on the prairie that I completed the manuscript.

Maureen O'Neal is an editor of talent and good taste. Her enthusiasm has kept me afloat, her editorial eye has kept me true, and her phone calls have made me laugh. I am indebted as well to Gina Centrello, Kim Hovey, Allison Dickens, and the entire Ballantine sales force. It is hard to envision how a book could land in better hands.

My agent, Deborah Schneider, has supported me with unfailing wisdom, comfort, and plain good sense. Words can't express my gratitude.

Jane Wood offered long-distance encouragement from London, and her over-the-top enthusiasm kept me smiling for days.

Many others have assisted in the journey.

The following have answered questions with patience and humor. While many helped with research, any error is mine alone.

In Los Angeles, I owe thanks to Ozzie Cheek, Kim Myers, John Kaye, Marie Coolman, Diana Faust, and Jennifer McNair.

In Virginia, I am indebted to Robert Reeves, Wayne Ferguson, Janine Casey, Meghan Wallace, director of the Amherst County Historical Society, Dick and Bill Wydner at the Amherst Mill, Sony Monk, and Sheila Gulley Pleasants.

I wish to thank Jacqueline Mitchard for aiding and abetting and a generosity that knows few bounds; Margaret Moore, whose friendship is a blessing; Ann Stevens for a careful reading of the manuscript; and Jebba Handley and Ginny Reiser, who at various times fed me, held my hand, and read the work in progress. Additionally, I want to recognize the contributions of Leona Leary, Pam English, Judy Rogers, Glen Ritt, Sylvia Brown, Susan Tillett, Kelly Bancroft, and Barnstable County Assistant District Attorney Michael Trudeau. I also want to recognize Sam and Donna Faulkner.

Lastly, I thank my mother, and Hillary, Hope, and Chris for the great gift of the unfailing love of family.

author's note

*a*lthough Amherst County, Virginia, does exist, Eden and her people reside solely in the author's imagination and bear no resemblance to any living persons or place.

Leaving Eden

Anne D. LeClaire

A Reader's Guide

A Conversation with Anne D. LeClaire

Lynda Barry *is a writer and cartoonist. She's the author of several books, including* Cruddy *and* One Hundred Demons.

Lynda Barry: Where were you and what were you doing when this story first showed itself to you?

Anne LeClaire: I was in the middle of a writing residency at the Virginia Center for the Creative Arts, which is situated in a rural town in the foothills of the Blue Ridge Mountains. One day I went into town to get a haircut and saw a poster in the local beauty shop advertising a *Glamour Day*, just like the one Tallie describes. "They make you look like a star," the owner told me as she trimmed my hair, summing up in this single sentence the magic formula. This started me thinking about the way Hollywood acts as a polestar in our culture, pulling us along in its wake, however much we deny its magnetism. I saw in my mind the young girl who would be Tallie, a teenager wanting to be transformed. It was just a glimmer, but enough to get me started, although at the time I thought it would end up as a short story. Out of this beginning—the daughter of a starstruck mother, deserted for a dream—a story was formed. I have to add that in the interest of research I did sign up for *Glamour Day*, but truly I did *not* end up looking like a movie star. More like a female impersonator.

LB: Was that first glimmer like a picture? Did you see Tallie in your mind's eye?

AL: It was actually more a feeling than a visual impression. When I looked at that poster, I felt the yearning a young girl might feel, an ache really, the wanting to be something more, more than a person's particular geography or circumstances suggested was possible. That sense of longing was central to the story as the work progressed: Tallie's longing for her mama, for a relationship with Spy, for a connection to her father, for information about how to become a woman, and, of course, her desire to be beautiful. Out of that initial sense of hunger, a visual did surface, and it was of Tallie standing in that beauty parlor.

LB: I love the Klip-N-Kurl! It seemed a perfect place for a teenage girl who had lost her mother (twice!) at such a critical time in her adolescence. It reminded me of a fairy tale in that way. Many fairy tales begin with an adolescent girl who has lost a good mother who has been replaced by an evil stepmother. I've often wondered if it isn't a way to tell the story of what happens to us when we hit adolescence and begin to separate from our mothers. That wonderful, beautiful, loved mother from our childhood seems suddenly transformed into an unreasonable, out-of-it, controlling old bag. Tallie didn't have a chance to have that crucial relationship with her mother.

AL: Exactly, Lynda. Even for the brief period when her mother returned from Hollywood, Tallie couldn't explore normal adolescent separation and independence. The few times she allowed herself anger, it felt too dangerous because her mother was ill. There wasn't even an evil stepmother to rebel against. So to continue the fairy-tale theme, Tallie had to create her own bread crumb path to negotiate her way to womanhood because she didn't have the road map a mother might provide. I don't know if I've ever told you, but I watched my three nieces grow up without a mother—they were eight, eleven, and fifteen when my sister died—and witnessing the confusion, pain, and significance of their experience helped me slip into Tallie's skin.

LB: That's one of the things that fascinated me about the book. There *is* no evil stepmother whom Tallie can hate. That's a tough position to be in, having your Natalie Wood–look-alike mother be forever preserved as good, perfect, young, and most of all, more beautiful than you'll ever be. It's also a tough position for a writer to be in, because a horrible person makes a writer's job a whole lot easier and the story follows a certain path. But no horrible person shows up directly in Tallie's life. I kept waiting for one and when I realized no horrible person was coming, I felt this odd sadness, a loneliness of being stuck in her position exactly. It was as if Glinda the Good Witch in *The Wizard of Oz* got the ruby slippers and then died with them on. She's the Good Witch, so how can you get mad about it? Our earliest love for our mothers is like that, like Glinda the Good Witch, like the original Eden. It was so lonely following Tallie through all her temptations and transgressions, knowing there wasn't anyone who cared enough to throw her out of Eden. In the end she had to throw herself out.

AL: It is lonely when no one cares enough to toss you out of Eden for your sins, or even notice them. But is it worse if someone tries to keep you stuck there? And you are absolutely right about it being easier for a writer if there is a wretched character threatening the heroine.

LB: **Beauty is a main character in this book. And as soon as I read Natalie Wood's name, I knew exactly what kind of beauty you meant. There is no way to be more beautiful than Natalie Wood. I know what it's like to be the plain-faced child of a beautiful woman. People always said my mother looked just like Ava Gardner and even now I can't look at a picture of Ava Gardner without getting a sad, empty feeling. It broke my heart to think of Tallie watching Natalie Wood movies.**

Was your mother beautiful? Your sister?

AL: My older sister was stunning, and people were always telling me how beautiful she was. I was the duckling to her swan. And I know exactly what you mean about that hollow feeling you experienced watching Ava Gardner. And about the desire to be beautiful. A lot of what I was exploring during the writing was this territory of desire. Not just the longing for beauty, but desire of all kinds. Where do our dreams and aspirations come from? How do our own experiences shape our desires? How do dream merchants like Hollywood and Glamour Companies form them? How do our dreams shape our lives?

LB: **And what happens when you get your wish? Tallie prays so hard for her mother to return and when she** does, it turns out she's dying. Did your sister come up for you a lot while you were working on this?

AL: Here's the odd thing. All the time I was writing it, I wasn't consciously thinking about my sister or my nieces, but when I read over the completed manuscript, I had that lightbulb experience of "My God, I'm writing out of my own history." I had a similar experience with *Entering Normal*. Like I'm the last to know. Does this happen to you, or are you very aware of where your material is coming from during the process?

LB: When I'm writing and it's going well, it's more like slow dreaming. Half of my struggle is to be able to stop thinking and just go along for the ride. I often tell myself, "Just be the stenographer. Your only job is to be the stenographer."

Someone once pointed out how odd it is that we can remember our dreams, we're aware of dream selves, but our dream selves seem to have no awareness of our waking life. What we call our "real" lives. You never say, "Man, I had the weirdest reality yesterday."

I think that may be part of why it's so often the case that writers are the last to know how close the story may be to their own experience. A story has no awareness of its author. Which feels very odd after living with a character for as long as it takes to write a book. They feel so real to us, but to them we don't exist, can't exist. And there's a great relief in that, somehow. To give yourself over and, for a little while, stop existing. I wonder if it isn't somehow a bit like flying a plane—

which you also do. Are writing and flying planes similar?

AL: I love your statement that a story has no awareness of its author. It feels odd—and a little sad—to think of characters that are so very real to me not even knowing I exist. I guess we humans want reciprocity.

About flying and writing: I've never thought about it before, but there is a connection in that both of them lift me out of my daily reality and present me with a different perspective of life, another way of looking at things. Both also require a great concentration, the kind of intense focus that is almost like meditation.

LB: When the writing is going well, it's a different state of mind. It doesn't seem to include a lot of thinking or planning. It is absolutely the best when it doesn't even feel like writing. When it's like the deep state of play you see kids go into sometimes. From an adult's point of view, the kid is playing with toys. But from the kid's point of view, the toys are playing with *him*. He doesn't have to plan out a story for the toys. As long as he's not self-conscious, the stories will happen by themselves.

I've always thought that self-consciousness was an odd name for that feeling because it's really conscious-ness of others. My very WORST writing experiences happen when I'm aware of "the reader," a reader who doesn't even exist because until the story exists there can be no reader, and as long as I'm concentrating on the reader there can be no story. My worst days are when I'm frozen into a state of worry about what the nonexistent reader thinks about my nonexistent story.

AL: But the trick is losing self-awareness, shutting out the critical mind. Then bliss. For me, writing flows when I don't plan it out in advance. The only novel I never got published was one I mapped out in detail first. By the time I sat down and wrote it, it was lifeless.

But to leap in, not knowing exactly where the story is going, takes trust, doesn't it? Some days I think writing is one huge act of faith. You set out with that glimmer and not much else, and trust if you write straight and true and with as much courage as you can muster, a story will result. That is what is required of us.

And I think the worst writing advice I've heard is that writers should have a particular reader in mind for whom they are writing. My experience has been that putting the focus on the reader (or editor or critic) lifts us out of the story and can lead to some god-awful pretentious prose.

LB: Plus, it's no fun.

We became friends in the early 1990s at an artist colony where we were both working on novels. The first thing I noticed about you was how much you genuinely loved to write. You had an exhilaration about it that I loved, and your way of talking about writing was so unpretentious compared to many writers I'd met. I was just starting work on a novel that became *Cruddy* and felt really shaky on my feet about it. You were so supportive and practical and helped me so much. I know you have many readers who would love to write a book but have no idea where to begin. What advice would you give them?

AL: Right back at ya', Lynda. Your humor and exuberance and honesty attracted me right from the get-go.

Advice to writers? Hmmm. I guess the old chestnuts: Take risks. Pay attention. Tell the truth as you see it. And write, write, write. Write not for fame or fortune or recognition, but because it brings you joy.

Reading Group Questions and Topics for Discussion

1. What is the significance of the title *Leaving Eden*? How does it work on both a literal and a figurative level?

2. Tallie's mother, Deanie, quotes the poet Robert Frost: "Home is the place that, when you go there, they have to take you in." How does this indicate Deanie's attitude about her hometown? In which ways does she stand out there? How are Tallie's feelings about Eden similar and different?

3. What is Tallie's reaction to Deanie's departure and subsequent return? How does Tallie feel inadequate compared to her mother? In which ways does she feel abandoned by her? How are mother-daughter relationships presented in the novel, including those between Goody and Deanie, Mrs. Reynolds and Sarah, and Mrs. Wilkins and Sue Beth?

4. "A person's as big as her dreams," Tallie recalls her mother saying. At the beginning of the novel, what are Tallie's dreams, big and small? How does she measure her dreams against the ones of those around her? Why does she adopt Deanie's dream as her own? Does she ever believe it's truly her own aspiration?

5. Tallie doesn't believe that anyone she knows, other than herself and her mother, has the capacity to dream. How is she proven right or wrong? What actions, both good

and bad, do Deanie and Tallie undertake in order to realize their dreams?

6. How does Tallie characterize the relationship between her parents, and how accurate is her viewpoint? Does the partnership seem imbalanced? What do you think attracted Deanie to Luddington, and vice versa? What role does Tallie play in their relationship? What is the dynamic of the family unit before Deanie's departure, and afterward?

7. What is Tallie's relationship with her father like both before and after Deanie's death? How do they both cope with their grief? Do you think that Tallie is stronger than her father? In which ways does Tallie need someone to take care of her? In which ways is she older than her years, and how is she younger?

8. Were you surprised to learn that Deanie's abandonment of Tallie was actually her death from cancer? What techniques does Deanie use to brave her illness? How do humor and laughter play a part? In which ways does imagination alleviate her pain? How do the people around her cope with her sickness and death?

9. How does Martha Lee serve as a foil to Tallie's mother? What does Tallie learn from their friendship? Does Martha Lee act maternally toward Tallie, or is she more of a nontraditional mother figure? What does Tallie admire about Martha Lee, and what would she like to change?

What aspects of Martha Lee's personality are reflected in Tallie's? In Deanie's?

10. Tallie compares everyone she comes in contact with to her mother. "Not like Mama" is her constant refrain. How does Deanie's presence guide Tallie in her day-to-day life and overall? In which ways does Tallie most miss her mother's influence? How do other women, like Martha Lee and Raylene, attempt to fill that void?

11. Tallie is upset when a social worker comments that she idolizes her mother. How accurate is his statement? Why does Deanie provoke such strong feelings in those who surround her? How does Tallie's trip to California cast Deanie in a more realistic light?

12. Tallie keeps many things to herself, from her feelings for Spy Reynolds to her plans to flee to California. How does her "secret self" compare to the persona she projects to the outside world? Do others in Eden—everyone from Deanie to Luddington to Spy to Martha Lee—also possess a hidden identity? How do they express or hide that facet of their personality?

13. Physical appearances play a pivotal role in the novel. How does Deanie's striking resemblance to Natalie Wood shape her life? How is Tallie driven by insecurities about her appearance? Why is *Glamour Day* so important to her, as well as to the ladies at the Klip-N-Kurl?

14. How does Tallie's makeover on *Glamour Day* affect her behavior toward Spy? What about Spy is so appealing to Tallie? How does her initial impression of him differ from how she comes to feel about him? Why does Spy, in turn, find Tallie intriguing? Does this surprise her?

15. Why does Martha Lee decide to attend *Glamour Day*? Why does she take Tallie's spot? What facets of her personality does this reveal?

16. Did the disclosure of Sarah's drowning surprise you? In which ways, both subtle and overt, does it affect Tallie's behavior? Why do you think Tallie skipped Sarah's funeral? How is this characteristic or uncharacteristic of her personality?

17. What is Tallie's initial conception of the Reynolds family? How do they appear to the outside world? How does their outward demeanor conceal secrets?

18. Initially, why doesn't Tallie believe the rumors that Sarah killed herself? What are the clues that point to Sarah's suicide? How does Mrs. Reynolds stand in sharp relief to Tallie's mother, particularly in relation to her children? How does Spy react to these forces and the emotions they unleash within him?

19. Why does Spy come to Tallie after he has been arrested? What compels her to make love to him? What is her attitude toward the possibility of having his baby? How are

her feelings similar and different to her mother's feelings toward Sasha?

20. Why did Deanie make a special trip to find Sasha? What do you imagine their reunion was like? Do you think Deanie would have believed Sasha's assertion, "It takes more than an accident of blood to make a family"? Why or why not?

21. What is Sasha's attitude toward Tallie when she shows up on her doorstep? Do you think that Tallie was surprised to discover an older sister? How does Tallie react to the secrets that Sasha reveals about their mother? Do you think that Tallie and Sasha will ever be in contact again?

22. What about her visit to Natalie Wood's grave evokes such a strong emotional response from Tallie? Why do you think that her father undergoes a significant change at this point in the novel?

23. "Wanting is a powerful thing," Anne LeClaire writes in *Leaving Eden*. How does LeClaire present the different forms of desire? How is desire a positive force in Tallie's life and in the lives of those around her? In which ways is it detrimental?

24. What propels Martha Lee to fall in love and get married? How do you envision her life together with Tallie's father? How do you think Tallie will adjust to having Martha Lee as her stepmother?

25. Why does Tallie initially begin to keep her book of sayings and advice? What does it grow into?

26. The last line of the book is from Tallie's journal: "The Queen of Cures is Love." How does this theme resonate throughout the book? What other lessons has Tallie learned?

© Sarah Fernbaker

a b o u t t h e a u t h o r

*a*nne D. LeClaire is a novelist and short story writer who teaches and lectures on writing and the creative process. She has also worked as a radio broadcaster, a journalist, an op-ed columnist for *The Cape Cod Times*, and a correspondent for *The Boston Globe*. Her work has appeared in *The New York Times, Redbook,* and *Yankee* magazine, among others. She is the mother of two adult children and lives on Cape Cod.